Sea of Snakes

Heidi Stark

This is a work of fiction. Any resemblance to real people, living or dead, organizations, places, events or locals, are entirely coincidental. Although if you do know four guys like Skyler, Zeke, Dom and Rake, please send them my way.

To the islands and the ocean where I found myself.

I will come home to you.

-HS

"Without the ocean, without loyalty, there is nothing."

Anonymous

CHAPTER ONE

Devon

The flight attendant peers at me from the aisle, her mouth moving while my music plays at full blast. She smiles at me, but it's forced politeness, her flat eyes defying her by communicating something more like she wishes everyone on this plane would fuck off and die.

It must be a tough job some days, trapped in a sky pencil with a bunch of demanding assholes. I can't really blame her.

I remove my headphones and sit up in my chair. "Sorry, what?"

"Would you like a beverage?" she asks, enunciating each syllable, her gaze and body language clearly trying to convey she wants me to hurry up and either order or not. I don't know how many times she probably has to repeat the same questions over and over, constantly drowned out by earbuds and headphones and the dull hum of the plane's engine.

"Just a Diet Coke," I reply.

She nods and then cracks open a can on her cart. She scoops some ice into a plastic cup and hands both the can and the ice-filled cup to me. "Here you go."

"Thank you." I smile back, mirroring her with my own fuck-you gaze, and roll my eyes as soon as she attends to another passenger. I only ordered a soda so I could get the plastic cup.

As soon as she moves beyond our row, I reach down and pull three flight bottles of Jack out of my carry-on bag and open them one by one, placing them on my fold-out tray.

My father hears the *click-click* sound of the opening of the bottles, and it rouses him from his nap. "Devon, you're not meant to do that, you know. It's against flight regulations."

I give him a sideways glance and then proceed to slowly pour all three bottles into my cup without breaking eye contact. I raise the cup to my lips and take a long sip, enjoying the taste as the amber liquid streams down my throat, creating a pleasant and familiar burning sensation.

"Since when have you ever given a shit about following the rules, Frank?" He lost the honor of being called Dad a long time ago. "Seems a bit late to start now, don't you think?"

He snorts because he knows I have a point.

My father and I have a strange, strained relationship. He's not a good person, and god knows, neither am I, but I've decided for various reasons to keep him in my life rather than completely expunging him. As an adult, we're past the point where I really feel he can hurt me anymore. Plus, we made an agreement a while ago that I'd go on a 'family' vacation with him once per year.

My trust fund is riding on that little requirement. Yes, I have a trust fund. Judge me. I couldn't care less. But I don't have access to most of it yet. Maybe I never will, because he keeps changing the rules surrounding it. Hell, knowing him, maybe it doesn't even exist anymore. I wouldn't put it past him to have spent it all already.

I'm not entirely sure why he keeps stringing me along like this. Sometimes I think it makes him feel like a better person having his daughter in his life. Or maybe he just likes to exert control over me because he can. He certainly did when I was a child, and maybe he just wants to carry it on into my adulthood the only way he knows how. I've thought about telling him to go fuck himself many times, and I might do that one day, but for now, we're stuck with each other for one week every year.

That's why I'm here, on a plane with my father, flying to a tropical island. While I like the ocean, these types of colorful, kitschy tourist destinations are totally not my vibe—it's hard to pull me out of the grungy stickiness of a city that's jam-packed with dive bars and a good music scene—but I let him pick the destination this time. He was strangely insistent on this specific location, which is weird because previously he's let me choose. Said he had some business to do.

I'll worry about that later, though. Right now, I just want to make it through this plane flight and get to the hotel. Maybe I'll even find some excitement on this vacation.

I take another long, satisfying sip of my whiskey, and wipe my mouth with the back of my hand. Sinking back into my chair, I replace my headphones and close my eyes.

CHAPTER TWO

Skyler

"You teaching a lesson today?" Zeke glances at me from the other side of the living room as he pulls a tank top over his head, grazing it past his closely cropped dark hair.

I don't think I've ever seen him wearing anything on his top half other than a tank top. I can hardly talk, but I do manage to pull on an actual T-shirt from time to time, occasionally even a polo.

He has no interest in dressing to impress anyone, though, ever. His imposing, muscular body and tall frame do that on their own. The way he's built, he could probably walk around naked and get anything he wanted. Which I've actually seen him do a few times, now that I think about it.

"Yeah, a bit later on," I nod. "You guys want to meet me over at the break?"

The surf forecast is looking decent today. Nothing crazy, but it should be fun catching a few long ones into shore. It's always fun showing off in front of the tourists who are just learning, and who can barely get on a board, let alone ride a wave. Show them who's boss, who owns the place. Maybe snag a phone number or two. Living on an island has its advantages.

"Yeah, I'm planning to head out that way. Have some stuff to pick up for our next job. I'll see you out there." It's hard to keep Zeke out of the water, so I'm not surprised he's game to meet up. When he manages to pull himself away from work, that is. Surfing and work, Zeke's two vices.

"What about you, Dom?" I glance over at the burly guy who's sitting on an armchair that looks almost comically small for his expansive frame.

"Nah, man." He gestures at his muscular chest. "I'm going to get a tattoo, remember?" He had mentioned that, but I'd forgotten. So much going on lately that it's been hard to keep track. "The snake on a surfboard."

"Oh, sweet," I nod. "Then we'll all have them finally, although I'm surprised you found a space to put it. But I'm glad you're getting it. The mark that shows everyone who we are, and what they can expect when we're in the ocean."

"Fuck yeah! I'm excited about this one." He grins.

"Two to four weeks off surfing though, bro, while your skin heals. I don't know how you'll manage that." I can't remember a day that Dom hasn't been in the ocean since I've known him, let alone two full weeks away from it. He'd go insane. The sea is part of him. It runs through his veins, almost as much as it does mine and Zeke's. Dom's technically a transplant from the mainland, unlike us, but you'd never know it to look at him or to see him surf.

"Fuck waiting for it to heal," he says with a scoff, curling his upper lip. "The salt will help it heal faster. Plus, I'm not that soft. You really think I follow doctor's instructions for shit like that?"

"Yeah, I guess not." I shrug. He has a point. Dom's not one for rules. None of us are. And he certainly isn't a stranger to pain and suffering. In fact, I'm pretty sure he's been through so much that he's grown to like it.

Zeke narrows his eyes and snaps. "Stop chit-chatting, anyway, you lazy fucks." He's clearly over this back-and-forth which ironically he started, and is ready to get back to work.

He's a very intense person, and it's something I both admire and detest about him. I don't give myself a lot of downtime, because there's money to be made and an island to protect, but Zeke takes things to the next level. I'm a fairly serious person myself, but sometimes I wish he'd lighten up.

"What time did you get done last night?" He glances over at Rake, who's lying back on the tattered couch with his cap pulled over his eyes. He doesn't respond as he's apparently dozed off, and Zeke walks over to him, rips his cap from his head and throws it across the room. "Answer me, you fucking slacker!"

Rake, startled, snaps to attention and rears his fist back, instinctively readying to punch whoever has woken him from his slumber.

"Knock it off, both of you," I call out.

"Why? You're worried you're going to get hurt?" scoffs Zeke. He's clearly woken up on the wrong side of the bed this morning. Or, knowing him, he didn't get any sleep at all. He probably worked through the night.

"I could easily take both of you."

I'm a good fighter, but so are they, and I don't need to show any sign of weakness, even around them. They may be like brothers to me, but sometimes I struggle to trust them, even though I trust them more than I do myself. They've never let me down so far. Whereas I've let myself down plenty of times.

"We've got shit to do, and can't risk another visit to the hospital before we go sort those assholes out. They were trying to cut in on us again and I'm sick of them pulling that shit. They're always trying to cut in on our business and our waves, and they're little piss ants who don't stand a chance, but they keep trying anyway."

"What's happening again?" Rake rubs his eyes as if they're taking their time adjusting to the light after his nap.

"Oh, for fuck's sake, man. Do we have to tell you everything three times? I need you to be more on top of things." Zeke sneers at Rake, who rolls his eyes in response.

"Stop antagonizing each other or I'll have Dom beat the crap out of both of you," I snarl at them while Dom cracks his scarred knuckles and grins.

It's typically Rake and Dom that carry on, bickering like a couple of idiots. It feels unnatural to take on a pseudo-parental role with them, breaking up their juvenile arguments. They're my age, after all. But Zeke and I both regularly seem to find ourselves in that position.

Something's up with Zeke today, though. I can feel it. He's hyper-critical and seems ready to lash out at the smallest thing. It's definitely not the first time Rake's had a power nap. He lives for power naps. Zeke knows this, and it's usually not a big deal.

"Mind telling us why you're so agitated today, Zeke? More than usual, I mean?"

His frown grows deeper. "The Brixtons, those slimy fuckers."

He spits out the name of our major rivals as his lips curl with rage. It's not too hard to get Zeke worked up about certain things, the Brixtons being one of them, but his fuse is ultra-short today.

"They really have been trying to cut in on our business. They intercepted our last haul, and I think they're trying to take our place. I know you don't think much of them, but I'm concerned we've been underestimating their strength and how far they're prepared to go to take over from us. They're not as weak as you seem to think they are, and they've been taking some big swings at our territory recently."

"How do you know it was them?" I raise an eyebrow.

The last haul was in transit only a few hours ago, and it seems like a quick turnaround to find out both what happened and who did it.

"One of their guys got sloppy down at the dive bar after a few too many shots. They told a few people, and word got straight back to me. They were downright giddy about it, apparently. Think they're the top dogs now."

Guess that's the advantage of having a dive bar on the island that opens at six in the morning. Some people just can't help themselves from heading down there first thing and over-sharing their life stories and other secrets. It also helps that we have some trusted contacts who spend a lot of time there gathering intel. Loose lips sink ships.

"Fuck that!" Rake, now fully awakened from his nap, stands up and clenches his tattooed fists at his sides. "Nobody takes our shit! Nobody fucks with us. We're the top dogs around here. I'm going over there right now."

He charges toward the door, but I reach up and grab him by the back of his tank top and pull him back into the living room.

"Easy now, Rake. I don't doubt you could take them by yourself, those pussy ass mother fuckers, but let's be strategic about this."

Rake's a good fighter and his height has definite advantages, but sometimes his judgement isn't the best. There's no need for him to charge into a fight by himself with ten or so guys who are likely armed and just as good at fighting as he is.

"Yeah, and I'm getting my tattoo done today," adds Dom, glancing at his chest again, apparently prioritizing his body art above our business interests. "I've put down a huge deposit and have already had to reschedule twice. They said they'll just keep the money if I can't come in today."

"Glad you're putting our business first, bro." Zeke glares at Dom, his rage at the Brixton brothers diverting to him. "Do we need to teach you about priorities? Because I'll fucking show you, boy!"

"You'll show me, *boy*? You sound just like your dad, talking like that." Dom's eyes glimmer cruelly at Zeke, who flinches almost imperceptibly. This conversation is going completely off the rails. The comment clearly stung. It's a low blow, and not entirely inaccurate.

"Gotta give me more credit than that. I'm not a completely evil piece of shit." Zeke runs his fingers through his hair and looks at the ground, his voice low. None of us has a father to be proud of.

"Hang on, both of you." I put my hand out in what I hope is a peaceful gesture. I need to de-escalate this situation, and we don't have time for this unproductive back-and-forth.

"Listen for a sec. I agree that Dom's priorities are off and he needs to sort himself out and soon. But, there's a benefit to thinking this through more carefully. Rather than rushing in there half-assed, and risking making a fool of ourselves in front of those shitheads, and compromising our credibility with Tane."

"Well, I disagree," says Rake, crossing his arms tightly over his chest, revealing ropy, well-developed muscles often overshadowed by his tall figure. "But I'll go along with it this time so Dom can try to turn himself into a pretty boy and make his body look better for the ladies."

Dom narrows his eyes and spits in Rake's direction, and Rake only just manages to dodge the saliva flying out of the other man's mouth.

"Fuck, you're a bunch of mongrels," says Zeke.

"Yeah, like you aren't," snarls Rake.

Both of them are right. And everyone's been on a knife edge lately.

CHAPTER THREE

Devon

After arriving at the hotel and checking in, I put my bag in my room, and don't even stop to check out the space.

Instead, I quickly apply a dollop of sunscreen to my face and shoulders and arms, then inspect the map of the hotel provided by the front guest agent and make my way to the bar.

That's where I naturally gravitate when I visit most places, but especially when I have to go on vacation with my father. Somewhere with a good drink, where I can drown out other people and their bullshit, and dull all the terrible memories.

While I'm not here for the architecture, I can't help but notice the grandness of the space as I move through the foyer, following the map's directions.

The high ceilings make room for elaborate chandeliers, and giant art pieces adorn the walls. Lively island music pipes in from invisible speakers, the area abuzz with people dressed in tropical attire, excitedly discussing their vacation plans. Discreet air fresheners shoot out some kind of floral fragrance, maybe hibiscus, and the salt from the nearby ocean also permeates the open-air space.

Down an expansive hallway, I see an oceanfront event lawn, where a crowd of hotel staff scurry around setting up banquet tables in front of a stage. I keep walking and make a left into another area filled with overpriced high-end hotel stores, and then a right which takes me outside toward the beach.

The humid air hits me as I walk outside and leave the comfort of the air conditioning behind. The sun beats down intensely from a cloudless sky, and even though I applied sunscreen, I know if I don't stay out of the shade I'll quickly turn into a lobster, or all of my freckles will connect.

After navigating the maze-like path, I find the hotel bar right where the map said it should be. It's an open-air bar, with seats surrounding it in a horseshoe shape, covered by a thatched roof. There are also standalone high-tops and other tables surrounded by hungry seagulls and other birds, but I always feel more comfortable sitting at the bar than being served by someone at a table. Being right beside the bar also usually means I can get my drinks more quickly.

Unfortunately for me, this bar is one of those spots that makes frilly tropical drinks. Things like mai tais with elaborate pineapple and cherry garnishes, which are at least boozy, and frozen monstrosities like Miami Vices and piña coladas. Gross. There's no way I'm ordering one of those garish things.

Instead, I order my signature shot of whiskey, and then on second thought I ask the bartender to make it two. He raises an eyebrow, not seeing a companion with me. I guess it's not a common request at a place like this, but then he sees I'm serious and pours me two shots, neat as requested. I quickly chug back both and ask for a third. He shrugs and half-grins as he grabs the bottle to refill one of my glasses. "Getting your vacation started off right?"

"Something like that." I smile and shrug. He's accurate. I need to get into vacation mode. I can barely tolerate my father when I'm sober, so I need to loosen up a little.

While I'm sitting here, I get a message on my phone and see it's from my friend Donkey, checking in to see if I've survived the flight with my dad. We call him that because he once accidentally sent a dick pic to his mom, and it's just kind of stuck. It's a silly name for a pretty serious guy. I send him back a picture of my whiskey shot.

He's one of my friends who also comes from a broken place and has endured so much pain in his life. We don't have a ton of superficial stuff in common, and it's like we've gravitated together because of the darkness we've each endured. While our specific experiences have been different, they've permanently changed both of us, and we recognize that in each other.

I've learned that darkness attracts darkness, and some might think it's sad, but I think it's quite beautiful. He's one of the few friends that I've let into my world, that knows some of what I've been through, and even then I wouldn't say we're *super* close. But he's really all I've got.

Chapter Four

Skyler

On my way to the beach for a quick surf, before I teach a lesson, I decide to cut through the bar. We're not really meant to do that, me in particular, but it's quicker and I don't care too much about rules. Besides, I'm not planning on sticking around.

Tony, the bartender on duty, nods at me. "Hey, Sky!" He calls out, waving as I get closer. He knows I'm not supposed to be here, but he doesn't care. I nod back and grin, pointing at the ocean, and he nods again.

As I walk past the bar area, I see someone who doesn't look quite like they belong. And that's a good thing because I don't think much of most of the people that typically come here. The girl hunches over her phone with her hand cupped around a shot of what appears to be whiskey.

At a glance, I can see she's not like all the other guests, each trying to outdo the next with their high-end fashion. The types that wear their diamonds down to the bar, order cliché drinks to take photos of for Instagram, and then complain when their priceless jewels get lost in the sand or the sea. The folks with metal detectors can make some really good money on the strip of beach in front of this and the other neighboring luxury hotels.

This stranger, on the other hand, is fucking stunning. She's wearing all black and gray, a fitted tank top and shorts, a contrast compared to all the bright, tropical prints people wear on their island vacations. Not what I'm used to seeing around here at all. Tony sees me looking at her and he winks at me from the bar, a cheeky grin on his face. I guess she stood out to him, too.

The other patrons are engaging in shallow chit-chat, probably about their hometowns and how they would never want to live on the island full-time. Boring jerks. It's actually disgusting hearing some of the ways they trash our home casually, barside when they think nobody local is listening. But she doesn't look like she's interested in interacting with anyone or anything other than her shot of whiskey and whatever's on the other end of her phone.

Just by looking at her, I get the vibe that she does what she wants without giving a shit about what anybody else thinks. Clearly not trying to fit in at this bar, anyway.

She's fixated on her phone and doesn't look up, but I can tell by her profile that she's absolutely gorgeous. She has high cheekbones and full, red lips. Smoky liner and long, dark eyelashes frame her eyes. Her red hair cascades down her back like waves of fire, and it's highlighted with streaks of pale pink that should look unnatural yet look perfect on her. Leaning over her phone, she shows off a hint of her cleavage. As I walk past her, I feel my cock twitch slightly.

I see a lot of pretty women at the beach, toned and tanned in their bikinis. I'm a good-looking guy, confident, and with a constant coming and going of tourists with loosened inhibitions on their vacations, I have access to all the pussy I want. So I'm kind of surprised by the effect this woman is having on me. There's just something about her that's captivating me at a glance. I'm not used to it, and it's an interesting new feeling.

I don't stop to approach her, though, because even though I have great flirting game, I'm almost late for work and my chosen brothers and I have caused trouble at this bar one too many times. We've been asked not to come back, at least for a while.

It's okay, though. She stands out so much that I'm fairly confident I'll be able to track her down later. There are only so many places you can go around here.

CHAPTER FIVE

Devon

I've been at the bar for about an hour, but now I'm finishing up a martini with a lemon twist. I've switched up from the whiskey shots for the time being, but haven't developed a sudden interest in fluffy cocktails.

And after all, a martini is what people drink when they're trying to maximize their booze intake without pounding shots.

What can I say? I like to drink.

I take a moment to stare out at the sparkling turquoise ocean directly in front of me and realize I've spent most of my time so far either looking at my phone or my glass.

The alcohol has given me just enough fuzziness around the edges so that I don't have to contemplate anything too serious or worry about how this week's going to go with my father.

My preferred state of being is numb. I find it makes everything much more tolerable.

"Can I get you another?" The bartender points at my glass and smiles.

"Yes, please. Extra lemon twists this time. And I'll have some truffle fries as well." He nods and goes to ring in my order.

Looking out beyond the fence separating the bar from the beach, there are a ton of people on the sand and in the water. Rows of umbrellas completely obscure some parts of the ocean from my view.

Wannabe influencers fly drones in the air above them while they jump up and down and pose and put on fake smiles. I can't help but roll my eyes.

The beach is overcrowded for my tastes, but there's some type of conflict starting up between some men with jackets marked *Conservation Police* and a guy who seems to have set up a tent structure near the shoreline, right in the middle of a bunch of tourists. They seem to be urging him to take it down, and he's not happy about it. A couple of other guys have come to defend him by the looks of it. There's a lot of yelling and animated hand movements from both sides.

As I look on with interest as more and more people gather around the tent, including a regular cop now, with a gun, I realize the scene reminds me somehow of being back home in the city.

It's somewhat soothing to know that I can find a bit of trouble, a bit of excitement wherever I want and that there's an underbelly, a realness and darkness wherever I go.

It's not all tourists here after all. There are people with actual problems beyond whether they got the room upgrade they wanted, or whether their diamonds are large enough. And I do like trouble.

As more and more people become involved in the conflict, voices rising and arms wildly gesticulating, I wonder if maybe this destination wasn't such a terrible choice after all.

———

The next morning

"What's on your agenda for today, dear?" My father glances up from his phone as I stab at pieces of melon and pineapple in the bowl in front of me.

We're sitting beachside at the casual breakfast spot at the hotel, and the sun is rising from the horizon, casting a pretty pink and orange glow across the sky.

I resist the urge to smirk at my father trying to act all conversational, as if we have breakfast together all the time, and as if he actually cares what I'm going to do today. Fake fuck playing happy families for a week each year.

He has some mega hotel points membership that results in us getting a complimentary continental breakfast each day. Which means I have to spend time with him every morning. *Oh joy, what fun.*

At least on trips like these, he lets me do my own thing during most of the day, and in the evening, aside from the odd dinner, he's usually also busy with his various other pursuits.

The whole breakfast thing makes me laugh. The hotel chain getting people to spend thousands of dollars per stay and then buttering them up with a miniature croissant, some granola, and a puny plate of fruit that probably only cost them a couple of bucks. Even rich people like getting things for free, no matter what it is, it seems.

I've perused the catalog of guest activities at our hotel and have absolutely no interest in weaving flower garlands, going on some stuffy architectural tour, or doing yoga with a bunch of pretentious assholes who only do that type of thing on vacation so they can post it on their stupid social media.

"I've decided to try surfing." It's the one option that looked remotely interesting other than sitting at the bar, which I also plan to do again later and for much of this trip. I figure that part is self-explanatory, so I leave it out.

I've never tried surfing, but it's always fascinated me and seems like a thrilling sport. Even though I haven't done it before, for whatever reason growing up I had posters of surfers on my walls in addition to the usual crap you'd expect to see a girl adorn her bedroom with.

Besides, I like individual activities where I don't have to interact with anyone else too much, and the ocean has always been a peaceful refuge for me when I've had the opportunity to be near it.

Surfing looks like something that will challenge my body, and I'm all about challenging my body, which is partially why I'm covered in tattoos and a few piercings. I'm not scared of pain or breaking a bone. Plus, it'll get me away from my father for a few hours, which is always a major perk.

"Mmhmm, interesting," he says, not sounding interested at all, as his phone rings. He holds out his index finger, indicating he needs to take the call, and walks off to a quieter spot, leaving me there to eat the rest of my meal alone. The way I prefer it.

He's been on his phone for most of this trip so far, and so it's been a sandwich of awkward conversations with me sitting there while he talks in low tones to someone who's probably sketchy as fuck. That's basically how dinner went yesterday, and how I expect the rest of our time together to go on this trip.

My father left the hotel late in the evening last night. I saw him through the window and I don't think he noticed me looking out as he departed.

I have no idea if he went to do some kind of shady business deal or cheat on his current wife with someone he met on a dating app for married men. Maybe he even visited a strip club or hired a sex worker. I could see him doing any of those things, the dirty philandering fuck.

It's not that I have a problem with sex work. It's more that my father is married and it doesn't impact him sticking it in other women at his leisure. Never has been concerned about that. He used to do the same to my mother, and if there's one thing I've learned in my life, it's that men never change.

He doesn't need to worry about me tattling to my stepmother, though. I drew the short straw when it comes to mothers, someone once said, and it's true. Abandoned by my birthmother, disowned by my adoptive mother, and my stepmother is even worse. Three strikes and I'm out, and I don't need any of them, anyway.

My current stepmother is like some trophy that my father parades around when he's trying to impress his business acquaintances. There's no love lost between us, and I'm sure she's pissed that he takes me on this mandatory trip once a year. He met her at a party where rich men go to meet much younger women when he was still married to my mother, and she's half his age, making her younger than me.

She looks pretty good, I'll give her that. She's always all dolled up with her face perfectly beat—in a makeup way, that is. I don't know if he hits her or not, but I wouldn't be surprised with his violent temper—and she dresses well, usually in tight-fitting sparkly dresses. On his dime, of course.

My father doesn't return for the rest of breakfast, so I head back to the room by myself to get ready to ride some waves.

A couple of hours later

"I'm here for my surfing lesson."

"What's the name?" The woman in the white polo shirt with the surfing school logo on it looks up at me from behind the outdoor desk and smiles.

"Devon Duke."

The woman runs her finger down the list of bookings for the day. Her finger stops about halfway down and stabs the sheet of paper.

"Ah, there," she says. "I see you. They're still out in the water, but they'll be ready for you soon. Take a seat over there and someone will come to get you when they're ready for you." She points to one of the sun loungers beside the hotel pool.

I nod and head over to the striped chair. I lower myself into the sun lounger and lay back, the umbrella providing much-needed overhead shade, as I wait for my lesson.

I've changed into a bikini with a bright pink-orange rash guard over the top, and covered myself in what felt like a full bottle of sunscreen. There's definitely no shade to protect me out in the ocean when the sun's at its strongest.

Gazing at the rippling water of the swimming pool in front of me, I don't know how people spend all their vacation just lounging like this all day, every day. It seems boring after a while. I like to get out and explore things, mainly the bar scene, but I'm not opposed to the odd hike or other adventure.

I'm getting a little nervous about this surfing lesson, though, a little bundle of nerves making itself known in my gut. I rarely find myself outside of my comfort zone because I tend to do what I want when I want, and there's a certain pattern to that, but this is something I've never done and I'm going to be at the mercy of whoever is teaching me out in the ocean.

For once, I'm not going to be in control and I'm not sure how I feel about it. Oh well, better than hanging out with my father all day.

After ten minutes or so, a guy in a polo shirt with the same logo as the woman who checked me in approaches me.

"Ma'am," he says politely with a gentle voice. "Your instructor is ready for you now."

I stand up and turn to face the beach, and it's teeming with people.

"See that guy over there, in the red shorts with the tattoos, and the real big one on his chest?"

I squint and try to find the person he's pointing to. The beach is busy, and I don't see anyone matching that description at first, but then I see a guy emerge from behind an umbrella who fits the bill.

"Go meet him over there when you're ready. His name is Skyler."

I nod and head over to where he pointed.

The guy he directed me to is walking in the opposite direction, back towards the admin desk, and I have to call out to stop him.

"Excuse me," I say, and he looks back at me, a little confused. "Are you Skyler?" I ask.

"Yeah, I am Skyler." He nods, still sounding a bit mystified, looking me up and down.

This is weird. He's looking at me with the expression some guys give when they've been up to no good, and someone's hunted them down to confront them about it. Have I approached some random guy instead of my instructor? That would be a great start.

"Um, hi. I think I have a surfing lesson with you?"

"Oh," he says, nodding, recognition dawning in his eyes. "Great, I'll just have you sit over there for a moment."

He points at a few seats under an umbrella next to some surfboards.

"Sit on any of those, and I'll be right back."

I take a seat and wait a few more minutes as the pit of nerves continues to grow in my stomach. I hope this lesson goes okay.

He appears again, this time wearing a shirt. For a moment, I'm confused by his added clothing, and not really sure what's going on. Are we going in the water? Am I still having my lesson? But his energy appears to have shifted, and he's smiling at me now.

He does a demo of surfing basics, and provides some ground rules so that I don't dive off the side of my board and hit my head, and so I hopefully avoid plowing into a group of tourists.

While standing on the sand, he shows me how to get up on my board as if it were on a wave. Everything makes sense while he explains it, and he makes it look super easy. He's so confident and looks so natural.

I'm suspicious that he's done this for a while and so it might not be the same for me.

"You have a turn now," he says.

I comply, lying down on the board as he instructed.

He says excitedly, "A wave is coming. Paddle!"

I paddle as if I'm catching an imaginary wave above the sand, and he yells, "Paddle faster!"

I feel like a bit of an idiot, lying on the board with a ton of people around, pretending to paddle, but I do it anyway, my arms moving faster and faster.

"Stand up!" he yells.

I lift myself up slowly to make sure I get it right. I manage to stand on the board on my first try, no doubt because I'm on the sand, which makes it a lot easier than on the water.

"Good job," he says, and gives me a high five.

It's cheesy, but I return the high five. Hopefully, I'll be able to replicate getting on the board when we're out in the ocean.

"Now do it again." Is he for real? Ugh. I hate being a spectacle, and this is like my worst nightmare.

There are people everywhere on the beach, some sitting quite close to us, and I can see them watching. I'm used to being good at things in my comfort zone, and I feel embarrassed play-acting surfing in front of everyone.

We go through the process again, and this time when he yells, "Stand up!" I try to get up more quickly, to get this over with. In doing so, I trip and end up falling off the side of the board.

Luckily, I land on my feet on the sand, but I notice a guy behind me pointing and laughing in my direction and the instructor cracks up too. I can tell he's not laughing meanly. He's more amused by my clumsiness, but I still feel myself flushing a deep beet red.

I giggle nervously. Jesus, if I can't do this on the sand, how the hell do I stand a chance in the water? This is incredibly embarrassing. Why didn't I just go to the bar instead? That's more in line with my expertise.

"One more time," he says, directing me as if he doesn't want that memory of awkwardly falling into the sand imprinted on my brain before we try it out for real. I hesitate, and he says, "Come on. If only so I get to make you laugh again." He grins.

I comply, giggling awkwardly and feeling even more flushed, but despite my embarrassment, this time I stand up on the board without making a complete fool of myself.

"Awesome!" He grins and high-fives me again, so hard that my hand stings. "We're almost ready. Now, what are the two things that you need to remember?"

"Don't dive off the side of the board and hit my head."

He gives me a thumbs-up and nods. "Yes! And?"

"Don't surf into groups of tourists."

"Haha yes, look in the direction you want to go and focus on the gaps." He claps his hands and bounces on the balls of his feet, grinning. "Okay, we're ready to get into the water."

He shows me how to carry my board, and then peels off his shirt, and I have to keep my jaw from dropping because it turns out his body is glorious. I didn't notice it when he first walked towards me, mainly because I was squinting into the sun, but the guy who is about to take me on my first-ever surfing lesson looks fucking good. Whoever assigned him to me needs a big thank you, because I get to stare at this majestic individual for over an hour while he teaches me how to do this whole surfing thing.

The strange thing is, he looks slightly familiar, but I can't put a finger on it. It's like I'm seeing someone out of context and can't quite place them because they're doing or wearing something totally different from what I'm used to. I definitely haven't seen this guy shirtless before, because I'd remember all of his gorgeous body art.

I love a man with tattoos. It usually means they have an interesting or at least funny story behind each one, are not stuck up or 'too good' to mark their bodies, and are into a certain amount of pain. Just like me.

He's not the tallest guy, several inches above my own five-foot-five, but he is muscular as fuck, which I guess you'd expect from someone who surfs every day.

He has an arrogant lopsided smirk and a cheeky grin, and although he's wearing sunglasses, I imagine his eyes to be playful, silently mocking me and my lack of surfing skills.

His deep tan shows he's clearly a local, born and raised on the beach. He has the slightest hint of stubble framing his face, his cheeks ever so slightly pocked, his face and shoulders covered in a subtle smattering of tiny dark brown freckles.

If I'd known he came with the lesson, I might have signed up for extra sessions just so I could perv at him a bit more. Maybe I still will. Luckily it's near the start of my vacation so I have the opportunity to schedule more time with him if I choose.

I find it hard to avert my eyes from his rippling physique, but I follow his instructions on how to get into the water and onto the board.

The water is cool and refreshing against the scorching sun. He climbs onto his board in one smooth movement. When I get waist-deep, I hoist myself up and flop awkwardly onto my stomach while he watches.

"Is that how you get onto your board?" He cracks up, but I can tell that he's teasing and being playful.

"No! It's just how I did this time." I grin back, feeling a mild flush creep onto my cheeks.

As we paddle out toward the break, to my surprise, he somehow hooks his foot onto my surfboard and says, "I got you."

From his own board, he starts to drag me around on mine with what seems like great ease. I've never seen anything like it. I wasn't expecting it, and it's incredibly hot. His strength and his prowess in the ocean are blowing my mind after only a couple of minutes. I watch his shoulders and back muscles competently propel us through the water as he tows me out to the break, and I feel a pleasant twinge between my legs. This guy is making me wet, and it's not because I'm literally in the water.

As we paddle out to the lineup where surfers wait to take their turn catching a wave, or rather as he tows me out with his powerful muscles that are getting me all hot and bothered, he turns his head toward me. "How old are you, then?" he asks, grinning. "Must be like... late twenties?"

Not afraid to ask questions other people might find inappropriate, I see, although he's being kind with his guess. Interesting. I like a man who doesn't give a crap about etiquette and niceties. Someone who feels comfortable enough in his skin to ask cheeky questions that he wants the answer to, without worrying about offending someone. I'm the same way, generally. On the other hand, he might just be flirting with me like he probably does with all of his students.

"Ha! Trying to get a bigger tip with your flattery?" I joke back.

"Oh, you're giving me the tip? Thought it worked the other way." He winks at me playfully and his eyes sparkle in the sun, his sun-kissed skin crinkling at the corners.

Damn, he's really cocky. And he *is* flirting. But that was a pretty forward thing to say, so maybe I misheard. Maybe that means something else here.

"Sorry, what?" It's not often that someone has me a little tilted sideways.

"Nothing, I'd just be happy to give you any kind of tip you want," he says, shrugging and turning around to face the rolling, gentle blue waves as they head towards the shore. "Restaurants, bars, things to do, anything. Follow me," he says, starting to paddle without me this time.

"Not giving me a tow anymore?" I ask. "I have good upper body strength, but I also like being dragged around by strong men." Two can play this game.

"Nah," he turns to wink at me again. "I reckon you've got this. Plus, that costs extra."

He laughs and paddles off more quickly now, his muscular shoulders, back, triceps and biceps continuing to mesmerize me as he uses them to slice his board through the water. His body is a canvas for surf and island art and tribal patterns, and as I watch him I want to know the story behind each of them.

He gets further away from me, and I realize I'm meant to follow him and not just stare at his gorgeous body, so I also start paddling.

I meet him out near where the other surfers are congregating. He's already chit-chatting with a couple of them like they're old mates, which they probably are. I don't pay too much attention, though. I'm laser-focused on him and my board and trying to remember all the things he taught me back on the sand.

"So how old are you really?" he asks again, smiling at me with his straight, white teeth. He has nice teeth, besides everything else I've seen so far. He sits up on his board, his legs dangling over either side. "I truly thought you were in your late twenties, but from your reaction, I'm guessing early thirties. You don't look it, though."

"Thirty-five," I say, cautiously. I don't normally share personal information with anybody unless I really need to. But it's like he's disarming me with his cheeky grin in the middle of the ocean, and it seems like an innocent question. Which is weird, because I rarely think any question is truly innocent. Everybody has a motive, an agenda.

He presses his lips together and nods, seemingly impressed by my answer. "You look great. Wouldn't have guessed it." Sweet of him to say, maybe an attempt to fuel my confidence and maybe catch a wave. "Well, then, how old do you think I am?" He grins at me and gestures at his face and body, and I let my gaze follow his hands across his hard physique. "Come on, I won't be offended."

I feel shy to guess. I take a closer look at him and realize he's one of those people who could be within a thirty-or-so-year age range. It's like he's asking me because he knows he looks way younger than he is. I would have guessed closer to late twenties for him, too, but maybe he's much older and that explains his wisdom and cockiness.

For someone who rarely gets frazzled, I'm still feeling a little giggly around him. What the fuck is wrong with me today?

"Um. I don't know. You tell me," I say, feeling a stupid smile spreading across my face.

"Truly, you won't offend me." He winks again, trying to coax out a guess, but I'm having trouble getting the words out.

The last time I acted like such a schoolgirl, I was one, and even then I was on the surly side. What the hell is this man doing to me?

"Alright, I'll tell you," he says, after I continue to not be able to speak the English language any longer, and instead resort to a simple shrug. "How about if I said I'm ten years older than you?"

He paddles off and motions for me to follow him again. I catch up to him.

"You're forty-five? Well, I would have guessed younger," I reply. He really does look good for someone in his mid-forties. "Late twenties or something."

"That's why I said I wouldn't be offended," he says, grinning. "I feel great and I take care of myself."

I can definitely see that's the case, but I don't reply out loud and instead just keep following behind his surfboard. *Shit girl, pull yourself together. You have some surfing to do.*

After we get out to the break, where quite a few more surfers are gathered, we continue to chat until the swell picks up again. He tells me a bit about muscle memory and fight-or-flight responses, and how important it is to keep riding a wave as far as you can without bailing, so your body doesn't get used to fleeing from a perceived threat partway through every time. I like how his approach is science-based besides the more general instruction I was expecting.

"Alright, start preparing yourself," he says, spinning my board so I'm facing directly toward the shore.

As we float there, I get the impression he's looking at me from behind, checking me out. I don't mind that at all. It makes me feel a little heat between my legs even though the water is keeping the air cool around us.

His hand grazes my ankle as he rearranges the leash that he wrapped around it earlier, untangling it and moving it to the side, preparing me for the next wave. It's an insignificant gesture, but it's almost like he's taking ownership of me, making sure I'm arranged just the way he wants me. I imagine that's what it would be like if he tied me up and controlled me, leashed me in a way. I don't think I would mind that one bit, and my pussy clenches at the thought. Who knew surfing was going to be fun *and* sexy?

He taps my board and says, "Alright, get ready!"

Oh my god, it's happening.

I position myself on the board as he instructed, and then hear him yelling. "Start paddling! Start paddling!"

I feel the swell of a wave coming up the back of the board and there's a sudden, powerful rush of water beneath me. I think he shoved the surfboard from behind to make sure I got on the wave because suddenly I'm flying across the water.

"Stand up! Stand up!" He screams the instruction at me and I go into the mode of trying to figure out where to put my hands, my feet, and most importantly, where to look.

Look where you're wanting to go, he'd said. *Don't look down, don't look at the people in front of you, look for the gaps.* So I do my best to put all these things together at once, pulling myself up, and suddenly I'm standing on the board.

I'm surfing! I put my arms out to keep my balance and then remember I need to stay low, so I bend my knees and try to lean so that I'm facing in the right direction, looking in the right places.

Oh my god, what a rush! I look towards the shore as I coast along the beautiful turquoise water, the slow, rolling wave propelling me. It's an inimitable feeling, like nothing I've ever experienced before. I ride the wave for what feels like a decent length, until it eventually dies, and I flop into the ocean with the grace of a fainting goat. Oh well, I technically surfed. I'll take it. What an adrenalin rush!

I paddle back out to where he's floating alongside some other surfers, chatting away casually, and he gives me a high five so hard that it stings my palm and sends a shock down my arm. He likes to hit hard. I wonder if that extends to spanking.

"Yeah, girl!" he cries. "You did it! Nice work!"

A couple of people who he's chatting with also call out and clap. I know he's just doing his job, but it's been a while since anyone's told me I've done a good job of anything, so this seems foreign but also kind of nice. He helps me attempt to catch several more waves, some resulting in spectacular wipeouts and others more of a success.

I keep paddling back to him each time, readying myself for the next wave, and as I do, I realize the waves are unique. They're never the same. You can't recreate them. You can't chain them up or put them in a cage. The waves are free. The waves are impermanent. Yet the ocean is permanent and powerful. I think I'm already in love with this new hobby, although I'm not very good at it yet.

And, as I continue to take sneak peeks at his body throughout the rest of the lesson, I realize I'm also in a bit of lust with Skyler.

CHAPTER SIX

Skyler

A few hours later

"You should have seen the girl I took out for a lesson today, Dom. You missed out." Rake and Zeke both nod enthusiastically. Rake lets out a low whistle from his spot on the living room couch.

Dom flicks on his lighter, waving the flame as a slow grin spreads across his face. "Hot, like fire?" We all nod.

"Sweet! Nice tits, ass or what?" Dom stretches as he asks, showing off his new tattoo. Like all of us have, it's a surfboard, and he's incorporated some hibiscus flowers. Apparently, he thinks the ladies will find it pretty. I guess it looks good even though it reminds me of a design you could get on collectibles at one of the many local souvenir stores.

"I mean, yeah, all the above. But she was different from the other ones we usually see."

"I can concur," Zeke nods. "A fucking knockout. Don't think she noticed us. She was too busy trying to stand on her board and follow Skyler's instructions. But we noticed her, that's for sure."

We all grin at the thought of the pretty lady. Often we'll tag along while the others are giving surfing lessons, and have a bit of a laugh when our students wipe out. Good backup in case anything happens while we're out there, too. Although most people know who we are, and wisely keep their distance, the odd rival group will occasionally look for trouble mid-lesson. Usually, nothing a good smack across the head with a surfboard can't fix.

"Different how?" Dom raises an eyebrow. "And, more importantly, did you ask her out?"

"I don't know how to explain it. Just... something about her I can't put my finger on. And no, I didn't ask her out. You know I get shit from management when I do that."

"Ah, you're fucking chicken." He laughs at me, mocking me as usual, and I punch him in the side of his chest, probably a little too hard, right where his tattoo wraps around. He doesn't flinch, but I see a flash of pain in his eyes. Good, nobody calls me a chicken.

"Fuck off, I have a plan," I explain. "Waiting until I'm technically off the clock. She knows where to find me."

I'm hoping she'll just rent a board and 'happen by' while I'm out there on the water in the next day or so. She seemed interested in me, especially when I casually mentioned I was single, just to test her reaction. I saw the look on her face, like she was intrigued and wanted to find out more. So I wouldn't be surprised if she rents a board and tries to paddle out there by herself in case I happen to be there, too.

It would be a good reason to strike up a conversation without my corporate overlords getting mad at me for breaching their policy about guest relations. It's a stupid rule, but I put up with their bullshit for various reasons.

Rake looks at me with a sneer, clearly skeptical of my plan. "I still think it's ridiculous we haven't branched out on our own. We don't need someone making us clock in and out, working these jobs that pay peanuts when we could be running the show ourselves. You could totally run a surfing business like that, Sky."

"Thank you for your confidence in me, but I'll give you two reasons, bro," I say, even though I've explained it to him several times before. "One, it's a fucking good cover story that helps to disguise some of our primary business activities. Because, like you say, it doesn't seem to make any sense. How can someone accuse us of doing what we're really doing when we're working jobs like this, apparently 'to get by'? And then second, you can't go out on your own and get a steady flow of customers from the luxury hotels. They're the ones that we want to know more about. They're the ones we get intel from. It's so easy, you know? They think we're there to teach them how to surf on teeny tiny waves so they can go home and tell their friends how cool they are. When really, we're taking our time out there chatting away, mining them for any information that could be useful."

It's surprising what people are often willing to tell you when they're out of their comfort zone. And how all the little tidbits they share can end up being very helpful when you add them all up.

"Also, *tit*-bits." Rake grins deviously. Such a one-track mind when it comes to the ladies. "You're devious, bro." He laughs as if he's heard none of this before, slapping me on the back with his long, ropy arm. It stings, but I don't let it show. It's my rule not to show weakness.

Anyway, I can handle it because I'm just as tough as he is. Sometimes more. And you only have to explain things to me once, unlike Rake.

"I don't have the patience for it, though," says Dom. "Having to like... be all nice to people. Not use swear words around them. Be patient when they can't stand up on the fucking board. Keep quiet when they accidentally surf in front of locals who've waited all day for a wave. Not laugh out loud when they wipe out on a tiny one."

I can't help but laugh. "Yeah, you'd be a right dick. One-star Yelp reviews for you."

Zeke snorts because it's true.

Dom scratches his head. "What the fuck is a Yelp review?"

I can't help but snort this time. He has no idea what's going on. No social media, and if he wants to look something up, he's absolutely useless at finding it. I usually have to help him. But he's skilled in other ways, I guess.

He's our muscle. He's loyal. And I've found in life that loyalty is all that really matters.

CHAPTER SEVEN

Dom

M y phone rings, and glancing at the caller ID, I see that it's one of Tane Brown's men. Or goons, as we call them behind their backs.

Tane is a scary man, not because of his muscles, but because of his power. Old money, also from this island, but he currently lives on a larger one just up the chain.

Zeke and Skyler get the calls involving the more strategic operations of our business, but I get the ones where muscle is needed. I don't take it personally. I know my strengths.

We're responsible for doing what we can to protect this island, as well as assisting Tane with certain aspects of his business operations here, and it's a job we take seriously. Skyler's dad was officially in charge of protecting this island before us, and it's been handed down to him.

A legacy. He's almost considered royalty around here in certain circles, although he'd never put it that way. Zeke's dad was involved too, in his time, working with Skyler's dad.

This island has deep roots that are very intertwined, for better and for worse.

"Yeah, what's up?" I answer the call, keeping my voice low.

"Dom, man. We have a job for you." It's not uncommon to receive an assignment from Tane's guys, although they haven't called me for a while. I'm curious to see what they have on their minds. The voice on the other end is clipped and to the point.

"Oh yeah? What kind of job?" I try to act casual, but I'm hoping it's something that allows me to use my fists. Those are the kinds of jobs I prefer, and it's been a little while since I last got to hear the satisfying crunch of my knuckles connecting with a human skull.

I turn my fist over that's not holding the phone and examine it. My tattooed knuckles are also covered in scars, and I enjoy thinking about all the reasons why.

We've been doing this for a while now, protecting this island. As much as I like to use my strength, Skyler and Zeke like to use their brains. Both are born leaders, not that Skyler sees himself that way, but he underestimates himself. And Zeke, so organized and analytical, always making sure we stay together and work as a team.

And Rake... well, Rake just likes to tag along for the ride and make himself useful where he can. He might come across as the funny one in our group, the class clown, but there's a depth to him that not everybody sees, and he's also stronger than he looks.

"It's a girl." The voice on the other end of the phone is cryptic.

A girl. Not something we typically deal with. We prefer weapons and roughing up locals who don't play by Tane's rules and the informal laws of the island. Occasionally transporting other goods that need to pass through here.

"We don't harm women, too much at least. You know that," I say. They know that's one of our own rules. We might occasionally pay a visit and instill fear in a female if they fail to repay a debt, but it's not normally our style to do anything beyond that. We have no problem punching a man's face in if he breaks one of the island's rules, though.

Tane's into some incredibly shady shit, and there's nothing he won't do. He knows our group has boundaries, but he tries to push them occasionally. Maybe this is one of those times.

"It's a protection job," says the clipped voice. "We need you to hold her for us. She's collateral for a debt."

"What does that entail, exactly?"

"Like I said, we need you to hold her for us." The voice pauses. "You can do whatever you like with her while she's with you."

"Oh, really?" I respond. Now he has my interest. "How long do we need to keep her for?"

I wonder what the other guys are going to think of this.

"No more than ten days," says the voice. "That's how long our associate has to repay his debt."

"How is this 'associate' connected with this girl?" Skyler's been teaching me to ask more questions rather than just accepting information at face value. I'm trying.

"You ask too many questions. But it's her father."

"How old is she? An adult, I am assuming? We're not babysitters."

"Yes, an adult. Not that it's any of your business, but he crossed a contact back on the mainland and is here on what he believes to be a business trip. His debt has been on-sold to us, and he's evidently having a little trouble accessing funds, as his primary asset source has been frozen."

"I see." I need to know more. There must be an end game to this. Tane wouldn't ask us to help if he didn't have a grand plan, or if he simply intends on disposing of her after the time is up. "And if he doesn't repay it? What happens then?"

The voice is clinical. "She'll be auctioned off to the highest bidder. And I have a feeling she'll attract a high price. Maybe higher than the value of the debt. We've already received some interest. Even if the debt is repaid, we might reassess our next steps."

Jesus, these guys are ruthless. We make sure to do just enough to stay on their good side, but we try to avoid getting involved with the human trafficking and hard drugs that they also control across the island chain.

"Oh, so she's attractive?" He's really piquing my interest here. Numerous buyers bidding on a woman. I wonder how someone determines the price to purchase a human.

This isn't something we've done before, harboring a captive, and it's definitely on the cusp of what we're prepared to do. I wonder what Zeke will have to say. Skyler is slightly more mellow than him, but they both tend to be overly cautious. Whereas I'm usually up for anything. And, well, Rake is up for anything involving a woman.

"You'll see," the voice on the other end lets out an icy chuckle, causing a shiver to creep up my back. I have no doubt that Tane's men are evil, just like him. I'm no angel myself, but my soul is just dark, whereas his simply doesn't exist.

"Do you expect anyone to come looking for her?" I glance at my free hand again and crack my knuckles. I wouldn't mind an excuse to use my fists, maybe curry a little favor with our captive to give her reason to be grateful to me. Nothing like a damsel in distress who owes you their life.

"That's for you to worry about," says the voice. "But again, she's yours to do with as you please while she's with you. Just don't do anything that will... lower her market value too much, if you catch my drift."

"That leaves a lot of options." I can't help but grin.

The person at the other end of the phone directs me to stay tuned for further instructions, and then they end the call.

It's been a while since I've been around a woman. I tend to avoid them. Sure, I'll have a little casual fun with a random woman now and then. No strings attached, a one-time event where nobody catches feelings.

But that's where I leave things. Because ultimately women are dangerous, and from my experience, they inflict nothing but pain.

CHAPTER EIGHT

Devon

The next day

My father went out again last night. Once again, I saw him leave from the window of my hotel room. But we'd agreed on having breakfast every morning while we're here, and there's no sign of him.

The past couple of mornings, he's knocked on my door and we've walked down to the restaurant together. I figure maybe I didn't hear today's knock over the loud music I've been playing since I woke up. He must have gone down ahead of me. I've been enjoying the contrast of blaring heavy metal with the fancy sensibility of this grand old hotel. Makes me feel like a rebel, doing something that would be frowned upon by the other guests, and that's one of my favorite feelings in the world.

I head down to the restaurant, expecting to see him at one of the dining tables, but he's not there.

I approach the host stand, and the host beams at me. She's way too perky for this early in the morning. The sun has barely risen.

"Did Frankton Duke check in for breakfast?" I ask.

The host checks her guest list twice, squinting at the document. She juts out her bottom lip, shrugging. "No, ma'am. He hasn't checked in yet."

How odd. "Can I check in without him and grab a table? He must have gone to the gym or a meeting or something."

"Yes, why of course, ma'am."

The host smiles, grabs a menu, and escorts me to a table directly in front of the beach.

This time of day, it's more peaceful. Just small groups of tourists taking photos of the sunrise while the beach services workers set up umbrellas and sun loungers in neat rows. Much nicer than the over-crowding that develops later in the day. I guess it's not the worst view in the world, and I'm starting to appreciate and even enjoy the sound of the waves gently crashing on the shore.

It reminds me of my surfing lesson and the rush that I got when I got to stand up on some waves. Also reminds me of my surfing instructor's incredibly hot body.

I have breakfast by myself. They bring me the whole yogurt, gra-nola, fruit and pastry extravaganza while I scroll through my phone and send Donkey a picture of the beach view. He texts me back with the view of his apartment, a grungy city alleyway. It gives me a pang of wanting to be back there, with the blaring car horns and alarm noises and general grittiness.

Surprisingly, my father still hasn't turned up by the time I'm done. I try calling him, but it goes straight to voicemail. Odd. Maybe he's on a business call. I text him just in case, asking him where he is, but there's no reply. This is super confusing.

There's no check, seeing the breakfast is complimentary, so I get up from the table and head back up to my room.

Well, at least I didn't have to make small talk with him over break-fast, I guess. He's probably doing some dodgy deal somewhere and forgot to tell me, or maybe he stayed overnight with some woman. It wouldn't be the first time he hasn't followed through on a plan.

Still, I can't drown out a nagging thought in the back of my head that maybe something bad has happened to him.

CHAPTER NINE

Rake

"So we're getting a girl?"

The thought of having a woman under our roof makes me smile as I sit at the kitchen table with Zeke, who's working on his laptop, and Dom, who's eating a sandwich.

"And we can get her to do whatever we want while she's with us?" I steeple my hands together in the style of Montgomery Burns. "Excellent."

Zeke grins an evil little grin. He comes across as way more mature and professional than I do, but underneath, he's got a sick, twisted mind, just like me. He also likes the ladies almost as much as I do.

"That's what they tell me."

"I'm sure we'll find plenty of ways to have some fun with this situation. Especially if she's hot."

The thought of having a captive, especially a female, sounds interesting to me. We haven't done anything like this before. It sounds like it could be fun having a hot piece of ass living under our roof who has to do whatever we want.

Dom's phone beeps and he pulls it out of his pocket to check it.

"Well, well, well. One of Tane's men sent through a picture of her." He lets out a low whistle as he examines the image. "Fuck, she's really hot. A complete smoke show."

"Seriously?" I crane my neck to look at his phone, but he turns it away so I can't see.

"Nah, bro. You have to wait. Sucker! In the meantime, this one's going in my spank bank." He grins at me.

So unfair. But also totally something I would do, so I can't really blame him.

I try to grab for the phone one more time, but he's not having it, and despite my long arms, he's so broad I can't reach around him to get to it.

"Fuck you and your big rectangular body!"

He shrugs in a mock apology.

Fine, I don't need to see her yet. If Dom says she's hot, I believe him. He's very picky when it comes to women. Too picky. I'm here for a good time, not for a relationship. I'll wait it out, and then she'll be mine.

"When's she arriving?" I ask. "Or do we have to go get her from somewhere?"

He shakes his head.

"She arrives tonight. She'll be dropped here."

"And then she's going to get dropped right on my dick."

I grin and feel my cock twitch at the thought.

"Settle down, buddy. You're not going to just rip her clothes off on arrival. Plus, I have first right of admission, seeing they called me about this little opportunity we have spread out before us."

"Just like she's going to be." I grin, and then bite my bottom lip at the thought. "This is going to be fun." I wiggle my eyebrows.

Dom snorts. "I know you'll give her a warm welcome."

"Oh, I'm planning on it." It's been a while since a girl has been in this house, and I'm hungry.

CHAPTER TEN

Devon

I take the stairs up to my room, and something just feels off when I pass through the entrance. I can't explain it. My hypervigilance kicks in as if there's a weird energy in the room that wasn't there before, and a shiver runs up my spine.

My alertness can be heightened by tiny changes sometimes, supposedly an after-effect of past trauma according to a short-lived therapy journey, but I can't remember ever not feeling this way. Perhaps it's just that a room attendant came in and left some fresh towels or something, but I can't shake the nagging feeling that there's a presence here, although I can't see anything untoward.

Heck, it's an old hotel. Maybe there are ghosts.

I move further into the room, and as I go to look in the closet and under the bed like I always do, a gloved hand reaches around from behind me and covers my mouth.

"Don't scream," says a gruff voice, "or I will kill you and your father."

Fuck. I've always worried that one day this would happen. That one of my father's shady business deals would go south and I'd end up bearing the repercussions of his poor decisions. I guess today's the fucking day.

Gnashing my teeth, I attempt to bite the hand that's pressed against my mouth, but the glove is thick and even my sharpest teeth can't pierce it.

I feel an object pressed into my back and I assume it's a gun rather than a hard cock, but you never know. Either way, it's not wanted.

"You're going to follow me out to the waiting car. Don't call out and don't attract attention. Just walk normally and smile and look pretty, or I will kill you and I couldn't care less who sees. And then I will kill your father, and I will make sure it hurts."

There's a chill in his voice that sends a shiver down my spine and sheds any doubt that this man will keep his word.

"Do you understand me?" he asks.

I nod, and let out a muffled, "Mmhmm."

I'd normally fight, but my deepest instinct is telling me not to. As much as I disapprove of my father, I'd rather not see him being flayed alive or having his intestines pulled out in front of me. That would be distasteful, even though he might deserve it for some of the things he's done.

Another man suddenly emerges from the bathroom. He's tall with a scarred face, and he's pointing another gun at me.

"I'm sort of sad you're behaving yourself, sweetheart." He winks at me and smiles, revealing yellowed, sharp teeth. "And to think, I was all prepared to have a little fun with you to get you to be more compliant."

I try not to react as he pulls a knife out of his pocket and flips open the blade.

"Put the knife away for now, man," says the man who grabbed me. "We've been directed not to reduce her market value unless we really need to."

The yellow-toothed man sighs and puts his blade away.

"Market value?" I sputter, as the gloved man lowers his hand from my mouth.

"Don't ask questions," he snarls. "Come with us, and like I said, no trouble from you. Pretend you're just going on a nice outing with two of your closest friends."

"My closest friends are better-looking." I can't resist.

The yellow-toothed man snarls at me and lunges in my direction, but the guy with the gun nudges me forward and motions for him to back off.

They lead me out of the room, and I continue to feel the muzzle of the gun against my lower back as we make our way down the spiral stairwell.

I comply with their instructions and try not to draw any unnecessary attention to our little group. I stop feeling the gun against my back as we move into a more public area, and then through the main driveway and into a waiting vehicle.

My brain is working in slow motion. Am I making the right decision, not making a scene? Going with them without putting up a fight seems risky, but having my brains splattered across the walls of this grandiose hotel isn't how I wanted to spend my vacation, either.

The yellow-toothed guy hops into the driver's seat, and the guy who initially grabbed me sits next to me in the back.

As we drive off from the hotel, the guy next to me grabs a blindfold and ties it around my face. He doesn't do a great job of securing it, and I realize he hasn't fully obscured my vision. What a newbie. I could have done better myself. I quite enjoy blindfolding people for... reasons, not that these two would be my choice for that type of activity. Gross.

"Sit on your hands or I'll tie you up," he says, gesturing at me with the gun.

I comply, because he still has a weapon and the guy in the front clearly wants to hurt me. Plus, it might be useful to have my hands free later. He places a large rectangle of duct tape over my mouth, attaching it firmly.

We spend the journey in silence. Out of the bottom of my blindfold, I notice the guy next to me put the gun on the floor in front of us. It's a shame he didn't put it on the center console between us, or I could have grabbed it and shot him in the face. Then again, the guy driving has a gun and a knife, and I'm sure an in-car shootout could get messy.

Given they attacked me from behind and stayed behind me on our way to the vehicle, I haven't gotten a good look at him, but I have a feeling that's the only weapon he's carrying. I tend to trust my gut, and it's kept me alive for thirty-five years so far.

It feels like we speed up on some type of highway for part of the trip, and then the car pulls into an area with a lower speed limit and the odd speed bump, maybe a residential neighborhood.

After what feels like somewhere between twenty minutes and an hour, the car slows. It's super disorienting being blindfolded, and I'm not familiar with the island beyond the hotel, so it's hard to say exactly how far we've traveled or how long it's been.

The yellow-toothed guy with the knife and gun stays in the car and leaves it running, and out of the bottom of my blindfold, I can see that the guy next to me leaves his gun on the floor of the back seat as he comes around to retrieve me from the vehicle.

He yanks me out of the car, holding my wrists behind my back, and drags me away from it. We walk for what must be a minute or so, and I can't hear anything except for our footsteps and the tweets of unfamiliar birds.

He pauses briefly, maybe to check his phone for directions.

I seize the opportunity to turn to him. Using my limited field of vision below the blindfold, I pull my knee back and then thrust it into his junk as hard as I can. He bends over in surprise and agony, letting out a loud groan.

I guesstimate where his head is and I headbutt him with all the force I can muster. I feel momentarily dizzy as our skulls connect, but I quickly regroup, pulling the blindfold off and punching him as hard as I can in the face. Dazed by the headbutt, he doesn't respond quickly enough to stop me or defend himself as I strike, and I feel great satisfaction as my fist splits his lip apart, and bright red blood oozes from his mouth.

"Why, you little bitch!" he yells, his eyes flickering with rage.

For a moment, I worry that he's going to try to kill me, but his phone beeps and it seems to remind him what he's here to do.

"Come with me, you little slut," he growls. "I'll make sure you're punished for this." He narrows his eyes, and they glimmer cruelly, like glinting black beads. "I'm just sorry that I'm not the one who gets to do it."

He's much bigger than me, and while I can usually put up a decent fight, he somehow grabs my arms and yanks them roughly behind me again. He uses his leverage to drag me down a poorly maintained sidewalk.

We are in some kind of residential neighborhood, but the houses look to be spaced relatively far apart. Probably more than yelling distance from what I can see. The guy we left in the car is almost certainly the closest person to us.

Where the fuck is this lunatic taking me, and who is going to punish me? He pulls me along forcefully, and I cry out as I feel my shoulder move in a direction it probably shouldn't as we cross over a potholed driveway full of broken asphalt and overgrown weeds. He laughs, clearly enjoying being rough with me while he can.

Dragging me up the path, we approach a house, and he knocks on the door.

Why the fuck is he taking me here? Am I finally going to die because of my father? I figured that would eventually happen. I just didn't think it would be today.

CHAPTER ELEVEN

Zeke

There's a knock at the door, about half an hour after Tane's goons were scheduled to arrive for the drop-off.

I peer out the window and see a stocky man holding onto a woman with a large rectangle of duct tape across her mouth. He grasps her hands behind her back to keep her restrained. I open the door and gesture for them to come in.

"This little bitch made me bleed," the man growls, shoving her roughly through the door in front of him.

She tries to wrench out of his grasp, but he tightens his grip and she winces.

"Do whatever you want with her. Just keep her alive, for now."

Her eyes grow large.

His lip looks freshly split, and he's sporting a facial bruise that I recognize as the shadow of a newly forming black eye. He subconsciously lifts a hand to touch his lip and grimaces. As soon as he lifts his hand, she tries to wriggle free. Rage flares in his eyes, his pupils dilating into evil little dots, and he grabs hold of her wrists again with both hands, twisting. She flinches in pain, but clenches her jaw as if willing herself not to cry out or show weakness. Very interesting. It looks like we might have a tough one on our hands.

"To be honest, I couldn't care less if you break that rule, the stupid little cunt. Rape her and cut her tits off for all I care." Jesus.

Her eyes widen again at his words. Tane's guys are ruthless, just like him.

I glance at her more closely. It's hard to get a good look at her with the duct tape on, but somehow she looks familiar. I just can't quite place her.

I run my eyes over her chest at the mention of her tits. They're perky and full. My cock twitches, not at the thought of chopping them off, but of doing a variety of other things to them with my hands and my mouth and maybe even my cock.

"How long are we keeping her for again? Has anything changed about the assignment?" I ask. Sometimes Tane's plans adjust at a moment's notice, so I want to be crystal clear about what he expects from us. Nobody wants to piss off Tane Brown.

"Ten days, and if the debt's not repaid, we will sell her. There are already some interested parties," he says, a sinister grin appearing on his face.

Her eyes narrow at the man.

"It sounds like the potential buyers have some *very* interesting plans for her."

Glaring, she tries to shrug him off, but both of his hands remain wrapped firmly around her wrists. She frowns, and her chest rapidly rises and falls. She's doing her best to act tough, but there are certain signs of fear that are more difficult to hide.

"I suggest you tie her up or something," he snarls. "And hide your knives and other weapons. She probably also bites, the feral little bitch. Might want to leave the duct tape on for the next few days."

"Dom, get in here," I call out to the adjoining living room. "Bring the rope!"

Dom appears at my side, rope in hand. He always has one handy.

"Tie her up to the chair so she can't wriggle out of it." I point at one of the wooden chairs tucked into the kitchen table.

The man who brought her here shoves her into the seat facing the window so her back is to us, as if he doesn't want to make eye contact with her again, and she plops down heavily. Dom's talented with knots, and he's soon got her tied up from behind in a configuration that even Houdini would have trouble escaping from.

"Alright, I think we're good. We can take it from here." I gesture at our captive, who sits silently in the chair, not able to see us.

"Await further instructions," he replies. "We will be in touch. But like I said, she's yours for the next ten days." He pauses, and a grotesque smile spreads across his face, revealing a mouth full of little grayish teeth. "Think of her as your personal property, to do with whatever you want. And I mean *whatever*. I personally recommend inflicting a lot of pain. The bitch deserves it."

He narrows his eyes as he gives one last glance in her direction, and exits through the front door.

She shivers visibly as Dom closes the door behind the goon and locks the three deadbolts that keep us secure. He inputs a code into a fourth locking system, just to be on the safe side, glancing back to make sure the girl isn't turning to try to see the code. Good, the last thing we need is her escaping on our watch. Tane would make our lives hell if we let her escape. Dom watches out the window as the man exits down the driveway.

Satisfied that the goon has left, Dom approaches the girl. "Let's get a proper look at you, then." He turns the chair around, revealing the face of our brand-new captive.

"Holy shit!" I'm usually calm, but I can't help but exclaim aloud when I see her face.

"I know, she's hot. I told you," Dom replies. "Same as in the photo."

We both move towards her to get a closer look.

"No, no! You don't understand. Rake! Sky! Get in here, it's her!!"

Dom raises an eyebrow at me, clearly not used to me being this excited about... well, anything, really.

He rips off the duct tape, revealing more of her face, causing her to flinch and instinctively press her lips together.

"The photo definitely didn't do her justice. She's absolutely breathtaking." He gazes at her, talking about her like she's not in the room.

She has big blue eyes, full lips, angular cheekbones and a smattering of freckles across the bridge of her nose. Her hair cascades in fiery red waves, streaked with pink highlights. I hadn't noticed her hair the last time I set eyes on her, because it had been wet, making it look like a much darker reddish-brown and obscuring the highlights.

She glares at us, appearing almost more pissed off rather than scared, although she's probably wondering what the fuck she's doing here.

"I can hear you, you know." She scowls at Dom, and then turns to me and further narrows her eyes. "And who the fuck are you, anyway?"

"What's going on?" Rake yells as he and Skyler both come running in. They stare at her, and Rake breaks out in a massive grin. "Oh fuck, it's that same girl. From the surfing lesson. The smoke show!"

Skyler laughs in surprise and shakes his head. "Well, well, well. What are the chances?"

"What are you talking about, man?" Dom is so confused he may as well have question marks flashing in his eyes.

"She's the girl I took out for a lesson the other day," says Skyler. "Hi, what's your name again?" He sucks his teeth, screws up his face and clicks his fingers as he tries to recall. A lightbulb seems to go off in his brain. "Devon! Your name is Devon. Hi again," he says, smiling as she blinks at him in surprise. "I believe we've met."

Recognition dawns in her eyes. "What the fuck is going on? What am I doing here? And are you a surfing instructor or a kidnapper?" Her voice rises as she snarls at Skyler.

"Technically, you were dropped off here. We have merely received you," says Skyler, smoothly. "And besides, they say anybody can be anything they want to these days if they put their mind to it. So why can't I be both?"

She narrows her eyes as he grins at her, his gaze trailing the length of her body from head to toe, soaking her all in.

CHAPTER TWELVE

Skyler

I can't believe it's her. The hot girl from the surfing lesson, of all people. I'm excited to see her again, but this wasn't quite how I was expecting to meet her for the second time, technically third, if you count the time I first saw her at the bar.

I was hoping to get her number, take her out for some drinks and work my charm on her, and then fuck her senseless. Maybe even a couple of times before she left the island, as all tourists inevitably do. But now she's here in my house, our captive. I feel my cock twitch in my shorts at this unanticipated turn of events.

I haven't had a woman as my plaything before, under my control, in my house. It was one thing dominating her out in the ocean. I'm used to that feeling, and it's a turn-on, but this is something else.

I never fancied myself a kidnapper or someone who receives people and keeps them against their will, but here's this sexy little thing and it wouldn't hurt to have some fun with her while she's here. During the lesson, I could tell she was into me. So cute and flustered any time I said anything flirty. Being locked in my house might change things, but I guess she doesn't have a ton of choice about that. And it's certainly not up to us to let her go. Tane would lose his shit and the consequences would be deadly. May as well make the most of this situation.

My cock jerks again as I think back to her lesson, and how I got to stare at her gorgeous ass as she waited for me to throw her down the waves. There are things I want to do to that ass, badly. I've definitely jerked off to the image of her that's stuck in my mind more than once. And now it's looking like I might get to play with her after all, just not the way I expected.

I look around at the other guys, wondering what we should do next.

"Place her in the room," Zeke instructs Dom.

Zeke always knows how to take the lead and always has the next move in mind. He's been that way for as long as I can remember. My dad saw that quality in him more than he ever did in me, that's for sure. I don't hold it against him, though. Zeke is way more like my brother, my father's favorite son, than I could ever be. It's not his fault I don't measure up.

Without untying her, Dom picks her up and carries her, chair and all, into a room at the end of the hallway. He undoes the rope, has her stand up, removes the chair, and closes the door.

"What the fuck are you doing?!" she asks, whipping around and screaming as the door closes in her face.

CHAPTER THIRTEEN

Devon

I don't know what the fuck is going on.

Those creepy kidnappers dropped me off at this random house, and my surf instructor is here! Did he plan this? That seems like a weird marketing move, kidnapping your surfing clients. But then again, I've known for some time that many people will do pretty much anything for money or pussy. I figure one of those things must be involved.

It seems like a far stretch that he'd go to the effort to abduct me after teaching me to ride waves. And it can't be a coincidence that my father was missing this morning and still hasn't returned my calls. Well, actually, I wouldn't know if he had at this point because the kidnappers took my phone when they grabbed me.

I have no way of contacting anybody, and my father is the only person I know on this island. Well, he and the surf instructor who's now apparently holding me captive. Even if my kidnapper hadn't mentioned him, I'd put money on my abduction having something to do with my father. I just don't understand how my surfing instructor is involved.

Speaking of which, as weird as this situation is, Skyler is still extremely hot. And so are the other three guys that just received me from the kidnappers.

There's a super muscular one who tied me up and carried me around, chair and all, who seems quite serious and is clearly very strong. I noticed he has what looked like a fresh tattoo, some kind of surfboard with flowers on it. Hibiscus, I think.

A tall one with longer, curly hair and sparkling, playful eyes. He has a large scar running along his back and up across his shoulder.

And another one with cropped dark hair that seems to be very intense, watching my every move.

Between Skyler and the quiet, observant one, I'm not sure exactly who is in control, but the other two guys seemed somehow deferential to them.

Are they all kidnappers? I'm guessing so, seeing they just locked me in a room against my will. Why me, though? What do they want with me? Ugh, this is not how this vacation was meant to go. I should have trusted my gut and told my father I wasn't going to play happy families anymore. Trust fund be damned.

I look around the room for any way to escape, but I don't see many options. Peering out the window, it seems to be reinforced with some kind of thick material. I pound on it, but it doesn't budge. Nobody can see me from here. The houses are spaced too far apart and whatever this coating is on the windows, it's pretty opaque.

There's a simple bathroom off to the side, with just a toilet and a basin, a small shower, a basic bar of soap and a near-empty roll of toilet paper. No toothbrushes or pills or nail scissors, or anything else I could fashion into a weapon to use on anyone, including myself. In the main area, there's a weird stain on the ground in one corner; it's a rusty brown color and I shiver as I realize it looks like old blood that's oxidized over time.

It brings back memories of my childhood home, of the horrors that I saw. I immediately try to shove them down because I need to stay focused on how to figure out what the hell is going on and get out of here.

What do they have a room like this for in this house, anyway? Maybe I don't want to know. Maybe they're going to kill me in here. Murder me and chop my body up and bury it in the backyard. I doubt anybody would ever find me.

And god knows my worthless father won't come looking for me. He's the only one who really knows where I am at the moment.

I guess Donkey technically knows I'm on this island, but he'd have no clue where to look. He'll probably assume I've run away to join a circus, because, let's face it, that sounds like something I'd actually do to escape my life and start afresh. Ugh. This is not good.

Walking over to the door, I tug on the handle, but it doesn't move at all. I bang on it as hard as I can until my fists hurt, but it's heavy and thick and I doubt they can even hear me.

"Let me out, you fuckers!" I yell as loudly as I can. "Big men, shutting a girl in a room because you're too scared that if you let me out of here, I'll chop your balls off!" They don't reply. "What are you running here? A torture chamber?"

I pound on the door again, causing my wrists to sting, but they continue to ignore me.

Fuck. I hate being trapped. I can handle just about anything, and I have had to endure an incredible amount of pain in my life, but being shut in a room makes me claustrophobic. It feels like I'm caged. I always said I'd have to make sure I stay out of prison because I wouldn't be able to handle being locked in a jail cell with no way out. I'd turn into a wild animal. Surprisingly, I've managed to keep out of lockup my entire life. But here I am, trapped in a weird room in a house by four hot guys after being kidnapped by a pair of goons. Sigh.

Looking around, there's literally nothing in this room for me to break out with. I check again, walking the perimeter, just to be sure.

From what I saw when I arrived, to what I've found in this room, this is such a guy's house, an austere crash pad. Things were a bit of a blur when I was dropped off here, but when the burly guy carried me to this room I saw a kitchen and a living room and a long hallway. There didn't seem to be a ton of decorations or personality to the house. Just like this room. Utilitarian, with nothing that I could use to try to bash the door or window in.

Judging from what's happened to me today, I'm sure these guys have weapons, but they're definitely not in here.

I sit down, because there's literally nothing I can do but wait and see what happens next.

Taking a deep breath, waves of exhaustion crash over me. Being kidnapped saps the energy out of you, I guess.

Chapter Fourteen

Dom

"What are we going to do with her, guys? Ten days is a long time to keep someone. I mean, I can think of a few things I'd *like* to do, but we haven't done this type of thing before."

We're sitting in the living room, all processing that we have a new houseguest. It was different hearing about it as an idea than actually having her here in the flesh. The very smooth, sexily tattooed flesh. We've done some fucked up things, but harboring a captive is new. "Yeah, I know."

Zeke runs a hand down the back of his neck, a pensive expression on his face. "It seems like more trouble than it's worth, honestly. She's clearly a firecracker judging by what she did to that goon who dropped her off. She's lucky she's still alive after doing that, based on some of the things we've seen Tane's men do before. Maybe we just keep her in the room the whole time."

"That sounds overly sensible and way not enough fun." Rake juts out his bottom lip. "We can't keep a girl in our house for ten days, a hot girl especially, and just leave her in that room. What a waste. Can we have her join us for dinner?"

"As in, you want her to sit down with us for a family meal? That sounds like a terrible idea." Zeke crosses his arms over his chest and furrows his brow. I can tell he's thinking of the best next move.

"She needs to eat, bro." Rake shrugs.

"That's a good point." Zeke shrugs back.

"But if she chops your dick off, that's on you, man," says Skyler.

I laugh. "Let's find some middle ground. I can tie her up and we can feed her. See how that goes, maybe? That way, we might all get to keep our dicks."

"Alright, let's give it a go." Zeke nods. "You can do the honors with the rope, of course, Dom. But let's leave her in there for a bit, first. Hopefully, she'll tire herself out from banging on the door and trying to escape."

We all glance up at the camera footage playing live before us. Luckily, the space she's in is soundproof, but we've been watching her try to escape since Dom placed her in the room.

She has no chance, but it's fun watching her try.

CHAPTER FIFTEEN

Devon

Two hours later

The door opens, and the serious, intense one comes into the room carrying a plastic cup of water and a snack bar. He's shirtless and completely covered in tattoos.

God, tattoos really are my weakness. And they adorn his torso, arms, and rippling back. He's incredibly attractive, and just my type. I resist the primal urge to lick my lips.

"Did you get eyes for Christmas?" He smirks at me as he hands me the water and the snack.

"I, uh—." I take the items from him, not quite sure what to say. Is he flirting with me? Are captors allowed to do that?

"Didn't your mother tell you it's rude to stare?" He continues to smirk, a sexy lopsided one, his eyes observing my every micro-expression.

"She told me to play with men sexually to get them to do what I want. No, she didn't tell me it's rude to stare." My mother was a whirlwind of interesting parental advice.

"Like what you see?" He raises an eyebrow.

I really do, but I try to play it cool. "Not bad. Have seen better."

In reality, he's one of the most perfect specimens I've ever laid eyes on. His six-pack is clearly on display, with chiseled obliques that form a compelling trail I'd quite like to follow with my tongue. A peen ravine, if you will. His broad chest and his muscular arms that I imagine wrapping around me, and that he could easily use to hoist me over his shoulder as he carries me to the bedroom to further manhandle me. I want to feel his weight on me, pressing down on me and dominating me. I want to feel like I can't breathe because he's on me, having his way with me.

Jesus. This man is holding me hostage, but all I can think about is seeing him naked. What is wrong with me? I'm warped.

"We could have a good time, you and me." His eyes run over my body.

"Leave me alone," I say, but my pussy betrays me once again as it clenches under his gaze.

He smirks again, and it's sexy as hell.

"Anyway, we figured you might also need some clothes while you're here."

He goes to the doorway and retrieves two shopping bags.

"Rake picked them out, so I can't make any promises that you're going to want to wear them. But they're all yours."

He hands the bags to me and leaves.

I look inside, and they're both full of clothing. A couple of pairs of very short black shorts, some black and gray tank tops, and weirdly a purple T-shirt with a sequined unicorn on it. I roll my eyes as I pull out some panties and bras that are my size but skimpy and very sheer. It's obvious a guy picked them out, and they're not very practical, but they'll have to do.

There are also a couple of bikinis, both super cute, one solid and one patterned. What the hell do I need a bikini for, trapped in this room, though?

And a black dress, knee-length with a plunging neckline, exposed back and cute puffy skirt. Maybe it's for when I host my own captive prom-for-one. I snort at the thought of putting on the dress and parading around this room.

At the bottom of one bag is some deodorant, soap, a toothbrush and toothpaste, as well as some foundation, eyeliner, mascara and some tubes of lipstick.

Who the heck is this Rake person Zeke mentioned? I'm strangely touched, and very confused, by this gesture, and by the attention to detail. What has my father gotten me into?

An hour later

After what seemed like another long stretch of time, the big burly one and the intense one who brought me the water come and let me out of the room.

The big one expertly binds my wrists in front of me, already seeming far more competent than the guy who blindfolded me earlier. This time, he doesn't carry me, and we walk down the long hallway with rooms off to either side, and then through the living room with a couch and armchair and a large TV. The walls are painted a pale lemon hue, and the paint has flaked away in some areas. The floor is some kind of hardwood, dotted randomly with random grains of sand that have been tracked in. He leads me to the basic wooden dining table in the kitchen where the other two are already sitting.

I'm exhausted from banging on the door and window, my fists bruised and my throat sore from yelling, so I don't resist. I really hope they're going to feed me because I'm also ravenous. There's a serving dish of some type of heat-and-eat pasta on the table, along with a few paper plates and plastic forks. This is a bachelor pad through and through.

The other guys are talking and barely look up as I sit down.

"You snaked that guy good, man!" The tall guy excitedly waves his hands around at Skyler, in some kind of mock reenactment.

Skyler smirks. "I know, right? He deserved it, the fucking newb. Tried to cut in on me earlier."

"Yeah, saw that. You showed him who's boss."

"Don't we always?" They all nod.

"What does snaking mean?" They peer at me, as if they were so lost in their conversation they forgot I was here. The height of hospitality for their new female captive.

Skyler snorts at me. "It's a surfing term. And we extend it to other areas of our lives."

"You'll have to explain more. You know I'm new to this whole surfing culture," I say, glancing at Skyler and narrowing my eyes.

"Well, you're going to have to study up, sweetheart. I don't have time to school you," he says. Ironic given he did just in fact school me in surfing.

I guess I'm not paying him this time. Maybe that's the difference.

"But just this once I'll tell you all about snaking. It means paddling around another surfer to give yourself the right of way over a wave. It's not something that many people are brave enough to do. But we're known for it, and we can do it because we dominate the ocean around here. There's nobody as strong as us when it comes to surfing on our home turf, and there never will be. This is in our blood, and we get to take it when we want it."

"Doesn't that piss people off? I don't know much, but I can't imagine that's the height of surfing etiquette."

He scoffs. "Do you think we could care less? We don't care if people think it's cheating or unethical or greedy or rude or all the little moral complaints people have when we do that or anything else. We take what we want, and we'll continue to do that until we die."

I look around at them, all seated around the table. They act very comfortable with each other and look to be around the same age, but I suspect they're not actually blood-related by their appearance. They're all incredibly in shape, tanned, and with very muscular bodies despite their differences. One of them is much taller than the others, another is really brawny and rectangle-shaped, and the one with close-cropped brown hair is a fraction bigger than Skyler. The common thread is that they're all fucking hot.

Despite being immersed in surfing talk when I first sat down, they're all returning my gaze now. I guess that's only fair because I'm staring at them, too. Their eyes reveal a combination of curiosity and hunger. Each of them observes me intently, like predators about to surround and capture their prey. Although in this case I technically was delivered to them like a meal from DoorDash.

"Is this really necessary?" I shrug my shoulders and eye my bound wrists. "Or is it just some kind of kink you have? Tying up women you don't know?"

"We saw what you did to that guy, Devon. We're not taking any risks." It's the controlled, intense one, and he's glancing at me as if he's trying to anticipate what I might do next.

"Scared of a girl?" I bat my eyelashes at him and he snorts.

"I wouldn't say scared," says the rectangle-shaped, burly one. "We just want to get through dinner as smoothly as possible. Zeke agreed it was a good plan."

"Zeke's your name?" I glance at the one who seems to be in charge alongside Skyler. "Is that short for Ezekiel? Are your parents religious or something?" I raise an eyebrow, and the others snicker.

"Ezekiel, haha! Tell her, Zekey!" The tall one apparently finds this hilarious.

I thought it was a simple question with what seemed to be an obvious answer, so I'm a little confused by this response.

He sighs. "Well, it's not that deep, actually. When I was younger, like a tween I guess you could say, some of my friends and I found a few bottles of Zyquil and drank so much we started tripping. We got caught, and I guess that's what I became known for. And I suppose it just kinda stuck."

I snort.

"Yeah, our boy was over here tripping on cold medication. Big man on the island!" The tall one's voice goes up into a falsetto, mocking his mate. Skyler rolls his eyes, and the burly one snickers at the exchange.

"Fuck off, I was eleven!" Zeke growls in the tall guy's direction, and he laughs back at him.

"Oh. Well, that wasn't what I was expecting," I say, trying not to laugh.

"You ask too many questions," says Zeke, frowning and narrowing his eyes.

"Hit a nerve, I see." I laugh cruelly. I might be bound and being held captive, but this is mildly entertaining. "What about you? What's your name?" I gesture at the tall one.

"Rake." He grins.

I laugh. "Why? You've got a skinny cock?"

The burly guy and Skyler both snort.

"No, fuck you." He glares at me, a flush creeping up his neck. "I'll show you just how big it is."

"Can't wait to see it. Do you keep it in the Museum of Tiny Things?"

I smile sweetly and bat my eyelashes at him this time. Secretly, I actually wouldn't mind seeing what he has in his pants. He's fucking gorgeous, all bronzed and muscly. I want to climb him like a tree. But I'm not going to tell him that. He is my captor, after all.

"Really though, why? I need to know."

"Because I'm tall." He shrugs.

"What? Skyscraper and Big Bird were already taken?"

He grins. "Something like that."

"Wait, Rake? You're the one that got me some clothes and things today?"

He frowns. "Yeah, why? You don't like them? Do they fit okay?"

"Everything's my size. And my style, actually, except for the weird T-shirt. I was just surprised, that's all. Not sure what I'll wear a bikini for while I'm stuck in a room being held captive."

"It's for just in case." He grins and winks at me. "You never know what you'll feel like wearing. Maybe you'll put on a fashion show for us."

I roll my eyes. "No, not going to happen. And you?" I point at the burly one. "Let me guess, Rectangle Man?"

"Dom." His face is expressionless.

"Is that because you're dominant in the bedroom?" I say, deadpan. "Seeing your names are apparently all so literal."

"Well, yeah, I am very dominant in the bedroom. You'll find out." He winks at me. "But that's a coincidence. It's just short for Dominic."

"Very creative." I roll my eyes, although I'm secretly having fun interrogating them about their names. "And of course, Skyler. That seems like a normal name?"

"Yep, named after my father. Unfortunately." He shrugs. "But I'm stuck with it now. Just like you're stuck with us."

"What he's not telling you is he's basically royalty on this island because of his dad," says Rake.

Do nods. "Yep, it's true."

"Sometimes we don't get choices." Skyler frowns, and under his tan, he seems slightly flushed.

"You have a choice, to feed me." I try to steer the conversation towards the pasta on the table because I'm starving and I'm really hoping they'll give me some food.

"Are you hungry?" asks Skyler, his tone changing. "I have something to put in your mouth." His eyes twinkle mischievously.

I roll my eyes. "Like I've never heard that one before."

"Oh, lots of guys wanting to shove their dicks in your mouth?"

"Plenty. But I'd actually quite like some food."

"Feed her, Rake," says Zeke. "Seeing you were so insistent she has a meal with us."

Rake stands up, picking a fork up from the table and coming to stand beside me. He picks up a bite of pasta with the fork and reaches out to place it in my mouth.

I take it in hungrily, not sure if or when they're going to feed me again.

"Got any hot sauce?" I ask, glancing over towards the fridge which is closest to Dom. The pasta is good, but I put hot sauce on everything and this could use some heat.

"You're very comfortable, asking for things when you've just been kidnapped," says Skyler, smirking.

"You're very comfortable, teaching me to surf and then locking me in a room for hours," I say, my eyes narrowing at him. "I figure I get to have one nice thing happen today."

He rolls his eyes. "Dom, grab it for her, man." The muscular man opens the refrigerator door and starts poking around, then turns back empty-handed and shrugs.

"Dom's too much of a pussy for hot sauce, so he doesn't know where to look," says Zeke, smirking at him. "Look in the door, second shelf down. There should be about four bottles."

Dom roots around in the area indicated by Zeke and retrieves all four bottles. He peers at each of them. "These look too fucking spicy for me. Why would you do this to yourself?"

He brings them over and places them on the table.

"Clearly she likes it hot." Rake wiggles his eyebrows at me and winks.

"What one do you want?" Zeke asks.

"Whatever one's spiciest."

Zeke grabs a bottle of deep red sauce and holds it up. "You sure? This is ghost pepper."

"Slather it on me, baby," I reply. "As much as you can."

"Okay then, your funeral." He shrugs, upending the bottle and letting a few tablespoons of the sauce onto the pasta. "That good?"

"Perfect," I grin. Rake returns to feeding me the pasta, and I enjoy the sensation of deep heat as it spreads throughout my mouth.

"Mmm, much better," I smile.

Dom stares at me, his eyes large, and shakes his head. "Won't be sucking any of our dicks tonight. I can tell you that much!"

I can't help but snort at Dom's exclamation. He's almost sweating watching me eat the hot sauce. He clearly *is* a pussy when it comes to anything spicy. Interesting. So big and strong and can't handle a teeny-weeny chili pepper. Good to know.

Skyler watches me closely as I eat the pasta by the forkful as Rake feeds it to me, a smirk plastered on his face, his eyes glimmering. I can't tell whether his gaze is mocking me or mean. He's hard to read here, and not as playful as at the beach. "Look at you gobbling that down, you greedy little slut." Well, okay, wasn't expecting that. He's clearly not the charming guy I thought he was.

In a break between mouthfuls, I respond. "Wow. That's lovely. I thought you were a nice guy, Skyler! Gentlemanly, even. You were so different out on the ocean."

"The water calms me." He laughs, his eyes gleaming. There's a coldness to them now, though. Not the sparkly, friendly gaze I'd seen during the lesson. "And besides, I was trying to get into your pants." This time, his laugh is full of mirth.

Well, there we have it.

"Oh, so you're a fuckboy then? That tracks." I realize all the lines during the lesson, the way he looked at me, were all part of his orchestrated act. I meant nothing to him, just a piece of pussy that he'd probably try to bang while I was on vacation. He probably does it all the time. What an idiot to think I was anything special to him, that we had any type of organic connection. "A lazy one, by the sounds of it," I snarl.

Rejection, not feeling special, is something I'm very much used to, but I've never found a way to handle it well.

"Now you've been handed to us on a platter, and I get to do with you what I want without even working for it. So I'll spare you the pickup lines and the flirting and take what's mine."

Blood surges to my head and starts thumping at my temples. "What's *yours*? I'm not yours to take."

I accept another bite of food, but this time I turn to face Skyler and spit it directly at him. Some of it lands on the table, but a big chunk lands on his face, hot sauce included. His eyes darken, and I cackle, even though this might be my last meal.

Sometimes you have to take every scrap of power you can muster. Sometimes, when you have the least hope, you need to take the greatest risk.

The other guys' eyes grow wide and their jaws drop.

Not bothering to wipe his face, he moves closer to me and grabs my throat with one of his powerful hands, cutting off my air supply as he leans in.

"Never, ever do that again. You're going to be punished for that, you dirty little bitch."

He shoves my head back as he lets go, and I still feel his touch lingering on my throat and jaw as I take in a gulp of air.

"How should we punish her, guys?" He looks around at the other three, and all eight eyes turn to me, roaming my body as if they're all planning their own little adventure.

"Can't decide by yourself, Skyler? Need help from your friends to come up with a good idea?" I give no fucks, and I want a reaction. To take my power back.

"We approach life just like we surf, Devon," says Skyler, his voice cold as he explains. He grabs me by my bound wrists and pulls me close to him so that his breath cools one side of my face. "We ride together, in a pack. We dominate, and we take whatever we want."

"So you're snakes in the water and on the land? Basically, just cutting in front of everyone else who deserves to be there and stealing things, including peopIe?"

I narrow my eyes at him. I want him to be full of rage at my words. In this moment, my only goal is to antagonize him so that he snaps.

He growls. "You got it. Because nobody deserves to be there as much as us. Why? You don't like that?"

"Oh, I like real snakes." I look him up and down. "Not boys who say they're animals like it makes them cool or badass or whatever the fuck you and your buddies here do it for."

The energy seems to change in the room, and all four guys turn to glare at me.

Skyler pulls me roughly to him, by the chin this time, until our eyes are mere inches away. I breathe in and his scent is all man, sandalwood and sweat and salt.

"Don't you ever call me a fucking boy again. You hear me? I'm a man, and I will take what I want from you whenever I want."

I don't know how his demeanor can so quickly turn from easy and flirtatious to icy and cruel. One of his personas seems like an act, and I haven't quite picked which one it is. And I'm not entirely sure which version of him I prefer. He's being a real jerk, but something about his coldness is doing it for me. He reaches down between my legs, brushing his fingers against the cloth of my shorts that separates him from my body. I feel a strong twinge between my legs as he cups me there, and runs his powerful hand from my inner thighs up against my lips and to my stomach.

"Do you understand me?"

As I feel myself throb in response to his touch, I jerk my body away from his hand, but my chin stays wrapped in the vice grip of his other palm and fingers.

Looking him straight in the eyes in what hopefully conveys my defiance, I reply, "Don't touch me unless I tell you to."

The truth is, I want him to keep touching me. Even after everything that's happened today. After all, I've touched myself plenty of times, thinking of him and our time out in the ocean, and ironically, this included him tying me up with my surfboard leash. But I can't let him know that. Can't let him know the effect he had on me then, or the effect he's having on me now. My pussy is aching with desire, craving to see what he could do to me, and I can't give him that satisfaction.

"You're not in charge, girl," he says, sneering, but he drops his hand. Maybe he's not the badass, cruel guy he thinks he is. Or maybe they all are.

The power imbalance is starting to feel real, sitting here with my hands tied, not knowing what's going to happen next. I need to get things on a more even footing and make them scared of me. I want them to think I'm angry, full of rage, and dangerous, so I raise my voice and try to puff myself up to appear as large as possible. "Fuck you. Do what you want. I'm not scared of you."

"Is that an invitation, *Devon*? Because I'll teach you a fucking lesson for what you just did. Spitting food at me."

"You think I need to be taught a lesson? I did nothing to be here!" My chest starts to rise and fall erratically. "I didn't put myself in this position!"

"Well, it turns out your father did," says Skyler, cruelly. "So we'll be taking care of you until you get sold to someone because your rich daddy hasn't paid his debt. You've inherited his shortcomings, it seems, just like we all have."

Something inside me snaps. Blood is pounding so fast through my temples that I literally see red. "I don't know why I'm here. Stuck with you. You're a fucking asshole! You're all fucking assholes!" I yell as loud as I can, and it feels good to get it all out. "I bet whoever I'm sold to is better! I should never have come to this stupid island!"

"You think you're too good to be here?" Skyler glares at me. "I hate stupid bitches like you, with your entitlement dripping off you. So many tourists coming and acting like they're better than the people who grew up here, who work so hard to keep the island safe and make sure people have nice vacations. I'm good at reading people, and you're not a typical tourist, I'll give you that. But you're still one of them, and you'll never be one of us."

"I would never want to be *anything* like you! And you think you know all about me, don't you?!" My voice is rising further, which I didn't know was possible, and I feel my nostrils flaring. My heart is beating so hard it feels like it might burst through my chest. Skyler's really gotten under my skin with his judgmental assumptions. Layered onto the fact that he's *holding me captive*.

"You know what? I think I do, love. But tell me who you think I believe you are." He smirks, which only infuriates me more. What a condescending jerk.

"You think I'm some stupid rich bitch who grew up in a life of privilege? That I somehow started life rungs up an imaginary ladder ahead of you." I pause, and he nods. "In some ways, I've had massive advantages. I'm not denying that. But I've had hardships, too."

"Oh, tell me your sob story." Skyler makes the boo-hoo gesture with his hands, curling them up and rotating them in front of his eyes. "Like your mother didn't buy you the prom dress you wanted and made you pick something else? You're really trying to compare yourself with the four of us, and the shithole lives we've had, the challenges we've faced, the enormous strength and focus and just refusing to stop that has gotten us where we are today? Really? Fucking rich girl problems. I'm not going to beat around the bush and indulge you about the trials and tribulations of growing up with what must have been an easy life. Jesus, you've probably got a trust fund or something."

"Fuck. You." My voice is low and quiet, a distinct contrast from moments before. He's hit a nerve.

"Oh fuck, you do, don't you?" He cackles cruelly, his eyes dancing with amusement and resentment. "Rich little baby girl here's got a trust fund!"

What a far fucking cry from the guy who taught me to surf. That guy is dead to me now. He never existed outside of my mind, anyway.

Chapter Sixteen

Skyler

Her eyes flash with anger in a way that I didn't expect when I mentioned her having a trust fund. There's no doubt she's feisty, but this is something else. An inner rage that has been building her whole life.

She takes a deep breath, her yelling outburst apparently on pause as her voice lowers. "Yes, I was adopted by people who have money. I won't go into how shitty they are and how much they've fucked up my life, as most parents do. But my life didn't start there."

"Well, you sure look like you come from money," I say, as my eyes trail her body from head to toe. "And you're staying at one of the fanciest fucking hotels on the beach. Well, you were until you were dropped off here. I know how much those rooms cost per night! What's wrong with it? Thread count not high enough for you? Is that the crisis that you're facing? Boo fucking hoo, bitch! Some of us have actual problems. All you fucking tourists do is come here and ruin our shit and ratchet prices up for the rest of us."

"I'm sorry I fucking stayed in a hotel that my asshole of an adoptive father paid for." She narrows her eyes at me and frowns. "For your fucking information, I was born to a sixteen-year-old girl who refused to tell anybody who the father was, but I can almost guarantee he wouldn't have been able to afford one night in a hotel like that." A cloud of what seems like sadness passes over her face, and her voice lowers so I can barely hear her.

I lean in closer.

"There was wild speculation about all the men it could have been, people who looked like me, boys in the neighborhood who she was close to and partied with. But when I eventually got my birth certificate and managed to track her down, you know what she did? She told me his name, she told me he raped her, and then she completely stopped talking to me. She tossed me aside *for a second time*. For being the child of rape, something I had no control over. She thought I was something to be ashamed of before I was even born, and even worse afterwards. Do you know how that feels?"

I take it as a rhetorical question and, while my mouth is slightly open, I don't move to respond. It seems too dangerous. What she's saying is resonating with me too hard.

She continues. "So no, there were no tantrums about prom dresses. But I didn't grow up with people who looked like me. I grew up with people who were using me to fill a void in their life. Who had the means to 'acquire' me like a fucking object. Who criticized me when I didn't 'fit in' and look like them and do the things they wanted me to do the way they wanted me to. Did I have 'things'? Yes. Did I need those things? No. I have no roots. I only have people who discard and abandon me, over and over again. I have nothing and no one. I came from darkness, from evil. A despicable act. And I can never shake that."

Abandonment and being unwanted, and in my case, second best. For her, a legacy of darkness casting a shadow over her entire existence.

In mine, feeling like I couldn't measure up to expectations, and couldn't do justice to my legacy. God, my dad thought so much more of Zeke than me, and he wasn't even his blood son. He saw him as a leader. He just saw me as weak. Her words bring a flashback to the last thing he ever said to me before he died, when he asked me why I couldn't be more like my brother or even Zeke. The words and actions of parents can be like knives that twist and turn inside you for the rest of your life, sometimes when you least expect it.

Just for a moment, I see the pain in her eyes, palpable and raw, as if she's reliving those moments vividly in her mind. A single tear threatens to burst from each of them, but she blinks hard.

For just an instant, she looks vulnerable and like she might shatter into pieces, shards of her present and her past projecting themselves across the room. For just that moment, she looks lost.

But just as suddenly as that look had appeared, it is gone, and turns once again to rage.

"So fuck you and your judgements." She is screaming now, contempt on her face aimed squarely at me. "You're just as bad as the people you look down on, who you criticize based on your own assumptions and prejudices. You think you're so fucking badass with your stupid surfing." She spits out the word, and I feel a shiver pass through my body.

I'm angry, I'm irritated, and maybe a little turned on.

"Grow up and fuck off out of my life." She projects her voice and her yells reverberate around the sparsely furnished kitchen. "I never want to see you again! Let me out of here!"

As if to punctuate her sentence, she stands up, her wrists still tightly bound, and she storms out of the kitchen, through the living room and into the hallway, crashing into the half-open door with her shoulder.

It flies open so forcefully it cracks against the hallway wall and smashes back on its hinges on a furious rebound.

The other guys and I look at each other while we hear her stomp to the end of the hallway and into the room where we've been keeping her.

Jesus. Maybe I went too far. She's putting herself back in captivity just to get away from me and my words.

I don't normally waste time thinking about other people's feelings. Or my own. It's a useless waste of energy and I'd rather focus on generating a profit or being out on the water. It's annoying because I know I won't be able to stop thinking about what she just shared. I wasn't expecting it, and I'm not used to people taking me by surprise the way she did. I really thought I had her pegged, and that she was like so many of the people I see visiting our island with their Instagram problems and TikTok tragedies, just in different packaging. It's clear that she has a bit of an edge to her, but I still thought she was one of *them*.

As it turns out, she's a black rose with a black heart.

For sure, I've dealt with tough women before. Ones I grew up with that could kick my ass, the way my mother and my aunt actually used to. I have the scars to prove it. But I didn't know that someone as beautiful as her could be so scarred, so tough. I don't like the way she's making me feel.

I sigh. For now, I need to push her out of my mind. After all, I have plenty of work to do.

Rake glances at me, a smirk forming on his face. "Already having girl problems, Sky? Only take you what, a couple of hours?"

"Just a dumb bitch pretending to have real problems," I say, rubbing my hand across the stubble on my jaw, and realize I have food on my face still. "Nothing I can't handle."

But as the words come out of my mouth, I realize I'm not so sure. On either count.

Chapter Seventeen

Devon

Stomping down the hallway, my wrists still bound, I realize I have nowhere to go except for the room where they've been keeping me captive. I stand there for a while, trying to figure out my next move. There really aren't many options in my current predicament.

I walk back into the kitchen, where they're still standing.

"And one more thing," I say, narrowing my eyes at Skyler. "You have food on your face, and you look stupid."

Rake and Dom both snort, and Zeke shakes his head and sighs. I swear the corner of one side of his mouth turns up a little, just for a second, before going back to neutral.

Skyler glares at me, then walks to the kitchen counter and wipes off his face with a cloth.

As soon as he wipes away the food, his expression seems to soften slightly. It's like he angered quickly and then got over it within moments.

I, on the other hand, am still feeling quite fired up by my own cathartic yelling. I probably overshared, but it felt good to get it out. Those were things I carry deep inside, and that I haven't let out in a long time. And that was only the start of my darkness. There's plenty more where that came from.

The other guys are all continuing to stare at me. Dom's mouth is slightly ajar, and Rake is looking between Skyler and me with amusement, probably wishing he had a bag of popcorn. Zeke squints at me like he's trying to read me, like he's wondering what my next move will be.

I want these guys to think I'm violent and have a deep hatred of them for taking me captive. It might be helpful if I just pretend to lose my mind completely, to shriek and howl as if my life depends on it. Because it actually might. But I'm tired and they haven't killed me yet, so instead, I glance at each of the guys one by one, taking them in.

Instead of anger, my gaze betrays me, drifting down Skyler's taut body as I remember how turned on I was during the lesson. Looking at him now, I can't help but feel arousal again at the tightness of his torso and his tattooed, athletic body, and the explosion of emotions he just brought out in me.

Maybe I really do want him to take me, to dominate me, and do whatever he wants with me. My pussy clenches at the thought, just like it did when he took me out in the ocean. Maybe I want all four of them to do that.

Oh, god. I need to push these thoughts down so I can escape. Not keep thinking about trailing my hands over their abs and down into their pants. I have never felt so conflicted or distracted by a man, let alone four of them.

"Maybe you shouldn't be mad at us. You should be grateful to us," says Zeke, narrowing his eyes at me.

"How so?" This is a plot twist. "I should appreciate you for holding me against my will? I have issues, but that's beyond even me."

"You're the one with the piece of shit father who would literally give you to the most evil man on the islands to pay off his debt and save his own life. Maybe he's the one you should harbor resentment toward."

I expect to feel anger at his words, but a wave of deep sadness washes over me instead.

"But you could have let me go," I blurt. "You didn't have to hold me captive against my will."

"What kind of message would that send to everyone on the island? Let alone how it would impact our relationship with Tane Brown?" Zeke is pragmatic as usual. "We'd lose all credibility on the island and beyond. Probably lose responsibility for protecting this territory, too."

"Sounds like you're stuck with me, in that case."

"It's kinda true. You have a point. We can't just let you go, and personally, I don't want to just yet. I think we all likely feel the same way. You need to stay here until it's time to hand you over." He glances around at the other guys and they all nod.

"It would have been easier if they just brought me here for you to kill me." I'm half-joking, trying not to hang onto their comments about this Tane Brown guy and what's meant to happen to me when I leave this house. I need to change the subject. "Why are you staring, Rake? You've never seen a woman before?" I glare at him because he's been eyeing my tits for what seems like ages.

"Oh, we've seen plenty," he replies. "But they rarely last long here. We tend to... uh, break them, I guess you could say."

"You're bullshitting me."

"That's not his style," says Skyler, smirking. "He's honest to a fault."

"Yeah, for example, you have really nice tits," Rake says, grinning, his teeth grazing his bottom lip, animalistic, as his eyes fixate once again on my tank top-covered breasts.

I roll my eyes and try to pretend my nipples aren't pebbling under his gaze.

"Well, lucky me then, I guess," I say, glaring back at them and jutting out my chin. "Because, as it turns out, I'm unbreakable. I'm going to take you down one by one and get the fuck out of here, and there's nothing you can do about it."

They look at each other, smirking. They have no idea how serious I am.

Just as much as they need me to stay, I need to find a way out of here.

CHAPTER EIGHTEEN

Skyler

The unpredictable, crazy fucking bitch. Spitting food at me. The height of disrespect. I haven't felt such rage in a long time. She's lucky I didn't knock her out right there at the dinner table.

She's also fortunate she didn't try that with Dom, or she might not even be alive right now. My temper is quicker than his, but he's also a brute force and sometimes can't control himself once he gets going. One of his massive hands squeezing around someone's windpipe can do a lot of damage. I've seen it many times. That's what makes him such a good enforcer.

After dinner, we put her in the soundproof room again. She doesn't put up much of a fight when Dom carries her back to the room, unbinds her wrists and closes the door. I think she knows she went too far, spitting food in my face. And even though she shared some of her dark past with us, we can't overlook her doing that.

We'd been thinking about inviting her to watch TV with us for a bit tonight to test the waters, but clearly, we can't trust her, and this is her punishment. Solitary confinement. I'll come up with something even better soon, maybe even something that will provide some pleasure for me.

I did relent and throw a pillow in there, and a blanket that she won't be able to use to harm herself. We may be holding her captive and punishing her for her unacceptable behavior, but I'm not a complete monster.

With her safely locked in the house and Dom on duty to watch her on the security cameras, the rest of us head out for a surf while the sun sets. "Don't let her out, don't visit her. Just leave her the fuck alone to wallow in her punishment," says Zeke, warning Dom as we leave.

We take over the surf break nearest to our house, and when we recognize a few acquaintances of the Brixtons, we make sure to cut in front of them.

Being a snake in the ocean means you know your power and you use it. You cut in front of other people because you can. Because you're better and stronger and they know it, so they let you. It's about exerting your abilities rather than shying away from them, showing people what you can do that they can't, and making them submit.

It's the perfect way to wind down from an eventful day, and the ride back gives us time to plot out how we intend to approach our captive for the rest of our time with her.

"When do we get to play with her?" Rake grins as we head back to the house.

"Soon, Rake, soon," says Zeke.

"Dom says he gets first dibs, though, because he got called by the goons first." He frowns. "He might even be getting what he wants right now."

"He'd better fucking not be. I'd kill him," says Zeke, his eyes flashing. "We all need to tread carefully here, or she could do a lot of damage to what we've worked so hard to achieve."

"But I want some time alone with her," says Rake, a dreamy expression on his face.

"It's alright, we'll all get a turn." I make eye contact with Rake in the rear-view mirror and can see the desire in his eyes. It's going to be hard to keep him away from her.

CHAPTER NINETEEN

Dom

I watch her on the cameras for a while. She paces around, still trying to find a way to escape even though it's futile, pounding on the door and window with her mouth open in a scream of frustration when she doesn't find any way out. I can't hear her but have no doubt my new friend is swearing like a sailor in there.

I also see her try to destroy the blanket that Skyler gave her, but she's unable to shred it with her bare hands.

She throws all of her new clothing around the room and examines the bags they came in, but doesn't seem to find a way to turn them into anything useful. She ends up slamming the pillow into the wall a few times as she continues to yell, and then she finally flops down onto the ground, putting her head on it and crossing her arms tightly over her body as she frowns at the ceiling.

Watching her have her little tantrum, I'm turned on. She's so pretty, lying there all frustrated. Her mouth is slightly open, her nostrils flared, and as her chest rises and falls, so do her gorgeous tits. There's a good angle of her cleavage from this camera, and I reach out and trace my finger along her delicate curves on the screen.

I can tell she has a lot of fight in her, and I can only imagine that she fucks like she fights. The thought of it makes my cock jerk in my pants. The way she banged up that goon's face before he dropped her off, I have mad respect. He was much bigger than her, and she's clearly very brave. Spitting food at Skyler was a ballsy move as well, especially with her hands being tied, rendering her somewhat defenseless.

As I watch my precious, angry little captive, I stroke myself. I want to wrap my arms around her and squeeze her as tightly as I can, carry her everywhere I go while she kicks her legs and pounds her fists against my back and screams. I want to fuck her, hard and fast, while she drags her nails across my chest and back, and puts all of her rage into bucking her hips as my cock slides in and out of her.

It's tempting to get a little closer, to open the door and see what happens if I go in. She's clearly feisty as hell, but I'm not scared of her attacking me. I just know there's a chance something might go wrong and I end up hurting her while my brothers are out. If she does attack me, I'll have no choice but to defend myself and sometimes I get into a zone where I just see red and I lose track of who and where I am. Then all bets are off, and there is some damage that can't be fixed. It's just me and her in the house, and nobody else here to pull me off her if that were to happen, and I can't trust myself that it won't.

There'd be hell to pay from Tane Brown and his men if we killed her, that's for sure. But that would be after my brothers deal with me first.

No, I'll have to wait to play with my feisty one. This time at least.

CHAPTER TWENTY

Zeke

The sky is pitch black when we get back to the house, the tiny sliver of waning crescent moon obscured by clouds.

I get out of the car first and start walking toward the building while Rake and Skyler take care of putting the surfboards away. My body initially relies on muscle memory to guide me down the dark driveway, but my eyes soon begin to adjust.

I don't refer to this place as 'home' because there's nothing homely about it. We're a bunch of guys who couldn't give a shit about it looking nice where we live. There are no throw pillows or *Live Laugh Love* signs here. We want a place to crash and to get business done. We don't love that our enemies know where we sleep and work, but it's all we've got. Living on a fairly small island makes it hard to hide. We're saving for something bigger and more secure, more like a compound, but still have a way to go before that will be possible. In the meantime, this will have to do.

At least our enemies are in the same predicament. Except for the ones that live further afield, in big cities on the mainland that we're less familiar with. But our location has its perks from a business perspective, too. When people from elsewhere visit and try to mess with us, they quickly find out that they're on our turf and that we have a distinct home-court advantage.

Approaching the front door of the house, I hear a rustle in the bushes to my right. I know the sounds the wildlife makes here—the scurry of a lizard, the nesting of a native bird, the subtle creep of a mouse. I can immediately tell the noise came from something much larger, and we don't have bears or big cats on this island. It was most certainly made by a human, almost definitely a man. Again, growing up here has some advantages.

I pretend everything is normal and that I haven't noticed him. As I near the door, just as expected, a bulky figure rapidly emerges from the bushes and lurches toward me. The guy is quick, but so am I. As he leans forward to sucker punch me in the side of my head, I grab his arm, pulling him past me and throwing him off balance.

As he stumbles, I take the opportunity to shove him away from me and downward.

He grunts as the center of gravity of his large frame tips and he thuds heavily to the ground. He's a lot bigger than me, so I don't waste time. I join him on the ground and pummel him, my fist connecting with his face in a frenzy, and I hear the satisfying crack of what I assume to be his nose breaking. He puts his hands up defensively, but I easily push them away and continue to smash him in the face.

"Please, stop!" The man cries out, saliva and blood and a tooth flying from his mouth, and as the moon emerges from behind a cloud, I get a better look at his face, which is now bloodied and beaten.

"Zeke!" I hear Rake's voice as he approaches from the roadside. He towers over the man, who takes my pause as an opportunity to hold his hands defensively over his face. He seems in no shape to fight back. "Who the fuck is this guy?"

"Some piece of shit who was hiding in the bushes waiting to ambush us when we got home. Wherever he's from, he's a weak link. Can't defend himself for shit, and tried to set me up with a sucker punch to the head."

I pry the man's arms from his face and push myself up to standing so we can both get a good look at him in the moonlight.

"Please! Please! No more," he says, tired and beaten, his face bloodied. "That's enough! I'm sorry. Just don't kill me!"

"Who the hell are you, and why the fuck are you here? Who sent you? And why shouldn't we kill you?" Rake snarls at the man.

The man stays quiet, his chest rapidly rising and falling, fear in his eyes.

Rake kicks him hard in the ribs and the man's body jolts.

He grunts out loud.

Rake rears his knee up, preparing to stomp on him.

"Fuck! Stop!" He begs Rake, eyes pleading, but to no avail. Rake stomps on the man, hard. He probably didn't need to keep going, but when people threaten our brotherhood or our business, Rake has no mercy. This time there's a loud, unmistakable crack as the flat of his foot connects with the man's torso. There goes a rib. Dom will be proud when we tell him. The man cries out in pain and grabs his side.

I glance toward further movement on the driveway as Skyler joins us, and the man's eyes grow bigger as he sees we're now a group of three.

"Okay, okay!" He screams, putting his hands out to protect his body. "The Brixtons sent me to give you a warning!"

"Oh yeah? What kind of warning? Be on the lookout for guys who can't fight?" Skyler raises an eyebrow, smirking at the man.

"That they're taking over your partnership with Tane Brown and his guys."

"Yeah, right," Skyler scoffs. "Because they have guys like you doing their dirty work?"

"The fuck they are!" Rake spits on the man, and then stomps on his shoulder. He cries out and grabs his shoulder with his other arm.

"You give them a warning back from us." I hiss in his face. "If you or anyone else from their stupid gang comes around here again, we won't just be snaking you and your boys out in the water. We'll take everything that's yours and make it ours. Your little gang is a joke, you hear me? You're like a fucking nursery rhyme. Coming around here trying to give us a 'scare'. Fucking pitiful. Do you feel equipped to relay that message? Better equipped than you were when you tried to attack me just now?"

I raise my arm back, readying to punch him again, and he flinches and then nods quickly. "Yes, sorry. I—please, just let me go. I promise I'll never come back."

This whole incident has been so sad for this guy that I just might believe him. Having to go back to the Brixtons with his tail between his legs. If I were him, I'd probably get the first flight off the island and never come back. I'd be too ashamed to ever show my face again.

"The fuck you won't. Get the fuck out of here." Rake kicks him as he gets to his feet, and he falls again.

He drags himself back up and then glances over his shoulder one more time to make sure there are no more incoming kicks or punches before he scurries off, limping, no doubt to report back to his leaders.

"A warning." Skyler scoffs. "More like a warning for those jokers to never try that again."

"Yeah, clearly not sending us their best and brightest. I'm just glad that didn't go differently, and that they didn't get to the girl." I frown.

If they'd made it inside and taken our captive, it would undoubtedly have put our longstanding arrangement with Tane at risk. He has to be able to trust us implicitly without groups like the Brixtons having a chance at undermining us.

This guy clearly didn't stand a chance. But our timing was fortunate on this occasion, and next time it might not just be one person they send.

CHAPTER TWENTY-ONE

Devon

*T*he music thumps inside our multi-storied home, the bass rever- berating off the wall as I try to sleep. But I know I won't be able to. There's too much noise between the thumping music and the chatter and raucous laughter of adults who've had too much to drink.

I curl my knees into my body, my arms tightly wrapped around them, trying to make myself as small as possible, to render myself invisible.

I hate it when my dad has parties like this. When everybody gets drunk and high and self-entitled to do whatever they want.

I fantasize that I'm wearing pajamas that have magical powers, that help me stay unseen and safe. But I know that's not the case. I've known for a long time that life isn't fair that way.

'Devon. Deeeeee-von.' I hear my father's sing-song voice that he puts on when he's drunk, accompanied by the deep tones of other men chatting as they make their way up the stairs. I know what's coming because it's not the first time it's happened and it won't be the last. 'Devon.'

I flinch as my door creaks open, and I immediately smell the whiskey fumes and cigarette smoke emanating from the men that enter with my father.

'Here she is,' he says, with what sounds like pride in his voice. 'Come and have a look at her.'

I squeeze my arms even more tightly around myself, trying to turn into a little ball.

'Devon, come and say hello to your nice new friends. They want to take a look at you.'

Squirming, I look away toward the wall, clenching my eyes tight. Hoping that if I can't see them, they can't see me, or that if I don't make eye contact, they'll lose interest and go away and find something else to entertain them.

'Devon.' My father's voice grows sharp. 'Stop being a little brat and be polite to my friends. Say hello.'

Slowly, I turn my face toward them, keeping my eyes tightly closed. I know what will happen later if I don't, because I tried that approach before and have the scars to prove it.

'That's a good girl,' he says, his voice softening. 'Now open your eyes and let them see you.'

Slowly, my chest rising and falling as I steel myself for what's coming, I open one eye and then the other. Two men stand there with my father, towering over me. They peer down at me.

'Hello there, Devon, is it?' one says, his gaze poring over me, taking me all in.

I nod, terrified, my body stiff with fear.

The other man smiles hungrily, reaching down to trace my jaw with his finger, which feels rough as it glides along my skin. 'You're a beautiful one, aren't you? Absolutely gorgeous. You were right, Frank. She's growing into a beautiful young lady.'

My father smiles as if my beauty is his biggest achievement. 'She sure is.'

One of the strange men sits down on the side of my bed.

'Alright, then. I'll leave you to get to know each other,' says my father, as if it's the most normal thing in the world. 'Be a good girl now, won't you, Devon? Now that your mother's not here anymore, it's your job to entertain.'

My dad laughs and stumbles away, sloppy as usual, and he closes the door behind him, leaving me with his two acquaintances.

I wake up in a sweat, a pit of nausea in my stomach, but relieved that this recurring nightmare stopped earlier than it sometimes does.

As my heart rate slows as I realize I'm not back there, locked in that memory, I look around in the dark. My brain fog starts to clear, and I realize I'm not at home or in a hotel or even in some random guy's bed. Instead, I'm a captive in a random house on an island.

Great. Now it's coming back to me. The guys shut me in the room last night as punishment. It was infuriating, having to lie there with nothing to do and nobody to talk to.

Just me, alone with my thoughts. That's the most dangerous place for me to be. With nowhere to go, no phone to scroll through, and no booze to create a warm, fuzzy numbness. There's no way to distract myself, to escape from the torment I constantly feel.

While being held physically captive is clearly less than ideal, it's what's inside my mind that scares me more.

Chapter Twenty-Two

Rake

"Knocky knock knock!" The door is thick and soundproof, so I don't actually knock, but open the door to Devon's room just a crack and call out to her. "Are you ready to be let out? Are you going to be a good girl for us today, or do we have to leave you in here as further punishment?"

I push the door open so I can see her better.

She's sitting up against the wall, legs bent so that her feet are flat on the floor, her pillow on her lap with her arms wrapped around it.

She looks at me. "Please, just let me out. It's fucking boring in here."

"If I give you a coffee, do you promise not to throw it in my face?"

Her eyes light up at the mention of coffee. "I promise."

"Alright, I got you iced coffee, just to be on the safe side."

I produce a plastic cup filled with freshly brewed iced coffee. Not taking any chances that she'll actually throw boiling hot coffee at me, or smash a glass or ceramic cup and use it to harm herself or me.

She takes the cup from my hand quickly, wraps her lips around the straw and thirstily chugs it down.

She sighs softly after a few sips. "Mmm, I prefer cold brew anyway. Especially in a climate like this." She takes several more sips until I hear the slurping sound that means she's reached the bottom of the cup and hands it back to me.

"Thirsty girl, huh?" I grin at her. "Taking it all in at once. Sexy."

She rolls her eyes. "I have a question for you," she says, eyeing me.

"I'm an open door," I say, even though nothing could be further from the truth.

"I noticed your back earlier. How'd you get your scar?"

"Shark attack," I answer without a pause and grin at her. "Great white. I fended it off. You should have seen it when I was done with it."

She eyes me skeptically, but changes the subject. "Is there any food? I'm starving."

"Well, that's kind of on you. You were being fed, and instead of being appreciative, you spat it all over Skyler. He's still pissed by your atrocious table manners, by the way."

"Oh yeah? Well, maybe my table manners are better when I'm not being held hostage by a house full of men."

"Touché." I shrug. "Listen, did you learn your lesson? If you come out to the kitchen and have breakfast with us, can we trust you not to stab us with a fork or assault Skyler's pretty face again?"

She rolls her eyes. "If I get to have breakfast and get the fuck out of this room, I promise not to attack anyone. For now."

"Alright, come with me." I extend my empty hand.

She glances at it suspiciously, but then reaches out her own and I grab it to help pull her up to standing. Her skin feels smooth in my hand, making me want to touch more of it.

"Come on, then." She follows me down the hallway, out through the living room and into the kitchen where the other guys are sitting at the table working out some details of a transportation job we're supposed to do in the afternoon.

When we enter the kitchen, they all look up.

"Devon's going to join us for breakfast. She promises to be on her best behavior. Don't you, Devon?"

She narrows her eyes as she takes in the sight of the three other guys sitting around the kitchen table. The far side sports a bench seat big enough for two, so with that and the three chairs, the five of us can fit. It's a tight squeeze, but we can make it happen.

"Come on, Devon, we'll sit over on the bench." I guide her around and she plops down heavily.

"This is a terrible idea," says Zeke, staring suspiciously at Devon as if she might suddenly pull out a weapon.

"Relax," I say. "It's fine. Now, are you going to apologize to Skyler, Devon? Once we get that over with, we'll feed you."

"Do you want a genuine apology, or can I just lie through my teeth?" She rolls her eyes and then glares at Skyler, who narrows his own eyes in response.

"Come on now, Devon. We could be making your life so much more difficult. And he did insist that you get a pillow and a blanket, even after you did what you did."

"That was your idea, Skyler? Super chivalrous of you." She rolls her eyes again. "Thank you for the blanket and pillow. I'll leave a positive review on Airbnb for your hospitality. Also, I'm sorry I spat in your face and hope none of the hot sauce got in your eye."

Skyler snorts. "That's a loaded apology, but under the circumstances, I'll take it."

"See? That wasn't so hard," I grin. "Now you can have some breakfast."

I go to the kitchen counter and load scrambled eggs and bacon onto a paper plate, along with a piece of freshly buttered toast. I bring it over to her with a plastic fork. We have proper silverware, but we're not stupid enough to trust her with a metal fork yet. Before I sit back down, I head back over and grab the hottest of the hot sauces from the fridge and bring that to her as well, handing her the bottle.

She looks up at me and raises an eyebrow. "Thank you," she says, and then liberally coats the eggs with the thick red substance. She devours the eggs and then begins to eat the bacon with her hands. "This is actually really good," she says, her mouth full of food, before inhaling the entire piece of toast within seconds.

"Glad you like it." I grin, absolutely thrilled that she enjoyed her breakfast, although I realize that hungry captives probably have a low bar for culinary excellence. "Fascinating fact about me. I actually went to cooking school for a bit. Didn't finish it, but I did learn how to make the perfect scrambled eggs."

Zeke clears his throat. "Oversharing with the captive."

"I'm entertaining our guest. It's only polite." I shrug.

She gives me a look, scrunching her face like she doesn't quite believe me, searching my eyes to see if I'm joking. "Alright then, Chef Rake. The more you know."

I laugh. "Something like that."

CHAPTER TWENTY-THREE

Devon

B reakfast was unexpectedly pleasant. I was starving, and probably would have eaten anything put in front of me, but it did really taste good. Better than the continental breakfasts I've been having at the hotel.

It was a revelation that Rake did anything other than hold women captive and surf. Humanizing, I guess. And remembering that I like hot sauce was oddly thoughtful. He also got me clothes and makeup and stuff, now that I think about it.

I obviously don't know them well at all, but I get the sense that maybe these guys don't hold women captive on a regular basis. They don't seem to know what to do with me. I'm just glad that they're letting me out of that boring room.

After breakfast, Skyler, Dom, and Rake leave to take care of something, leaving Zeke to watch over me.

He stays at the kitchen table, working on a laptop. He has an intensity about him while he works, squinting at the screen now and then and frowning as he taps away at the keyboard. Probably realizing I'm just standing there staring at him, he glances up at me. "You can go watch TV if you want. Check out the house. Just stay out of our rooms." He goes back to intensely focusing on his laptop.

I eye the front door, but it's well within his view, so there's no point in even trying to escape through it. I head down the hallway, through the living room with the couch and the TV and a video game setup. There are some plants on the windowsill. Interesting. I didn't figure these guys would be interested in houseplants. It's kind of reassuring to know they can keep a living thing alive, being their captive and all.

I wonder if this whole letting me roam around the house by myself thing is a test. If they're sitting outside, waiting for me to escape. They've got cameras in here. I've noticed a couple of them and am sure there are more I haven't spotted yet.

There are several doors along the hallway, presumably their bedrooms and maybe a bathroom, and then of course the door at the end that leads to the room where they're keeping me. I don't want to go back in there if I can help it.

Heading to the first door on the left, I try to open it, but it's locked.

I move to the second door, and it opens to reveal a bathroom. It smells of steam and masculine shaving cream and soap, like someone freshly showered. They all seem quite clean for guys, I guess. There's a laundry hamper full of clothing. There are toothbrushes in a cup over the sink and a half-used toothpaste tube. I'm tempted to do something gross to fuck with their toothbrushes, but I think better of it. Good to know they're there if I change my mind.

I open the medicine cabinets, but they're basically empty, with a couple of washcloths underneath the vanity and some extra shampoo. Nothing I could use as a weapon. They must have locked their razors away, which was wise.

I head to the other side of the hallway and try to open the door directly across from the bathroom, but it's locked as well.

I make my way back down the hall and try to open the other door on that side. Bingo. It's unlocked. Quietly, I turn the handle and open it and slip inside.

It's relatively organized and clean. Inside is a freshly made bed, with dark blue sheets pulled up to the pillows, not military-level precision with the bed-making but not messy either.

There's a window on one wall and I try to open it, but it's locked. No surprises there.

There are a couple of trophies on a bookshelf featuring figurines of men surfing. Engraved on each is *Skyler Kane*. Well, well, well.

I trail my fingers along a row of science books. They seem to have a common theme around kinesiology and psychology. Interesting. During my lesson, he did spend a lot of time explaining muscle memory and psychological blocks, encouraging me to see the wave the whole way through as far as I could take it. He definitely went above and beyond what I'd expect most instructors to cover, which is part of why I really enjoyed my lesson, other than looking at his hot body the entire time. And now I see why. He's clearly a big science nerd. That's kind of hot, actually. And then paired with a hot body and lots of tattoos. *Drool*.

On another shelf, I'm surprised to see some CDs. How quaint. They're a collection of country music albums, and I even see a Taylor Swift album in there. Oh, I'm going to give him shit about this.

In one of the room's corners, to the left of the bed, I see a guitar. I'm not an expert, but it looks fancy, with some ornate carvings on it. It seems to take pride of place in his room, on a special stand. Obviously, he's a talented surfer, and it looks like he's a bit of a musician too. From its placement, the guitar seems important to him. An evil thought passes over me, because they *are* holding me captive, after all, and I have a particular beef with Skyler after he's shown up in my life in two very different contexts. But I want to finish exploring the room first, so I look in the drawers and find nothing especially exciting. Just clothing, a tube of lube, and a box of condoms, the large kind. Interesting.

I see a few twenty-dollar bills in his sock drawer, and I stuff them inside my underwear. They might come in useful somehow.

I glance over at the guitar again. It wouldn't be very nice of me to damage it, but then again, it's not very nice for these guys to be holding me hostage, is it? It's tempting to test them, to see how far they'll go. Maybe if I can get them to truly snap, they'll be distracted and I'll find a way to escape. I quietly take the guitar from the stand and leave Skyler's room. I carry it to the end of the hall, to the room they've been keeping me in. The door's still unlocked, and I put the guitar inside for when it's the right time to carry out my evil plan.

I tiptoe back down the hallway and sit down on the couch and flick on the TV, trying to act casual. I find something to watch, a reality TV show. The couch is comfortable and offers a cozy reprieve after sleeping on the floor. I lie down and snuggle against a cushion.

———

I open my eyes and look around, confused by my surroundings yet again. They're different this time. Instead of being locked in my captivity room, I'm on the couch, and there's a blanket over me. I must have fallen asleep watching TV. Goodness knows how long I've been out.

Zeke is sitting at the other end of the couch. He notices me stir and glances over at me. "Hello there, sleepyhead," he says. He has his laptop on his lap, but for whatever reason, has made his way to sit next to me on the couch instead of continuing to work in the kitchen.

"I didn't mean to fall asleep," I say, sitting up and stretching my arms up high. I feel a little foggy from my unintended nap.

"It's no problem. You're cute when you're sleeping, by the way," he says, a softness in his eyes that I haven't seen before. He's normally so intense. "Beautiful, even."

I feel a flush creeping up my neck as I gaze back at him, both because of his unexpected compliment and because he's still shirtless. He is very hot. Like Skyler, he has an ageless quality where I guess he's probably older than he looks. Deeply tanned, and covered in gorgeous tattoos, he's only wearing board shorts.

He sports a silver watch on his wrist which I've noticed him glance at regularly, as if he lives his life on a tight timeline. His arms are sinewy, muscled and strong. He's athletic, with a smooth, well-defined chest. His jaw is strong and square, and his intensely observant eyes are an icy blue-green that reminds me of the ocean. He has straight, white teeth, but I haven't seen them much because he rarely seems to smile.

I'm glad the eye candy is at least good here, and that the guys who kidnapped me from the hotel aren't the ones keeping me at their house.

"What are you working on?" I ask, genuinely curious. I don't imagine he's typing out hourly reports on my activities.

"Protecting the island, and helping things get to where they need to go," he says.

"That's cryptic." I frown. "What do you mean 'protecting the island'?"

"There are things that need to happen to ensure we preserve this place and way of life as much as we can. There are so many tourists, no offense," he says, glancing at me and frowning. "People trying to fuck with the natural order of things. Some locals get distracted and get too big for their boots. It's up to us to help keep this island as close to what it should be as possible."

"How does that involve keeping me captive?" I narrow my eyes at him.

"We believe people should pay their debts." He shrugs. "And from what I understand, your father owes a massive debt with no way of repaying it."

"So you're okay with me being sold to the highest bidder? A human being sold?" I feel a surge of anger course through my body, as if he was describing me as some commodity to barter over.

A strange cloud passes over his eyes. "Well, no, not entirely. But sometimes we just need to do our job and not ask too many questions."

"How is that okay? Why don't you just let me go?"

"Because we made a commitment to keep you here, and we're going to follow through on that. We need to."

"Who are you keeping me for?"

"The man who runs the island chain. His name is Tane Brown. We work for him, but it's the only way we can keep this island the way it needs to be. He's powerful. Nobody crosses him." He sounds so practical, so clinical.

"Even when he tries to auction off *humans*?!" My voice continues to rise.

I throw the blanket off my body and stand up. My fists clench at my side and I feel my heart thump in my chest. Blood rushes to my temples. "Sounds like a cop-out to me! It sounds like you and your boys would do anything for money or to look good for this Tane Brown guy. Sounds like your moral code is sketchy as fuck!"

It's enraging, being this helpless to change my circumstances and I want to take it out on him, on all of them. I look around, but there's nothing heavy for me to grab within reach. I want to take something, anything, and throw it across the room. But I have something specific in mind. A little smile spreads across my face.

"Careful," warns Zeke. "Do you want me to lock you in the room again? Because I will."

"Fuck you," I hiss. "I'm choosing to go in there myself."

I storm off, out of the living room and down the hall to the end. I open the door and let myself into my den of captivity. Being careful not to lock myself in accidentally, I remove the guitar from where I placed it earlier and stomp back down the hall to the living room.

As Zeke looks on, his eyes growing large, I raise the guitar high above my head. He glares at me, his ocean eyes frosty. "Drop the guitar," he commands.

I smirk at him. My heart beats faster as I keep the guitar above my head, raising it even higher.

"Drop. The. Guitar. Do not test me, Devon."

Grinning, I bring it down as hard as I can in front of me, smashing it into the TV. The screen shatters, glass fragments flying everywhere. I turn slightly and continue bashing it on the edge of the entertainment stand. It splinters apart, piece by piece, as Zeke watches in horror. I yell each time I exert myself, smashing the guitar into the stand, over and over again. Finally, I stop, out of breath, just the long neck of the guitar left in my hand.

"You really shouldn't have done that," he says, frowning.

Just then, Skyler walks into the living room. I hadn't heard him come in the front door, probably because I was hosting my own demolition derby in their living room. He looks at me, and then at the remnants of his guitar in my hand and all over the floor, as well as the smashed TV, and his jaw clenches. He looks over at Zeke, who shrugs and mouths, 'Sorry'. His eyes darken, almost seeming to turn him into someone else.

"What the fuck is going on in here?" He runs over to me and grabs my wrist. His grip is rough, and I try to pull away, but there's no way he's letting go.

"Drop it." He's snarling, and I can feel his hot breath on my ear.

"Or what?"

"I'll fucking kill you." His eyes are like pinpoints of rage. He's seething. I believe him.

I keep holding the neck of the guitar, as if to taunt him, and he shoves me against the wall, placing his other hand against my throat and once again cutting off my air supply.

"I mean it, Dev. Don't fuck with me. Drop it." He loosens his grip on my throat and I gulp in a deep breath.

Sighing, I let the piece of guitar fall from my grip. He's unpredictable and has a mean streak, as I've come to learn. They all have a certain level of palpable intensity about them. But there's something particularly volatile about Skyler, and the guitar appears to be a real sore point. Maybe I shouldn't have set him off. I fear that it's too late. This time, maybe I've gone too far.

It could be because I know this will not end well for me, that this is where I'm going to die, here on this island at the hands of the person I'm sold to, or even one of these men. But I decide to continue poking the bear. "Why did that upset you so much? It's just a guitar, after all." I smile sweetly at him. "I'll buy you another TV if that's what you're worried about."

He flicks his hand out quickly and slaps me hard across the face, leaving me seeing stars and my jaw stinging from the impact. I knew he was furious, but didn't see that one coming.

"You fucking bitch." He growls at me, and it's primal. He's so close to my face that I feel his breath on my skin. A tiny drop of saliva lands on my cheek.

"Say it, don't spray it," I say, a cruel smile playing on my lips as I test the waters, to see if I can get him to snap further. I can't resist, even though this could be my undoing. But then again, maybe there's no better time to stop feeling the pain that's lingered within me for far too long. It sounds better than being sold to some psycho.

He slaps me again, this time harder, and I feel my teeth reverberate in my jaw. My lower lip splits against the roughness of his palm, and I feel a little trickle of blood beginning to form, like karma for what I did to that other guy.

His eyes grow large at the sight of my blood and it seems to snap him out of whatever enraged trance he was just in. He reaches out and wipes away the blood with his thumb, which he then licks clean. His eyes drill into mine as I watch him tasting me.

It's weird. He's just hit me across the face twice and yet now he's looking at me with what appears to be fascination and concern, maybe even a bit of remorse. I have a feeling that he didn't intend to make me bleed. At least for now.

"You going to hit me again?" I ask, batting my eyelashes and running my teeth over the wound on my lip, tasting my own blood.

"Are you done being a brat now?" His voice is gruff, but it's as if this is him extending an olive branch.

"Why would I want to stop? I'm being sold to a fucking sex trafficking person. What do I have to live for? Why don't I just antagonize you until you kill me?"

"Maybe that will be the outcome, especially if you keep carrying on the way you have been," he says, now eerily calm. "But I have some plans for you. A way of pushing you, of punishing you, and I intend on enjoying every moment of it. By the time I'm done, there will be no question that you belong to us. And that you want to belong to us, even beyond when your time with us is up. You'll be begging for more." His eyes are still angry, but they've taken on that mocking glimmer I've started getting used to. I'll take his mean over his angry.

"There's no way that's ever going to happen. I don't want to have anything to do with you guys, although it appears that I'm stuck with you for now. It's not like I have much of a say."

"You're right about not having a say." He winks at me, and I feel a chill pass through me. He removes his hand from me, still standing close enough for me to feel the warmth emanating from his skin. He crosses his arms over his chest, making his biceps bulge, and I'm momentarily distracted.

Fuck, why does he have to be so simultaneously hot and volatile? I don't think this is Stockholm syndrome because I am under no illusions that he and his brothers would hurt me in the blink of an eye if it came down to it. He's just shown me he would.

Everyone has a dark side. And nearly everyone will lash out when they're cornered, when they feel trapped. But the twinge between my legs is betraying me, a familiar throb starting every time he exerts dominance over me, like right now. A therapist could have a field day with this.

He smirks at me. "You are a real brat, you know that?" He frowns. "I'm sorry I hit you in the face, though. I shouldn't have done that. Guess I got carried away. Are you okay?"

"I've had worse." I frown, because it's true, and his eyes flash to mine with what seems to be concern. "What's the deal with the guitar, anyway? Why did you get so angry?"

He sighs. "Family heirloom, I guess you could call it. Handed down by my father before he died, from his father before him. Only thing my father ever trusted me with." His eyes display pain, but I get the impression this has to do with more than just the guitar. "One of a kind, irreplaceable."

"Oh. I see." *Shit.*

Even though they're holding me hostage, a shiver of guilt runs through me. They haven't really done anything more than keep me in a room. They've fed me and even given me hot sauce. It's not their fault that my father didn't pay his debt, that they're just fulfilling their obligations to this Tane Brown guy. It doesn't make what they're doing right, but it places it in somewhat of a morally gray area, I suppose. And I'm over here smashing up their most precious items.

I gaze at him. He's so close, I can see the slight ridges at the edge of some of his tattoos. I want to reach out and touch them, to trail my fingers along each one.

"Yeah. Anyway, you're going to clean up the mess you made, and then we're going to figure out what to do with you. Because you are going to be punished. But who's to say you can't enjoy it a little as well? I feel like you don't mind us as much as you say you do." He winks at me, his eyes twinkling the way they did back at the beach.

I feel myself flush. Fuck, it's like he knows that I'm becoming increasingly attracted to him and his chosen brothers. That the danger and mystery and violence that swirl around them is becoming intoxicating. I was trying to keep that little fact close to the vest, but something in his expression tells me he's onto me.

"You need to pull yourself together and stop acting out like this, though. I can't promise that Dom would have been as understanding had you pulled this little stunt on him just now. We've been incredibly nice and… tolerant of your little shenanigans until this point. But our patience has run thin. And what your punishment entails, and there most certainly will be punishment, is entirely up to whether or not you're a good girl."

The front door bangs and Dom and Rake appear from the kitchen. They glance around at the debris, glass and wood everywhere, and at the three of us who are already standing in the room. Rake lets out a low whistle as he surveys the scene.

"Jesus," says Dom under his breath as his eyes settle on the neck of the guitar.

"You're just in time, guys," says Skyler. "We have a punishment to dish out. Dom, as soon as she's done cleaning up, take her to the room and make sure it's locked properly. She's not allowed out again until we say so. This time she's not getting off so easy."

"I hope at least one of us gets to!" Rake grins, rubbing his hands together excitedly.

"Clean up." Skyler points at the fragments all over the ground.

Dom heads to the kitchen and comes back with a trash bag. I place fragments of glass and wood into the bag, and can feel their eyes boring into me, particularly Skyler's. They converse in inaudible whispers behind me, no doubt figuring out what to do with me, and I can't make out what they're saying.

I turn so that my back is to them, and place a sharp piece of wood into my bra.

Once I'm done cleaning up, Skyler takes the trash bag from me, snatching it out of my hand and walking it into the kitchen.

"Take her into the room, Dom," says Zeke, "while we figure out what to do with her next."

Dom nods and throws me over his shoulder like I'm light as a feather, which I'm not going to lie, is pretty hot. I make a show of pounding on his back and kicking my legs about as hard as I can, but he just laughs and carries me down the hallway.

"You're turning me on," he says.

I hear Rake crack up in the background, and Zeke snorts.

"In you go," says Dom, placing me down gently. "You really shouldn't have smashed up that guitar, you know. It wasn't nice. It was very important to Skyler."

"Holding people hostage isn't nice." I pout, crossing my arms across my chest. I see desire in his eyes as my arm-crossing unintentionally plumps up my breasts, creating more cleavage than usual.

"That's true." He shrugs, gazing at me with gentle eyes. "But life isn't fair. And we're still going to punish you for what you did to Skyler's guitar." He exits and closes the door behind him. I hear the lock click into place.

His approach was oddly gentle, understanding even. A rough, tough giant who could have thrown me across the room but chose not to.

I just can't figure these guys out. Maybe their punishment will tell me more about them and their true intentions. Because right now, they don't seem like hardened killers, although I don't doubt they could kill someone if they needed to.

They seem to have a morally ambiguous sense of right and wrong, and they might be prepared to get rough. They could have done much worse after I destroyed their precious property. But for whatever reason, they chose not to.

Half an hour later

"You will spend the rest of the day with Rake." Zeke announces my fate as he opens the door to my room of captivity, and leads me out into the living room where Rake is lying on the couch and Dom and Skyler are standing in the middle of the room. "And he will figure out the most appropriate punishment for you based on your behavior today."

My god. He's leaving me unattended with the one who's most obsessed with my tits, the one who seems most unhinged out of all of them. The one who's made it abundantly clear that he wants me. Either my body or my life, maybe both.

Rake winks at me and grins. "Let's get the party started then, shall we? I have plans for you. But first, please put on the purple t-shirt with the sequined unicorn on it."

Jesus. This is going to be a weird time.

Chapter Twenty-Four

Rake

I can't help but smile as my brother informs the group, including Devon, that she's going to be my plaything for the rest of the day. None of the other guys has got to spend any one-on-one time with her yet.

It's particularly exciting that I get to decide on the punishment. I enjoy punishing humans that deserve it, and finding new and exciting ways to do it. I like to think of myself as the wildcard of the group and I flourish in that role, always doing the unexpected. Dom likes to use his fists, but I like to mix things up a little more.

She's shown us a bit of her darkness already, but doesn't seem to realize darkness radiates within all of us. She needs to learn that bad behavior doesn't go without punishment. Even the ones who don't let on, who wear a mask that hides their real selves, experience pain. Everyone is bad in some way. Everyone dies. Sometimes I just make sure that people feel a little extra pain when they cross my path, because

I enjoy it. I have a feeling that maybe she already does too, but if she doesn't, she will learn soon.

Every woman I've ever met has let me down, starting with my mother, so I don't doubt that Devon will do the same at some point. But for now, I think she's cute and hot, and there's a way to punish someone that can involve a bit of pleasure as well, if you do it right.

I'm always trying to find that perfect balance, that little tightrope of pleasure and pain. Almost giving in, letting them go nearly all the way and then ripping it back mercilessly right before they reach their destination. It's a hobby of mine, you might say.

I think we could have some fun with this one, though, so my plan is to not go in as hard as I might ordinarily. She will be well aware that I've punished her when I'm done with her, but she'll still also be very much alive. I just need to make sure I don't break her. I want to be able to play with her more than once.

She stares at me, wearing the purple unicorn T-shirt just like I asked her to, and I know she's doing her best not to let on how scared she must be. I think she thinks I'm a bit crazy, and she'd probably be right about that. Her breathing has grown shallow and I see her consciously trying to slow it, to breathe deeply. Her cool-as-a-cucumber ruse is fooling nobody.

I return her intense gaze and tower over her, grinning in a way that I was once told makes me look slightly deranged which only encouraged me to do it more. Knowing she is a bit scared of me only serves to turn me on, and my cock grows hard in my pants.

I enjoy trying to terrify people just a little, and she seems like the type of person who tries to make out she's a badass. I mean, she kind of is one, but she's trying to make me think she's even tougher than that. It's a bit of a power trip seeing such a feisty little firecracker seem vulnerable and worried about what I might do to her.

I reach out with my thumb and touch her split lip, pressing on the minor wound so that it bleeds again. Reaching behind her, I grab her hair at the nape and bend down, pulling her to me and biting gently on her bleeding lip. I run my tongue over it, savoring the flavor of the blood that oozes from her. I smack my own lips and grin at her. "You're delicious." I wink.

She looks up at me, and her eyes grow large. God, she's gorgeous with her large eyes and long dark lashes. "What are you, a vampire? Drinking my blood? You're the second one of you to do that now."

I can't help but chuckle. "Something like that, my little... Devo. Something like that."

I'm quite pleased with the name I've just come up with for her on the fly. It seems perfect. My feisty little Devo, because she's a deviant, just like me. Devilish. I can just tell we're going to have a lot of fun together.

"I'm looking forward to giving you your punishment, by the way." I growl into her ear, still holding her hair close to the nape.

I see her body stiffen as if she's afraid I'm maybe actually going to hurt her. Maybe I'm laying this on a little thick. There are times I've been a little too rough, maybe bitten someone a bit too hard, but that's not on the agenda for today.

I've promised to keep her mostly intact during this little session of ours. Just enough to teach her a lesson and remind her that me and the other guys are the ones in control here.

"You know that you've brought this upon yourself." I growl like an animal, pulling her hair to the side so that her neck tilts, exposing her smooth flesh. I have the urge to sink my teeth into her, marking her, but instead, I lean down and lick her neck. She quivers under my tongue. Her breath grows shallow.

I flip her around so that her back is facing the wall, and I advance on her so that her body presses up against it. She looks up at me, pleading. She has nowhere to run, and she knows it.

I lean over her, a forearm on either side against the wall behind her. "It's okay, my little Devo. You're strong enough to handle what happens next."

This is probably the most scared I've seen her. She stills and I just stand there, towering above her, meeting her gaze.

"Alright, it's time," I say, after a few moments. I lean down, my arms still pressed against the wall. "Kiss me," I say as my lips graze her smooth, creamy neck.

"You want me to kiss you?"

"Yep. You heard me."

"That's my punishment?"

"Think of it as a gateway to your punishment. An appetizer, if you will." I grin at her.

"You've gone through all this because you want a kiss. Why don't you just take it?"

"Because I want you to give it to me."

She meets my gaze, and I see a look that I recognize, because I feel it too. Desire. I'm sure she must still be a bit scared, but she's not repulsed. Instead, she seems to be turned on by me physically towering over her, rendering her unable to move. The thought of her arousal at me dominating her, of me tasting her blood, causes my cock to twitch again.

She pauses for a moment, and her gaze travels to my lips. "Fine then, fuck it."

She stands on her tiptoes and pecks me on the cheek.

"That's how you kiss your grandma when you visit her over holidays," I say, smirking. I gaze down at her and bite my bottom lip. "Kiss me properly. Show me how you really feel. How much you want me."

"I don't want you, though." She sighs, but it's a weak attempt at a lie and her body betrays her. She eyes my lips again and licks her own, a primal response to her growing desire.

She leans in towards me, wrapping her arms around my neck, and the next thing I know, her lips are on mine.

She had a choice not to kiss me. I wouldn't have forced her if she had risked not doing it. But she didn't turn away, and she didn't try to run or stomp on my foot or kick me in the junk like she did to the guy who dropped her off at our house.

Instead, she looks me straight in the eyes and takes her version of control.

Her eyes close as uses her tongue to pry open my lips, entwining it with my own with urgency and hunger. She dips her tongue in deeper and begins to explore.

I lean back towards her, dominating her now, sliding my tongue through her lips and feeling her bite down just enough to feel her teeth graze against it. God, she bites, too. My cock twitches again. Our tongues lock in a spirited dance, wrestling for dominance.

I suck on the end of her tongue, wishing it was her clit, and she lets out a little moan. I wrap my hand tightly around the back of her neck, pulling her closer to me. She clings to me, her nails digging into my flesh. I growl and plunge my tongue further into her mouth. God, I want her so badly.

It's as if all of her anger and frustration and fear are being channeled into this kiss. It's electric. She's electric.

I increase the pressure of my lips on hers and nibble on her bottom lip to make it bleed again, just a little. Licking the blood from her gorgeous lips, I slide my tongue back into her mouth so that we can both taste it.

I lean into her, my body shaping against hers, my hardness pressing prominently into her mid-stomach.

This woman is intoxicating. I can't get enough of her, and this is only our first kiss.

I want more. I want all of her. Realistically, I could take her now and she wouldn't have a choice.

But instead, I unwrap my hands from around her body, detach hers from around my neck, and walk out the door, shutting it behind me. She might be the one locked in a room, but now I'm also captive.

CHAPTER TWENTY-FIVE

Devon

As much as I don't want to admit it, the kiss with Rake has gotten me all worked up. I'm a sopping mess, my pussy throbbing intensely as I think about the sensation of his lips on mine, of his tongue sliding into my mouth. The way he sucked on my tongue and used his teeth got me wondering what else he likes to nibble on.

But he's dangerous. Who knows if he will be so nice next time? And now he has a taste for my blood. I could feel his arousal through his pants, digging into me. It felt impressive, and I can't say I minded at all. As crazy as it sounds, I was disappointed when he left the room. Maybe he's all talk when it comes to punishments.

As hot as that was, I need to focus. I'm still a captive, and if I don't get out of here by the time five days are up, it's clear I'll be handed over to a man who's pure evil, and then potentially someone even more terrifying than him.

A shiver runs down my spine. I'm going to have to figure out an escape plan. To exploit their vulnerabilities. I haven't seen many yet, but they must have them.

Everyone has a fatal flaw, no matter how strong they might seem on the outside. I just need to figure out what can take each of them down.

Still, I can't stop thinking about the hardness of his cock when he pressed into me. It was clear that he desired me, that he was focused solely on me with his intense gaze, and I know he intends not just to stop at a kiss. For whatever reason, he stopped from going any further this time, and left me horny as hell. He's an absolute lunatic, unpredictable in a sexy way, and I can't stop thinking about his cock. Which isn't going to help me get any closer to escaping.

Flustered and more than a little frustrated, I lie down on the ground and wrap the blanket around me, resting my head on my pillow.

Half an hour later

I wake up to see that I'm still in the captive room and must have dozed off.

I keep thinking about Rake's mouth. His tongue, his lips. His hardness further down. Maybe I just need to relieve this pent-up tension. Maybe then I'll be less distracted, and more focused on getting out of this little predicament.

I think about what it would be like to tack on a second part to our interlude, to see his cock unfurling as it emerges from his pants. Sliding my hand inside my underwear, I find that, as expected, I'm soaking wet. Using gentle pressure, I tease my clit.

I take my other hand and slip two fingers inside my pussy, gliding them in and out of my slick entrance. I imagine what it would be like to have Rake's hardness, which I'd earlier felt pressed hard against my belly, slipping in and out of me, pounding into me over and over again. There's no doubt it would be rough, crazy even. There is no calmness when it comes to this man. He's chaotic, he's wild, he's fun. I bet he knows how to use it, too.

As I speed up both hands and insert a third finger, I moan. I wonder if he likes to go down on women. He's very skilled at kissing. I wonder if he'd suck my clit into his mouth the way he did with my tongue when we kissed.

I can't stop thinking about him. Or his brothers.

I want them to have me. I need it.

There is nobody else that has ever made me feel this way, to this degree. And now there are four of them. Four incredibly hot men.

I know it's dangerous. But I can't help it. I'm becoming obsessed.

A moan emerges from me as I think about fucking Rake while his brothers watch. Their eyes, watching his hard cock sliding in and out of me as I sit on it, slamming up and down. I imagine gazing back at all of them as I control his cock.

An intense orgasm tears through me, causing my entire body to shudder, my hips bucking against my own hand at the thought of these handsome, muscular, desirable men.

Satisfied and pleasantly tired, I clean up and then lie back on the ground and pull the blanket around me. I still don't know how I'm going to get out of this one. But I may as well indulge in some fun in the process. Maybe taking my punishment and giving, and receiving, a little pleasure will prove to be the key to my freedom.

They want me to be part of their group. For now. Maybe the days will run out and I'll find myself in the hands of some madman who wants to kill me himself, or terrorize me for the rest of my life. Maybe I'll antagonize these guys so badly they actually will kill me.

At least then my pain will float away.

CHAPTER TWENTY-SIX

Skyler

"**W**hat are you grinning at, you goofy fool?" Rake is sitting on the couch when we get home, a smile stretched from ear to ear. It's not rare for him to smile, but he's straight-up cheesing.

"Nothing," he says. "Just thinking about my girl."

"*Your* girl?" Dom snaps, narrowing his eyes at Rake. "I don't believe you get to call dibs on her, bro. As far as I'm concerned, she's *our* girl. Am I right, guys?" He looks at Zeke and me for support, and we both nod.

"Well, whatever. *Our* little girl showed me a good time earlier."

I feel a little envious, wondering what they got up to while we were out.

"What was her punishment?" I raise an eyebrow.

"I made her kiss me."

"Where?" I narrow my eyes at Rake. "What part of your body?"

"My mouth. Relax." He smirks at me.

"Oh yeah? And how was that? Did she knee you in the junk?"

"No, actually. She kissed me back. She wanted it. Wrapped her arms around my neck and shoved her tongue in my mouth. She's a very good kisser, too."

"And that's all?" The three of us stare at Rake, clearly all eager for more details.

He shrugs. "Yeah, I left her in there, and she was practically begging for more."

"You're an odd duck, man." Zeke snorts at Rake.

"That's not a punishment, Rake." My eyes narrow. "She broke my fucking guitar and you just... kiss her?" I glare at him. "I'm going to have to finish off what you started. She needs to learn."

"What can I say? Some things are worth waiting for."

"She's being sold off in a few days, man," says Dom, his voice sullen. "We don't have time to wait for anything."

"Way to bring down the mood," I say. But he's right, and I can't help but frown.

Our girl isn't going to be ours for much longer. She may not even be alive for much longer, and if whoever she's sold to does keep her alive, her life is going to be a horror movie.

"Do you think there's much we can do about it? We should at least put our heads together and think of a way to get her out of this situation."

I glance at Zeke, and can tell it's weighing on his mind as well. He's no doubt mapping out every plausible scenario and the pros and cons attached. I wish I was as creative as him when it comes to solving problems.

As if on queue, Zeke's phone rings. "Yep," he says, glancing at the caller ID and frowning as he answers the call. "Seriously? The timeline was adjusted?" We all stare at him, trying to figure out what's going on. "You're sure?" He pauses. "Okay then." He hangs up and sighs, looking at the ground.

"What's going on?" I ask.

"It was Tane's men. He's reduced the timeline. Meaning we have her for three days less than we thought."

"No way!" Dom growls. "Why?"

Zeke sighs again, his shoulders slumping. "Apparently, our Devon has proven quite popular, and a few interested parties have started a bit of a bidding war. It sounds like a few of them have some pretty sick plans for her."

"Oh my god," I blurt. "What the fuck are we going to do?"

"I really hope we figure something out, because I want to feel her lips on mine again. I want to keep her here forever." Rake's eyes take on a dreamy appearance, and it's almost as if he's floating. He grins and adjusts himself. "After we finished making out, I watched her on the cameras, and her hands were under the blanket, but I think, I really think she finger-fucked herself."

"What?!" Dom grins at Rake, his eyes growing wide. "For real?"

"Yeah, she did. She was really into it, too. I think I've fallen in love with our little Devo," he says in a sing-song voice, resuming his ear-to-ear grin.

Jesus, he's going to be devastated when we have to hand her over. He's obsessed. We're all obsessed. This girl is going to ruin us if we don't stay vigilant.

———

Later that day

She looks up as I enter her room. She's sitting with her back against the wall, a bored look on her face.

I couldn't get her off my mind, and I meant what I said about finishing what Rake started. Might as well let her enjoy herself as well, while she still can.

"What do you want? What have I done now?" She narrows her eyes at me.

I sit down next to her. "You must be bored sitting in here."

"Yeah, it fucking sucks. I hate it." She narrows her eyes at me. "Why do you care?"

"I just wonder what you think about when you're in here by yourself." I wink at her. "Do you fantasize about me?"

She snorts. "Yeah, sure. I sit here and jerk off while I think about you and your four friends." Her words have a ring of truth to them. She doesn't know what showed up on the cameras earlier.

"Rake's punishment was a bit lame, no?" He's so lucky he got to kiss her.

"Why? Think you can do better?" Her eyes twinkle at me, challenging me.

"Oh, I know I can. Want me to try?" I let my eyes trail down her body, and rake my teeth across my bottom lip.

Her chest rises and falls more quickly as her eyes roam across my body, as if she's taking inventory of each of my tattoos.

"Maybe." Electricity crackles in the air between us. She reaches over and trails a finger across a tattoo on my arm.

"It's going to be more than a kiss, Devon. And it won't be gentle. I can't let you off that easy."

"It has to be more fun than being trapped in here," she says, her lips pressing together as her eyes meet mine.

"Alright," I say, winking at her. "Your funeral."

CHAPTER TWENTY-SEVEN

"Stand up." Skyler's voice is commanding and serious, but his eyes are full of desire.

I comply, interested to see what he has planned. If I'm going to be a captive, in a house with four hot men, I'm going to at least try and get something out of it.

Knowing you might not be alive in a few days also makes it easier to throw caution to the wind.

His eyes slowly travel down my body, landing on my shorts. "Remove your shorts and your panties."

His confident direction is making me aroused. I slide my shorts and panties off in one movement, leaving me standing there, my lower half bare to him. Resisting the urge to cover myself with my hand, I stand there, exposed.

He groans. "Get over here. Stand over me."

I walk closer to him, and he grabs me, pulling me to him. He reaches around and palms my ass cheeks, sinking his hands into my flesh as he pulls me closer.

"Oh god, you smell so sweet, just like I imagined," he says as he inhales, my pussy inches from his face.

He drags me even closer, planting a row of kisses against my lips, taking one and tugging at it with his teeth. My breath grows faster, and I gasp as he nips at my lip now, sending a ripple of good pain throughout my body.

He laughs. "You like that, Devon? Do you like pain?"

My breath hitches.

He nips again and I squeal. "Answer me when I ask you a question. Do you like pain? Don't try to hide it from me, Devon. I can see that you do. Your pussy is soaking and I've barely touched you, you dirty little slut."

I nod, and he smiles.

"That's my girl. Get ready for more, we've only just started."

He tugs on my other lip, gently this time, and I quiver as he places another kiss right over my slit. His warm breath caresses my most sensitive spot, and I feel myself leaning into his soft lips with my own. My pussy throbs like crazy as I wonder what's coming next.

"Lie down, Devon. And spread yourself apart for me. I'm hungry."

I get down on my knees first, and then slide onto my back. I let my thighs fall open and reach down, spreading my lips apart, displaying my pussy to him.

He groans. "Oh my god, you're so beautiful."

He kneels down in front of me, bending his head and kissing me on my slit again. He slides a finger into me.

"And so fucking wet," he rasps.

I can feel my juices sliding out of my pussy. I've been craving this man and now he's touching me. It's all on his terms. But I don't want him to stop.

He licks me, from my ass up to my clit and a moan escapes my mouth.

"Jesus, you taste good." He lets out a growl, his husky voice causing my pussy to clench.

I gasp as he sucks my clit into his mouth. My whole body trembles as he flicks it with his tongue. And then his teeth sink sharply into my swollen nub. I cry out as sensations of pain and pleasure wrestle to take victory over my nerve endings.

He laughs. "Do you like that?"

I look down at him, not saying anything, trying to find the words.

He bites down on my clit again. "Oh my god!" I yell, my back arching as pain radiates through my body. It stings, but in a good way. Whoever said you shouldn't use your teeth when performing oral sex was wrong.

He yanks my thighs further apart, pulling against my muscle, and he plunges his tongue inside me, lapping at my arousal. I moan as he begins to fuck me with his tongue, sliding it in and out of my hole. I buck my hips in rhythm with his thrusts, and he reaches out, gripping my hips tightly to hold me still. I squirm as he continues to plunge his tongue into me, at his mercy, unable to meet his rhythm.

His eyes meet mine and he begins to lap at my clit, humming, causing little vibrations of pleasure to radiate throughout my body.

Without warning, he plunges three fingers into my pussy and bites down hard on my clit. I cry out and grab the back of his head, smashing it against my cunt. He laughs, sucking on my clit as he glides his fingers in and out of me.

I start to grind my hips against his face, and I feel the beginnings of an orgasm forming in my stomach. He increases the pace of his tongue, thrashing it against my clit and I feel myself getting closer.

My body begins to tense, pressure rapidly building and building. The instant before I come, he pulls away.

I narrow my eyes at him, my mouth open as I pant, catching my breath. My pussy aches for an orgasm, or to be filled with his cock.

"I'll give you a choice now. I can leave you here, or I can finish you. But no more tongue, only teeth." His eyes glimmer, and he bites his lower lip as he eyes my pussy.

His pants are tight and I can see that he's rock-hard.

I stare at his mouth, and as good as his tongue felt, I know that I have to have his teeth on me again, even if it hurts. And I definitely can't let him leave me here like this.

"Finish me," I pant. "Please."

"Are you sorry that you broke my guitar?" he asks. I'd forgotten that was why we were here.

"Yes," I nod furiously. "Yes I'm really sorry. Please, just finish me."

He smiles. "Good girl."

He descends on my pussy again, and I cry out as he nips his way up and down each of my lips, tugging and letting his teeth sink in further this time. They sting, a low buzzing pain.

He sucks one of my lips into his mouth and I feel suction as his teeth scrape across it. He's giving my pussy a hickey, marking me as his. I moan and grind against him, and he pulls my lip as far as it will go with his teeth.

He suddenly bites down on my clit and begins to nip at it. I squeal and he laughs. Bucking his head so that his teeth are basically fucking my clit, he growls, animalistic. His hot breath fans across my pussy. Jesus.

He slips two fingers inside me again and continues to nip at me, and I feel myself edging closer to orgasm. My swollen clit feels raw, sensitive. I cry out. "Please."

"Please what?"

"I need your tongue. Please," I pant.

He smirks. "Only because you asked nicely and because you apologized."

His tongue gently laps at my tender clit, soothing the pain. I moan as the pressure against my clit grows and grows, and he continues to thrust his fingers into me.

As he swirls his tongue over my bud, my orgasm starts building again, more quickly this time, as if it remembers where he left off.

He groans against me as he devours my clit, licking and sucking and swirling.

My hips buck and I lose all control as my orgasm reaches its peak, my whole body shuddering as a wave of pleasure crashes over me. White stars flood my vision as feelings of bliss course from my clit throughout my entire body, my pussy clenching tightly around his fingers.

He groans again, continuing to lap at me while I writhe under his tongue.

I cry out loudly, certain the others in the house can hear me, the door left slightly ajar, wondering if they're watching us on the cameras. I wrap my legs tightly around his head as he continues to lick my pussy while I squirm.

After just about longer than I can take, he removes his mouth and his fingers, my release dripping down my thighs and making a puddle on the floor.

He looks at the mess and smirks, then gazes at me, his mouth slick with my juices.

He climbs on top of me and reaches his mouth to mine, sliding his tongue between my lips to meet mine. He kisses me, hungrily, and I wrap my tongue around his, moaning as I taste myself on him.

I feel his hardness pressing into me, and for a moment I think he's going to remove his shorts, but he doesn't. Instead, as I lie there, he removes his mouth from mine, pushes himself up from the floor, and stands over me, his eyes trailing over me, a look on his face that I can't quite put my finger on.

He retreats, and I silently watch him leave, still regaining my breath, craving more of him. He reverses out the door, and I hear the lock click as it closes.

I am throbbing, tender, and raw. He has ruined me from the mouth of any other man. And I want to do it all over again.

Chapter Twenty-Eight

Dom

"You're on captive watch again, Dom," says Zeke, looking at me cautiously. "I know we all want to spend time with her, but I think you should keep her in the room. Last time we let her out to roam around, we all know what happened. We're still waiting for the new TV to arrive."

"Yeah, yeah. You think I can't handle her?" I was hoping to have some quality one-on-one time with our girl while everybody else was out. Especially if we might see her for the last time a couple of days from now.

"Dude, it's not a criticism. I couldn't handle her, either. We let her out for a moment, gave her a sliver of freedom, and look at what she did. Destroyed the most sentimental item Skyler has in his life. Had, I guess."

Skyler looks down. "Listen, it's only a guitar. But," he says, looking at us both, "Zeke's right. She's highly unpredictable. Stealthy, cunning. If she sent us a job application, we'd hire her in a minute. We should only let her out when at least three of us are here. I don't even think two is enough to control her."

Zeke snorts, because it's true. "So you got this, Dom? You did a good job last time."

"Yes." I sigh. "I can look after a captive in a locked room. I did it last time, didn't I?"

I flick my lighter on and play with it against the palm of my hand, riding the line between generating searing heat but without burning my flesh. Fire fascinates me, and it ever has since my life changed. It's probably weird that I've developed such a liking for it in the circumstances.

Clicking off the lighter, I frown. I'm so sick of these guys doubting me. I know I've let people down before, in the most unchangeable way, but I can look after this fucking girl.

"Yeah, of course you can," says Zeke, slapping me on the back twice, hard, as if he's reading my mood. "We trust you. See you later on."

They all leave me to it, and I pour myself a cool glass of water and take up a post by the camera monitors. She's sitting in her room, meditating or some shit. I know she's going crazy in there. I know she hates to be by herself with her thoughts, because I'm the same way, too.

The minutes tick by and I want desperately to be near her, to experience what Rake experienced. Watching her on the camera monitor just isn't the same. A kiss from the most beautiful, fierce, brave, angry woman I've ever seen. I want to do more than that, too. I want to play with her.

I sit, legs up on the desk that holds the camera monitoring equipment, flicking my lighter on and off, on and off, while she sleeps. So beautiful, so peaceful when she's not breaking things. So psycho when she wakes up.

Eyes still closed, she suddenly starts throwing her arms around and her mouth opens, her face grimacing. She flails about, and her legs are kicking now too. Clearly, she's having some type of nightmare.

I try to wait it out, but it continues after five minutes, and then ten. She's tormented, and I need to wake her up. To save her. I've been in this situation myself, too many times to count, and it's terrifying. Recognizing the signs of someone in the throes of night terrors, I can't just let her go through this alone. I didn't force this, and I need to go in there.

I rush down the hallway from my informal guard post and hurry to unlock the door. I bend down to attend to her, intending to wake her up, to soothe her in my arms, when she leaps up and screams.

Suddenly, I feel a searing pain in my lower torso.

"What the fuck?" I yell, grabbing myself and seeing blood start to flow from my body. She stabs me in the shoulder as I try to protect the first area she stabbed. "What the hell are you doing, you fucking devil!"

She cackles and reaches out to stab me in the face. I reach my arms out just in time to feel the edge of what she's holding slash me gently on my cheek. I grab her hands together. "Drop it, Dev!" I growl. "Don't make me actually hurt you."

"Who says I don't want you to?" She cackles again, sounding hysterical like some kind of unhinged witch. "Kill me, if you like. I'd rather that than what's going to happen. Do your worst! I don't need these dark thoughts anymore! I shouldn't be here, anyway."

At that moment, I see myself in her. I drop to my knees. "Oh, I'm so sorry, Dev. I'm so sorry. You do deserve to be here."

She suddenly swings around, her momentum carrying her wrists away from my grasp, exploiting my attempt to help her.

Her eyes are large, crazed, as she screams at me. "You can't keep me! I'm not yours! I'm nobody's but my own!"

She slashes at me with the sharp piece of wood in her hand and I feel it as it slices down my chest, impaling itself in my flesh, and she runs out of the room as my hands fly to where she just speared me.

The weapon is still sticking out, and I realize, as she flees, that it's a piece of Skyler's guitar. She must have grabbed it while she was cleaning up after her destructive episode.

I move to get up and follow her, as the door swings shut and I hear the click of the lock. The quick, clever little bitch. She's locked me in the room that she's supposed to be trapped in. She's fucking brilliant.

I pull the guitar fragment out of my chest and blood oozes out, but not anything I can't fix at home. Assessing the injury, I'm sure it's going to leave a decent scar. At least I'll always have something to remember her by.

Shit. I have to find her, but first I have to get out of this room.

Running my hands through my hair, I realize I'm going to have to explain this to the other guys. I had one thing to do while they took care of other important things, and this is how we ended up.

Losing the one thing that any of us have cared about in a very long time.

CHAPTER TWENTY-NINE

Devon

I rip myself loose from Dom's grasp and I run as fast as I can, swinging the door shut behind me and hearing the satisfying click of the lock that until now has held me captive. Ha! Two can play this game.

I run to the front door. My near-photographic memory comes in handy as I punch in the code, as fast as I can, that I've sneakily watched the guys enter, and unlock the deadbolts. I shove the door open and I sprint as quickly as my legs will take me, down the driveway and out into the street. My lungs feel like they're exploding as I run and run until I can't go any further.

Turning around, I see that nobody's following me. I just hope the other guys don't get home anytime soon so I can get a decent head start. I walk fast now, weaving through a few streets, so I'm not on an obvious path along what seems to be the main road.

After a while, I stop. Where do I go now? I don't know where I am, and I have nothing but the cash that I swiped from Skyler's room. No phone, no ID. I don't know where my father is. After attacking Dom,

I probably look like a crazy person. I look down and luckily there's no blood on me.

Counting out the money that I grabbed, it looks to be about eighty dollars. I realize my hands are shaking.

I'm free, technically, from my captors. But I feel far from free. I don't know where I am, other than on this island. I'm all alone.

If I run to one of these houses, who's going to believe my story, anyway? I'm a girl with pink streaks in my hair, covered in tattoos, with nothing but a bit of cash on hand. Fuck knows, but based on my experience, whoever I try to get help from might try to take me captive too.

I'm so angry. How did I get myself into this position? Why did I cave into my worthless father's insistence that we come to this island? I feel so betrayed. I wonder if he knew he would trade me as collateral for a debt, if that's why he was so insistent on coming to this place. Or if that just became an opportunity for him while we were already here. Maybe I'll never know.

I keep walking up the street, even though I have no idea where the fuck I'm going. As long as it's away from being trapped in a room, I figure I'm in a better position than I was earlier.

After a couple of blocks, I see one of the most beautiful, comforting sights I've ever seen. It's everything I ever needed right now. Absolute perfection has met me at this moment. Like a series of sunshine rays breaking through a fluffy white cloud, but the complete opposite.

It's the grungy, nondescript exterior of what most certainly is a dive bar. The perfect way to get my head straight, to give myself the courage to figure out my plan for escaping from this hell that I've fallen into.

Hell within a hell, the irony. Who would have thought a beautiful island could have such an underbelly of horror and evil?

As I approach the bar's entrance, I hear the familiar screech of heavy metal from the inside, and it warms my soul. There hasn't been enough music in my life lately, and this is going to be just what I need. I can feel it.

I yank open the heavy door from the outside. It creaks, and the handle is sticky. Some would say gross, but I find it comforting. Real people come here, people with sticky fingers and probably worse problems than that, or even than what I'm facing.

Once I'm inside, it takes a moment for my eyes to adjust. It's dark and dingy, just the way I like it, the walls and ceilings painted black to match my soul. There's a long bar on one side, and high tops running along the length of the bar itself, as well as the back wall. It's pretty busy, and I take a seat at one of the few empty barstools. There's no menu, of course. Just a row of liquor bottles and various beers on tap and in cans. Excellent, whiskey's all I need, anyway.

The bartender is busy and looks delightfully grouchy. I'm here for it, as long as he gets me drinks. After a few minutes, he turns to face me and nods to indicate he's ready for my order. "Shot of rye," I point to a bottle.

He nods, grabs a shot glass, and places it on the countertop. Taking the bottle from the back bar, the man pours until the glass is almost overflowing. When he places the shot glass in front of me, I immediately grab it and shoot it back, savoring the pleasant burn that runs down the back of my throat. He winks at me. "Thirsty?"

"Yep, parched. Keep them coming."

He laughs and refills my glass. "I'll keep the bottle over here on the bar. Just shout out when you're ready for the next one."

Excellent. He gets the assignment.

Now that I've established myself in this seat, I take a moment to look around at the other patrons. Mainly men, and some have their eyes on me. I avoid eye contact. I'm not here for conversation or to be picked up.

From my peripheral vision, I can see a few continuing to stare, so I order another shot in an effort to block them out. To block out everyone and everything.

I can drink. A ton. Always have been able to. I think of myself as being like a powerful mammoth. Would need a giant tranquilizer to take me down.

I've been told I go from zero to a hundred and sixty miles per hour at times, when I reach a certain tipping point, and that's probably true. By the time I reach that speed, I'm not aware, and it's blackout zone. Booze doesn't make me vomit or get hangovers anymore. Sure, I'll have unexplained bruises and scrapes, and sometimes my hands and feet even get a little tingly, but those are small prices to pay to block the demons out of my mind. Today, there's no need to deviate from the usual plan.

I sit at the bar and keep to myself, enjoying shot after shot of whiskey while I plan my next move.

I could go back to the hotel and my father, but that doesn't sound appealing, especially after being kidnapped the last time I was there. Tane's men would just come and retrieve me again, because they think I belong to them, and this time they might follow through on their parting words.

For all I know, my dad's done a runner and escaped back to the mainland. Or maybe they've already killed him. I try to think about how I'd feel if he did get killed, but I'm unable to conjure up any feelings about it. Sad but true.

I guess I could ask someone here to borrow their cell phone and call the cops. But then what would I say? Four incredibly hot men are holding me captive in their house, but that I'm at a dive bar of my own free will?

I've asked cops to help me when I've been in real trouble before, and that's never ended well. They can't be trusted. It might even put my father's life at risk if he's not dead already, although he *did* just use me as collateral to pay off a debt, so that's not my primary consideration.

It sounds like this Tane Brown guy is bad news, pure evil, and I'm sure he has the cops in his pocket. They'd probably just deliver me back to the house I've escaped from, or even to Tane himself. A shiver runs through me as I think about what type of punishment he might dish out.

To block out any further thoughts on this, I order another shot.

Then there's the airport. I could try finding my way there, but I don't have any ID or money other than the bills I grabbed from Skyler's room, and I'm burning my way through the cash with this whiskey. Donkey might be able to get some money to me, but an ID is going to take too much time and too many explanations.

The liquor has me feeling a little fuzzy and warm now. It's a comfy feeling, like I'm home. I'm getting bold. Maybe I could go back to the house and beat the guys up, one by one. But what then? Back to the same predicament. Tane still claims to 'own' me, and I'm still stuck on this island without a way to get home that doesn't involve contacting the authorities and explaining this whole situation.

Maybe I can convince the guys to take out Tane, but I have a feeling they would have suggested it if they thought they had a chance.

"Hey there," says a deep voice. I glance to my right and see it belongs to one of the other patrons who has now appeared beside me. He's a burly guy, about six-foot tall with close-cropped brown hair and a striped tank top. He stands side on, facing me, his forearm propped on the bar. "I haven't seen you around here before."

I'm not here to talk to anyone, so I pretend not to hear him.

"I said I haven't seen you around here before," he repeats, louder this time.

I sigh and turn to look at him. "Listen, you haven't seen me because I haven't been here before. I'm not here to chat, so if you wouldn't mind, I'd like to be left alone."

"Bitch," he hisses and narrows his eyes at me, and then makes his way back down the bar.

I order another shot, and I'm starting to feel much better now. I'll find a way out of this whole situation, I'm sure. Just need to get my bearings, figure out how to get an ID so I can travel, and then I'll be all set. Go home to my regular life and add this to the very long list of fucked up shit to look back on.

Three guys approach me now, one on either side and one behind me, flanking me. The one standing at my rear taps me on the shoulder and I swivel around on my barstool to face him.

"Excuse me?" I snarl at him.

I cannot stand when guys reach out and touch me in bars. Noses have been broken and wrists have been twisted for this. But getting in a bar fight probably shouldn't be my top priority right now.

"Just came to say hello," he says, smiling. "You don't look familiar."

"That's because you don't know me," I said. "I just want to be left alone, please."

I turn back around and take my shot.

The guys don't move away. "Please, give me some personal space. There's plenty of room in this place that's not right beside me."

They look at each other and smirk at me. "She's a real piece of work, isn't she," one says. "Thinks she's invincible." The others nod and smirk some more.

I feel funny now, suddenly. The whiskey had me feeling good, confident, but something's not right.

Everything is getting a bit blurry. The voices in the bar are coming and going and I can't make sense of what anybody is saying.

I wish Skyler was here. Any of my guys. They'd know what to do.

My field of vision begins to narrow, and I feel the guys standing around me press closer as everything begins to shrink.

CHAPTER THIRTY

Dom

Fuck. *Fuuuuuck!*

I pat my shorts pockets and, luckily, I have my phone. I grab it and dial Zeke. He's going to be infuriated.

"Dom? Everything okay?" He answers on the first ring.

"Shit, bro. I've fucked up big time. I came in to make sure she was okay and she tricked me and ended up locking me in here! She's fucking devious. I'll give her that!"

"Make sure she was okay? She was locked in an empty room. Why the fuck would you go in and speak to her by yourself, man? We talked about this, about not going in there. You trying to fuck her or something? She's here as our captive, not our houseguest."

"She was having a nightmare, and it seemed to just keep going. I was worried she was going to hurt herself. I guess she fashioned a makeshift knife and impaled me with it."

He sighs. "We'll be right there. Don't go anywhere."

A minute or two later, the door clicks open and I follow Zeke to meet Skyler and Rake in the living room.

"You alright?" Zeke eyes my chest.

"Yeah. The bleeding has stopped. She got me here and here, too," I say, gesturing to my torso and my face, "but those ones are more superficial."

Rake lets out a low whistle. "That sneaky little Devo."

"Well, glad you're fine but you've really fucked us now, bro," says Zeke, his anger palpable in his tone. "We'd better find her and fast, before Tane's goons get word that she's missing. And we'll sort you out later, you dumb fuck! I'm not surprised that she escaped. You're so fucking thirsty, drooling all over her like a love-struck schoolboy."

"She's pretty amazing, though, isn't she? Hot, too." A little smile forms on my face as I think about how clever she was with her escape.

"She's a fucking smoke show, but at the end of the day she's just a woman," Skyler narrows his eyes at me. "I enjoy looking at her, but it doesn't mean I think of her differently than any of the others that have made their way anywhere near us."

"You're in denial. You like her much more than any other woman, Sky. I can tell. Don't try that macho shit, I can see right through you." I glare at Skyler. "She is absolutely not like any other woman we've ever known. She's unique. She's our Dev."

"She stabbed you, man." Rake squints at me like he's trying to diagnose me with some form of crazy, pointing at my chest and my torso.

"Yeah, it was hot as fuck." I can't help but grin. I feel tingly just thinking about it. "I'm going to have a scar," I point at the cut on my chest. "Might ask her to go harder next time." I flick my lighter and stare at the flame, entranced, picturing her dancing in the flickering light. "Might get her to brand me."

"Damn you're a sicko, Dom." Skyler snorts.

"Nah, I kind of get where he's coming from." Rake has a dreamy look in his eyes. "Finally, a girl who enjoys inflicting and receiving pain. I think I've met my soulmate. I'm ready to have some more fun with her myself. I'd let her stab me, too."

"Okay, enough. We get it, she's hot. Dom's in love with her. So are you, Rake. Now we have to find her, and fast." Zeke's back to being all business, reminding us we really do have to find Dev immediately. "Let's split up. She has to be on foot. You two go left," he gestures to me and Skyler, "and Rake and I will go right. Let's meet back here in an hour if we don't locate her before that."

"We are going to find her," says Skyler, a curious look in his eyes, "and then she's really going to get it."

CHAPTER THIRTY-ONE

Skyler

"Well, well, well. Look what I found." I look up from my phone, which I'm using to text acquaintances about potential Devon sightings, and I gasp as Zeke carries her over his shoulder, through the front door.

Dom and I had just got back after having no luck finding her for the past hour.

I follow them into the living room where he lowers her gently onto the couch. She rolls her head upward in my direction, but she doesn't seem able to maintain proper focus. Her eyes are glassy, and she has a crooked half-smile on her face. She makes a move to sit up on the couch, but her motor skills are visibly impaired and she just flops back down again.

Nobody moves to help her as she lies there. We don't have time for princesses, and since her little disappearing act she appears to have gotten herself into quite a state.

"Fucking hell, where'd you find her, bro?" She looks relatively content on the couch, but the thought of her stumbling around the street like that, vulnerable, is concerning. Anybody could have taken advantage of her. Good thing Zeke found her.

"Down at the local dive," Zeke shrugs. "They said she was acting fine until her eighth or ninth shot and then suddenly started acting like this."

"Oh damn. Well, she can drink more than eight or nine shots without being like this, I'm fairly confident." I recall back to seeing her at the hotel bar. This girl can drink.

I'm struggling with the fact she ran away. It feels like a betrayal in some way, but then I'm also not in her shoes. It's not like we offered a solution to her problem. We're still failing, to think of one, and in the meantime she tried to take things into her own hands. I just prefer the idea of her wanting to be with us.

I shove the feelings down. I'll worry about those later.

"How did you know she was there?" I raise an eyebrow.

"One of the Barrett boys called me, they were down there, too." says Zeke. "Apparently, when she started acting funny, she was saying our names in a sing-song voice. I'm glad they were there. This could have ended badly. Sounded like a few guys were circling her like sharks, trying to get her to leave with them."

"Jesus," says Dom, his eyes flashing.

"Yeah, I owe some beers to the guys that called. She has really impressive drinking skills, they said. Must have the liver of fortified steel. But something was up at that bar."

"She got roofied, it sounds like." A wave of rage rips through my body as the realization hits me.

I was mad that she left, but that pales compared to what she's just been through. What some rapey assholes were likely trying to do. My heart crashes in my chest like it's about to leap out of my body. My head hums with blood, my fists clenching at my side. "I'm going out there to find who did this and I'm going to kill those fuckers."

Again, she tries to adjust herself on the couch. It's not clear if she's trying to sit up or just get more comfortable.

"I understand why you want to do that, and we will take care of it." Zeke, as usual, is calm even during a crisis, the voice of reason. "Right now, our priority is to look after Devon and make sure she's okay, and to protect her while she's in this state. We need to stick together right now."

Rake walks in and immediately notices Devon in her fucked up state on the couch. "Well, well, well. What do we have here? A Drunky McDrunkPants?" He approaches her, and even though she's clearly not in her normal state, his eyes roam her body. He goes to sit beside her and starts to trail his hand up her leg, his eyes full of desire. "Think it's time to have some fun with her. We've left her alone until now. I think she'd be up for it."

"Hey man, knock it off. She's fucked up. Get your hands off her."

Rake is generally a good guy, but then he does weird shit like this and it makes me question things. "Like that's ever stopped anyone before."

"Nah dude, don't." Zeke's voice has a warning tone.

He continues to slide his hand further up her leg, onto her thigh.

"Knock it the fuck off, bro," I say. I'm getting annoyed now.

"Why? She's fine. She'll be fine in twenty minutes. No harm in having a little preview beforehand."

I rush over to him and yank his hand away. He stands up and he's taller than me, and we stare at each other. He's looking down at me, glaring.

"Or what? You going to stop me?"

"Yeah, if I have to. We don't treat any woman like that. And definitely not Devon."

"Oh my god. You fucking like her! You like her a lot! Skyler's got a big fat crush!" Rake grins at me and makes a kissy face, rubbing his two index fingers together as if they're making out.

"No, I just like my pussy to be conscious, that's all."

"Yeah, yeah. I was only joking anyway. Wasn't going to do anything to her," says Rake, backing off. "Nobody hurts Devon, and we're here to protect her."

"Well, what you just did was fucking weird. Not funny. You're lucky I didn't knock you the fuck out."

"Guys, stop arguing over her and can someone get her a glass of water or something?" Zeke, again with the sensible suggestion.

We stop bickering to look over at Devon, who's finally managed to sit up on the couch. She giggles and then looks around as if she's trying to figure out where the noise is coming from.

"Hi everyone." She grins, her eyes sleepy and her speech slurred. "Did you miss me?"

Even like this, or maybe especially like this because it's showing us her vulnerable side, she's so fucking cute.

"Yes, Dev." I sigh and shake my head. "We did fucking miss you."

I walk over and sit on the couch beside her, and wrap her in my arms. I press my lips to the side of her head, kissing her gently.

Losing her for a couple of hours was terrifying. There's no way we can lose her permanently. I never want to let her out of my sight.

Rake was partially right. I do have feelings for Dev, but this feeling is way more intense than a crush.

CHAPTER THIRTY-TWO

Devon

I feel funny, like everything is a fog, but I'm still awake, still present.

The guys seem to be squabbling, and their voices are a blur. I don't know what they're saying exactly, just that they appear agitated. Deep, husky tones that rise and fall. Sexy voices.

Someone, Rake I think, touches my leg and I half-giggle. Not that I think it's funny, per se. It's just like everything is in slow motion.

Rake is really hot, but I can't move my body properly and I just feel really funny. I wouldn't be opposed to him touching me in all sorts of places, but not right now. Right now, I just need to relax until things get clear again.

I think Skyler and Zeke must stop him because suddenly his hand isn't on my leg anymore and I hear their voices cut through the blur. They're arguing. The words are still indistinguishable, but I can tell that it's them. Zeke and Skyler.

Did they just look after me? And protect me when I can't protect myself? Zeke, so intense and hot. Skyler, so complicated and volatile and hot. Rake, so quirky and hot. Dom, so strong and gentle and hot. Hot, hot, hot, hot.

Which one do I like the most? I can't pick. Why do I have to choose? Maybe I don't have to. What a time to be alive. Or maybe I'm not alive and that's why everything seems like a fog. Maybe I'm dead, and this is some weird version of heaven and hell.

So confusing. And I'm so very sleepy. I could just take a nap right here, if only the room would stop spinning.

I need to sit up, but it's really hard. Like, the hardest physical thing I've ever had to do.

My arms don't work when I try to prop myself up. I try again a few times and eventually manage to hoist myself up, ending up sitting with my legs sticking straight out in front of me.

This is so weird, it makes me want to giggle. I hear giggling. Who's laughing? Is that me?

My vision clears just a little. I see them all now, hovering around me.

"Hi everyone," I say, but my voice sounds funny, wobbly. "Did you miss me?"

Skyler comes over and sits beside me and suddenly I feel his arms wrapped around me. It feels good to be in his arms. Comfy, cozy. Like I belong.

I do feel like I belong around these guys. I wish I could stay with them forever.

I never should have run away. There's a reason I did, but I can't remember right now.

Because I'm so tired, so very tired and my eyelids feel like they have little weights on them. Little tiny dumbbells making me do eyelid curls to keep them open. I giggle again, and then the world goes dark.

CHAPTER THIRTY-THREE

Zeke

S eeing Rake put his hands on Devon pissed me off. He was just being a goofball, trying to get a reaction from the rest of us, but I still didn't like it.

I'm beginning to feel some type of claim over her, a strong need to protect her, which is rare for me and is really getting on my nerves. I need to view her as just another piece of pussy, or better yet, just one of the many objects that we move for Tane, and she just happens to be human.

That would make things a fuckload easier to get through the rest of our time with her and to reconcile handing her back over to Tane's men and her inevitable fate. I'm assuming that once the highest bidder gets her under their control, they'll either snuff her in some sadistic way just for their own perverted fantasies, or have her working for them in the sex trade in short order.

Her looks will last a while, so they could probably figure out some profitable uses for her for a few years at least. Or they in turn could on-sell her to god knows who, and could probably get a pretty penny given how hot she is. I don't know that I'll ever be okay with that, especially now that I've caught feelings. It's something I just have to find a way to get used to. It'd be better if I just cut the feelings off right now before they grow any further, but I fear I'm already too far gone.

In the meantime I'm stuck being around her, noticing her scent. She smells like some kind of flower, but not in a grandma way. I know nothing about flowers, but that it's not that lavender shit that old ladies wear. And she also smells like citrus, maybe lime. Plus a fuckload of booze. It's that unmistakable scent of whiskey, even when she's not drinking it.

The way she talks, shot after shot, doesn't normally phase her. From what I've heard, she could drink the island's entire whiskey supply without stumbling.

If she was roofied, which seems to be the case, if someone has slipped something into her drink, I'm going to find out about it. And I'm going to kill them. It's as simple as that.

The four of us haven't gone that far before, although we've come close. But if somebody has tried to take advantage of our girl by rendering her helpless, there's going to be hell to pay.

Oh god, I'm calling her *our girl* now. That can't be good.

She's in my head.

Skyler and Rake almost came to blows over her.

She's clearly in Dom's head, too.

She's tearing us apart from the inside.

We're all in too deep.

CHAPTER THIRTY-FOUR

Devon

*T*he Next Day

I'm pacing in the living room, trying to put the events of yesterday back together in my head. Skyler's leaning against the doorframe between the living room and the kitchen.

"He's okay. He wouldn't do anything too fucked up," he shrugs.

"I seem to remember him trying to fuck me while I was so drunk I was barely conscious." I remember Rake's hand being on me, and loud voices following before he pulled his hand away.

"Yeah, I don't think he was trying to fuck you. He did touch your leg, but he stopped when I asked him to. He says it was a joke, and he's so fucking weird I believe him. I agree that's not cool, and he'd better never try that again or there'll be hell to pay. I'll kill him, I swear."

"Yeah, if he tries again... well, I'm of good mind to pretend I'm drunk around him again to see if he does. And then I'll chop his dick off."

Skyler laughs. "Somehow, I don't doubt that for a moment."

This brief exchange with Skyler, it's almost feeling natural, like we're building a genuine rapport. Like he is a human being who really cares about me.

I need to tread carefully here. Just because he's acting nice doesn't mean I don't need to be careful around him. I can't let my guard down just because he displayed a random show of chivalry.

He has slapped me across the face before, after I antagonized him until he snapped. He almost bit off my clit as well, although I enjoyed that. I can't let myself get too close.

And besides, my time is almost up.

Goodness knows what any other guys would have tried if they were the ones who found me in my hugely inebriated state. I might never have made it home alive. I'm still surprised I ended up that way, and can only guess that someone put something in my drink.

My headache when I woke up was different from any hangover I've ever experienced, back when I used to get them, and my mouth was unusually dry. I'd say maybe I just drank too much, but I can drink a shitload without it impairing me in any way.

My capacity to handle liquor routinely shocks doctors. I've heard that they're trained to take the answer to 'how much do you drink?' and double, sometimes triple, it. In my case, I'm usually fairly honest, so they must think I'm superhuman.

Not that it's something to be proud of, but it comes in handy when creeps are trying to take advantage of you because you're a woman who's alone at a bar. Unless they roofie you, that is. There's not much you can do at that point.

It was probably those guys who kept staring and trying to talk to me at the dive bar. I should know better because it's happened to me before. That's why I usually drink shots, so I can take the liquor down before anybody fucks with it.

I guess those three guys all came up at once. I remember turning around when the one behind me tapped me on the shoulder before I had the chance to take a sip, and it's the last thing I can remember happening before I found myself on the couch back at the house.

That just seems so orchestrated and creepy. I'm surprised I don't hate men completely.

There's something about this guy, though. My Skyler. He's an incredibly attractive, horny man focused on his own wants and needs. I can tell that much.

He's a flirt, he's good-looking, and he's out to fuck. There's an intensity and a darkness about him. But for whatever reason, I'm drawn to him beyond wanting to touch his naked body.

His mind is a turn-on. It only helps that he's physically so fucking sexy. I can imagine what we'd do to each other, how we'd take care of each other's bodies, how he'd punish me with his cock. He's already shown me what his tongue, his hands, his teeth can do. A shiver of pleasure shreds through my body as I remember his teeth scraping against me, stinging me. I'm interested to see what might happen next.

Still, I don't think I can fully trust him. He's too volatile, and a good fuck is all whatever this is between us could ever be. It couldn't grow to be anything more than that, because he and the others are holding me captive for fuck's sake.

I need to be careful, to protect myself. Maybe he's really nothing special, just a hot guy. There are lots of guys around. I'm just reading too much into something that doesn't even exist. At least, that's what I need to try and convince myself of.

"Don't treat him too harshly though, eh? He's still one of us, and he's loyal." Suddenly Skyler breaks into my thoughts. I'd kind of forgotten we were still in conversation. I have too much to think about.

"He's been there for me when nobody else has, and I know how much he's been through. Despite his flaws, I wouldn't trade him in."

I return his gaze, skeptical, a little ball of something forming in my gut. But I have to respect the strength of their bond. It must be so nice knowing someone has your back at any time and accepts you, flaws and all, even loves you more for them.

I realize the feeling in my stomach is envy. When everything's so continuously fucked up, nothing suddenly feels fucked up anymore. It becomes normalized. Like anybody else who hasn't been through half of what you have would never understand.

If most people experienced just a fraction of what we have in their lives, they wouldn't be able to handle it. One of our dark experiences alone would be enough to ruin some.

But for people like Skyler and me, anything could happen, no matter how bad, and it would just feel like any other day. Unlike me, though, he has three people to ride all of the waves, all of the good and bad things life throws, right alongside him.

"I'll have my eye on him, but I kind of get it. Kind of." I shrug.

He nods and puts his arm around me, squeezing me to his side. I lean into him, enjoying the feeling of his body pressing into mine, and he smiles at me.

Rake enters the room. He looks at me, and then at Skyler, and drops his eyes. "Can I, um, talk to Devon privately, please?"

Skyler glances at me as if to see if I'm okay with that and I nod. He removes his arm from my shoulder and heads down the hallway.

"Can we sit down?" Rake gestures at the couch.

"Why? So you can try to fuck me while I'm barely conscious again?"

"Look, I'm really sorry. That's not what happened, but I can understand why you think that. I really just want to explain."

"Fine." I head to the couch and flop down, arms crossed against my chest.

"Listen," he says, sitting down next to me with one of his long legs folded under him. He turns to face me. "It was a really poor joke, and yes, I touched your leg. But I see that it's not funny and just added to a really unpleasant situation. I would never do anything to hurt you, Devon. Really, I'm not like that with anyone, and especially not with you. I need you to know that. I'm so, so sorry."

His eyes are pleading. He has terrible taste in jokes, after all, and I can't help but think he's telling the truth. I can't just lump him in with the guys that put something in my drink because I'm angry at them. It wouldn't be fair.

"Well, I'll give you the benefit of the doubt." I sigh. "You've been alone with me before and you didn't try to pull anything. You kissed me, but I kissed you back."

"You remember our kiss?" A small smile forms on his lips.

"How could I forget?"

"So you forgive me?" His eyes are large, pleading.

"Yes. And next time I get roofied, I expect you not to do that."

His eyes flash darkly, the corners of his mouth pulling downward. "There's no way that anybody is ever going to do that to you again. And when we find out who did that to you, we're going to kill them. I can promise you that."

His protectiveness makes my chest give a little squeeze and I smile at him. "Wow, did we just have an adult conversation where we figured things out? I mean, except for the murder plot bit?"

He smirks. "Yes, Devo. I think we did."

He leans over. "Do you mind if I put my arm around you?"

"I would like that," I reply. "And thank you for asking first. Consent is sexy."

He grins.

I lean forward, and he wraps his arm behind my back and pulls me close to him.

As I mold myself into his chest, he kisses me on the top of my head. "I would never, ever do anything to hurt you, my sweet Devo. Please know that."

My bad-joke-telling, quirky, tall and hot, loving Rake. He's really growing on me. I'm really going to miss him when I leave.

CHAPTER THIRTY-FIVE

Zeke

I can't get Devon's impending handover off my mind. I've run every scenario I can think of through my head, and nothing has an upside.

We either lose her, or everything we've worked our whole lives for, or both. And I don't think I can live with either option.

In an attempt to distract myself from my dark thoughts, I crack open a slightly cold beer from the barely working fridge, take a satisfying gulp of the refreshing ale, and carry it to my room.

I take a seat on my bed, which is made neatly as usual because I like it that way, and as I continue to drink my beer, my mind floats back to her. To her scent, and how fucking hot I find that combination that's unique to her. She herself is a unique combination of spitfire and beauty and mystery. She's strength and vulnerability and bravery all in one.

Seeing her lying there, reliant on us to take care of her today, made me feel something. My cock jerks in my shorts as I think about her sexy smile.

Jesus, why am I so attracted to her? She's hot, but this is about so much more than the way she looks. My cock twitches again.

Giving in, I slide my hand inside my pants to grab hold of my cock. I imagine shoving her onto her back on the bed—and I have a feeling she likes it rough, just like I do—and sliding my hardness deep inside of her while she gasps in pleasure and a little pain as I fill her up, her mouth ringed by those sexy, full red lips of hers.

I stroke myself as I imagine flipping her over and once again slamming into her, this time from behind, grabbing onto her waist as I ram myself into her over and over again, her tight pussy enveloping my rock-hard cock. Reaching around and rubbing her clit until she bucks her hips with pleasure, screaming my name. Hearing her little gasps and moans as I dominate her and hold her down until l finish.

I groan as the vision of coming inside her makes me release at the touch of my own hand. *Fuck*.

Wiping myself off with my shorts, I grab a clean, neatly folded pair from the dresser. I don't know why she, in particular, has got me so aroused. I don't normally head into my room to jerk off during the day when I'm meant to be working.

Sure, she's sexy as hell. But I need to convince myself she's just another pussy. I keep telling myself that I don't need her. That I can go find it from so many other places whenever I want. And I can get good pussy anywhere on the island. It's on tap around here when you look like I do. I'm sure watching me surf has some girls creaming themselves. But she's the only one that's got me feeling this way ever since I laid eyes on her. I can't even imagine going out and finding some random piece of ass just for the release. I only want her. I need her.

I need to stop thinking about her like she's going to be here with us forever, like whatever *this* is would ever stand a chance in the longer term.

There's no room for something consistent in my life. And this is only temporary anyway, her being with us. I need to get her out of my mind.

She's distracting me, she's confusing me, and I need to get back in the game or I'm going to fuck up our business. My brothers need me to stay strong, to be a leader. I need to forget about her.

She'll be gone soon, anyway. It's the one thing I can't fix.

CHAPTER THIRTY-SIX

Devon

There's been a change in the energy of this house. They're letting me roam around freely.

After everything that's happened, I have no intention of trying to escape again. Sitting at the bar, thinking through my options if I actually could leave, just showed me there's no real point, and that things could just end up worse for me. Of course, I reserve the right to change my mind. A captive's prerogative, if you will.

But things are almost comfortable here right now. We spend hours just hanging out, cracking jokes and watching bad comedy shows on the replacement TV that arrived in the morning.

I try to ignore the doomsday clock ticking in my mind, counting down to when I'm going to be sold to the highest bidder. Jesus. Of all the fucked up things my father could do, this may be the worst yet.

Dom teaches me how to play a particularly violent video game where we burst people's skulls open with a variety of firearms and other explosive weapons.

It also turns out that the plants on the windowsill near the TV are his, and he's somewhat of an expert at making them grow, even the really tricky ones. He talks to them sometimes, apparently. Says it makes them grow faster or something. He teaches me how to prune them with delicate shears, creating room for more growth.

He brings out boxing gloves and teaches me to punch, showing off the boxing skills he learned many years ago. He lets me hit him as hard as I can and laughs at my efforts to cause him any pain as I pummel him.

What a chaotically violent, brutish, gentle giant he has turned out to be.

Skyler shows me his country music collection, and we listen to a couple of his favorite songs on his CD player, each of us wearing an earbud from the same cord like a couple of 90s kids.

He even shows me the cowboy hat he keeps hidden in his closet, too embarrassed to actually wear it around.

I get him to tell me stories behind each of his surfing trophies, and he regales me with tales of the best surfers that ever lived on the island.

He tells me he would have played me a song on his guitar, but of course, I smashed it. I still feel bad about that, even though it was fun at the time.

The twinkle is back in his eyes again as he teases me about my musical tastes, the twinkle where the skin at the corners of his eyes crinkles. The twinkle that I fell in lust with back in the ocean.

Rake insists on giving me a grand tour of his bedroom. It's colorful, lots of red and green and yellow and black. He's into reggae music and has a Bob Marley poster on his wall, as well as lots of art featuring sequined unicorns. The T-shirt is starting to make more sense now.

He teaches me the difference between a unicorn and a pegasus, and we argue about the plural of pegasus. He says pegasi, I say pegasuses just to make him laugh.

Rake is messy, like me, his sheets unmade and his clothes strewn across the room in clean and dirty piles that meet somewhere in the middle.

He's funny and silly and makes me roar with deep belly laughs that result in tears rolling down my face and cramps in my abdomen.

Despite his randomness, and his ability to make me laugh, I feel like he's still the most closed off of all the guys. Behind his exuberance there are hints of darkness, and that he uses his humor and craziness to hide his pain. None of this stops him from being sexy as fuck. In fact, it adds to it.

Zeke is serious, as usual, but he lets me come and watch him work.

He shows me how he tracks activity on the island, surveilling particular problem spots by camera, and tells me how he figures out who isn't playing by the rules.

He tells me about growing up on the island and shows me some of the surfing photography that he's been doing as a hobby in his few moments of spare time. It turns out that Zeke is a talented photographer, and he even smiles while talking about it.

I enjoy spending one-on-one time with all four of them, and together as a larger group. It's just so easy, so natural between us.

They're all unique, and then they have this collective dynamic that's energizing to be around. I could get very used to this.

But I know I can't. Today was an anomaly, like a dream that I don't deserve.

Because nothing good lasts forever, and I'm about to be sold. Who knows if I'll still be alive this time next week?

CHAPTER THIRTY-SEVEN

Zeke

The next day

"I know we had a bit of a relaxing day yesterday, to let the dust settle. But we're still furious with your little escape mission, and you could have ended up in a terrible situation."

I glare at Devon. She needs to understand how dangerous that was, and how she put herself at risk of being attacked or worse.

"Uh, worse than being held captive while a mafia guy plans to auction me off to the highest bidder?"

"Yes, Devon. We're talking about people taking advantage of you."

"I repeat, worse than—." I cut her off by putting my hand up to silence her.

"We got the guys, by the way. They'll never be doing that to anybody ever again."

She glances down at my knuckles, which are swollen and covered in scratches. We'd all tried to clean up, so she didn't see the full extent of the blood covering us when we returned home.

They hadn't been too hard to find, with all of our contacts on the island, and they didn't stand a chance against the four of us. We crossed a boundary that we never intended to cross, and we disposed of the evidence in silence.

"Glad I took one for the team then, I guess," she laughs bitterly.

"You owe us now, by the way. We had to take care of your mess because you fucked up. By escaping and putting yourself in danger."

"Oh yeah. Owe you how?"

"We've decided on a way for you to pay us back." I gaze at her, observing her reaction. Making her wait to hear what she has to do to get back in our good graces. "Then we'll be square."

"Oh, really?"

"You're going to put on a show, just for us." The four of us had thought long and hard about the most appropriate punishment. Something that we could all enjoy equitably.

I like to watch, and the other guys do, too. So this should be fun. A way to get to know our little captive more intimately.

"What kind of show?" She raises an eyebrow. "Like *The Masked Singer* or something? You want me to sing for you? I'm not very good."

"No, not quite what we had in mind." I smirk.

"Oh, you've discussed this with the others, have you?"

"Yes, we reached a consensus after extensive consultation." The other guys shrug and nod and she smirks. They trust my judgement about everything, including women, but we all had a say in this idea.

"So, what kind of show?" Now she seems intrigued. Little does she know what we have planned.

"You're going to show us how you like to make yourself come." I lock eyes with her, so that she knows I'm completely serious.

"Why? Don't know how to give a woman pleasure?" She bats her eyelashes at me, the smartass, and I try to keep my face still but I end up smirking slightly. Goddammit she makes me weaker than I need to be.

"Watch it," I growl, grabbing her wrist. "Don't get smart with me, young lady."

I bring my face closer to hers and lower my voice, speaking each word slowly.

"I'm capable of giving you more pleasure and pain than you've ever dreamed of in that warped mind of yours. And I'm more than happy to cross the line between the two. So don't try me."

I see her eyes light up in a way that tells me she's not averse to a little pain. Good. I'll remember that for later. But for now, I will let it rest. I'm determined that she'll do this for us.

"Go on," I say. "This is non-negotiable. Make yourself come for us."

"You don't get to decide what I do with my body," she snarks, her eyes glinting with an expression I can't put my finger on.

"You let Skyler decide the other day." I wink at her. "It was quite the show."

Dom and Rake nod at her, and Skyler grins, baring his teeth.

Her eyes flash to me, and a deep red flush works its way up her chest and throat and onto her face as she realizes we all saw him chomping on her cunt like he was a starving man.

"That was different. I said he could. He was hungry."

Skyler snorts.

"Nobody's forcing you to do this either, Devon," I reply. "You should only do it if you want to. I just figured you'd like to do something to make us all happy. Seeing you're ours, and seeing we cleaned up your mess."

She looks from one of us to the other, as if she's trying to read us. Her lips part and I swear I can see her breathing increase. Is the idea of masturbating for us turning her on? I feel my cock jerk at the thought.

This is an interesting development. It looks like we've found ourselves a little exhibitionist. This could be fun. I really wasn't sure that she'd do it, but it seems like maybe she's going to call our bluff.

Her eyes flick between us as she seems to consider her options.

"Fine," she says, to my surprise. I see Rake's jaw drop in my peripheral vision. "But then you have to take me out for dinner somewhere nice."

The other guys and I exchange glances, and ultimately we all shrug. I mean, this could be a transparent attempt to escape from us again, but we have enough contacts on the island to take her somewhere she won't be able to leave. Plus, how far should she get on the island if she did?

If she runs to the cops, they'll just turn her back over to us. We do things to help them out, too, after all.

This sounds like a winning proposition. My cock twitches at the thought of her stroking herself, bringing herself to orgasm the way she likes best. I'm pretty good with my fingers, but I can always learn from the way a woman caresses her own body.

"For real?" Rake asks. "You'll flick your bean in front of the room full of us? That's hot."

I notice his pants are stretching across his own growing cock as he grins at her.

"That's one term for it, I guess," she replies. "And as for dinner?"

She looks at me inquisitively, presumably because I'm the one who suggested this little performance.

"Sky? What do you think?" We usually defer to him on anything that involves good food. We definitely don't extend the same courtesy to Rake because he inevitably picks the worst option even though he's the best cook. Go figure.

"Sure. What do you feel like, Dev?" Skyler asks, raising an eyebrow in her direction.

"My name is Devon," she corrects him, her eyes flashing. "And I feel like a steak with a big ass baked potato and all the fixings."

"You're about to jerk off in front of us. I hardly think we need to quibble about nicknames. We're basically family," Zeke replies.

She frowns at me, narrowing her eyes.

"And I know you like it when we call you nicknames. I've seen you smile when we do. So stop being stubborn and putting on an act. When Dom calls you Devo you practically cream yourself."

A small grin forms on her face and she flushes again slightly. We have caught her in her lie.

"I like a girl that likes to eat," Rake says, appreciatively, rubbing his belly.

I glance at him, noticing his pants only seem to have gotten tighter since she mentioned devouring a steak. He'd probably have her dinner served on his cock, given the chance.

"Alright, well, seeing you've promised me a banging dinner, I guess I'll put on your little show... boys." Her eyes glint cruelly as she calls us the one name that we're all sensitive to for various reasons. But we're willing to let it go, distracted as she jumps up on the kitchen counter.

We're all mesmerized as she makes eye contact with each of us while she peels off her shorts. She hooks her fingers over both sides of her panties and lowers them slowly. She throws them at Rake, and he lifts them to his nose, inhaling her scent.

She angles her hips up, and spreads her legs wide apart, revealing her pussy. Her folds are slick with wetness, and I realize that my request for her to perform for us is arousing her just as much as us, maybe even more.

She lowers a hand and dips a finger into her glistening opening, and then brings it up to her mouth, licking it clean and coating it in her saliva.

My cock jerks in my shorts as she moves her wet finger to her clit and rubs it, slowly at first. Occasionally, she slides a finger in and out of her pussy to coat it in her juices and then moves it back to continue focusing on rubbing her clit. She arches her back and lets out a soft moan as her finger increases its pace.

She slides two fingers from her other hand into her soaked pussy. I notice that Zeke's pants are as tight as mine, and Rake's cock is out, which I'm not shocked by. He's gliding his hand over his shaft while he watches her. No fucks given.

Skyler stands in the background. His pants are tight too, but he's trying to act cool about it. I figure he'll finish himself off later, won't give her the satisfaction of how hard she's making him.

"Do you have a cucumber, or something else long and hard?" Her voice comes out in a soft moan as she continues to massage her clit. "I want something inside of me so bad right now."

"I have one right here," says Rake, gesturing at his hard cock as he continues to stroke it.

"No, something from the kitchen," she says, shaking her head. "No dicks right now."

I hurry to the fridge, skeptical of what's inside, but I'm suddenly elated that Skyler has been on such a health kick lately because there, right in the vegetable crisper, is a very phallic, very large cucumber.

"Will this work?" I ask, picking up the vegetable and holding it in her direction.

"Mmhmm," she says, eyeing the cucumber. "Bring it here, please."

I walk closer and hand it to her.

As all of us look on, she takes the cucumber, spreading her lips apart with one hand and sliding it slowly inside of her, inching into her pussy.

Once she slips it in as far as it will go, she gently pulls it out again, her other hand roaming back to rub her clit. We all stare, transfixed, as she fucks herself with the cucumber.

Her pace of rubbing her clit with her other hand increases and her hips buck, thrusting the cucumber in and out. It's slick with her wetness, gleaming as she glides it inside of herself and pulls it out again, over and over.

She moans and begins to thrust it in and out more quickly. I feel like I'm about to come in my pants as I imagine it's my cock that's slamming into her as she cries out. She continues to rub her clit and her pace increases even more.

She cries out as her whole body rocks, her neck arching back, exposing her delicate throat as she continues to fuck herself with the cucumber, an orgasm ripping through her body.

Finally, the rocking of her hips subsides, and she slowly removes the cucumber from her soaking vagina, some of her juices releasing down her inner thighs as we all look on.

Glancing around, I can tell that we're all equally jealous of the cucumber. She lifts it up, examines it, and bites a chunk off the end. Okay, now I'm extra jealous. But I'm weird like that.

I feel my cock buck and realize I did in fact just release in my pants. She has a habit of making me do that. Fuck, that was hot.

I wonder if any of the other guys did the same, but I quickly shove that thought out of my mind because I want to think about the little show she just performed for us rather than their dicks.

"Damn," says Rake. "Good one, my little Devo," he says, grinning and putting his cock back into his pants.

She smiles at each of us as she jumps off the counter and collects her panties from Rake. "Glad you enjoyed it," she says. "Alright, now where's my steak?"

CHAPTER THIRTY-EIGHT

Devon

Two hours later

"You look goofy, just like you surf, bro!" The guys are laughing at Rake.

"Nothing wrong with surfing goofy! And you do it too, you idiot!" Skyler ducks as Rake throws a bread roll at him and it lands on the floor and rolls across the ground.

A couple of hours after my performance in the kitchen, they come through on their word and we're at a steak restaurant. It's a fancy place, with white tablecloths and waiters that scurry around in embroidered vests.

I'm sandwiched in a round leather booth between Dom and Zeke, with Skyler and Rake sitting on either end. This place isn't my usual scene, but I asked for it and even fucked myself with a cucumber in front of a roomful of hot men to get it. So I'm going to savor every moment. I try not to think about this potentially being my last meal out.

I'm wearing the dress that Rake picked out for me, as well as some makeup—foundation, mascara, bright red lipstick, and eyeliner. I am feeling good in my skin tonight. I feel beautiful and sexy. The guys have struggled to take their eyes off me, even more than usual, ever since I finished getting ready.

They're all wearing collared shirts, and by the sounds of their earlier bickering back at the house, they ended up sending Rake out to buy them because they didn't have any. They all clean up very nicely, although you can tell they're not used to dressing up by the way they adjust themselves awkwardly in their seats now and then, tugging on their collars and their buttons. It's very cute.

Their banter is free-flowing, and they clearly enjoy making fun of each other's surfing prowess.

"What does that even mean? Surfing goofy?" I sense that they're not talking about the Disney character. There's so much lingo around surfing, it's hard to wrap my mind around.

"It's when you surf with your right foot forward instead of your left. Like a giant goof."

"Oh, I think I'm goofy then, too."

Skyler laughs and winks at me. "You definitely are."

"See?" says Rake, grinning smugly. "Our girl is goofy, just like me."

Dom rolls his eyes, almost like he's jealous that Rake and I have something in common that he doesn't. These guys are ridiculous sometimes.

"It's alright, Dom. We'll teach you how to surf goofy, too," I laugh. I can't resist teasing him a little more. "You can join us cool kids."

It sets him off. "You?" His lip curls as he looks in my direction. "You can barely stand on a board. Don't you try to tell me you can teach me anything about surfing. You're fucking useless!"

His words sting. He may as well have slapped me across the face. Jesus. What the fuck has gotten into him?

"Woah, man, chill out," says Skyler. "She was just joking. Don't think she actually meant to take you out for a lesson." He glances at me. "Sorry, Dev. Dom's a little fixated on the thing we're trying not to think about tonight, and it's got him acting like a bit of an asshole."

"I see," I say, clearing my throat. I'm determined not to go down that rabbit hole right now, so instead, I turn to Dom. "Yeah, I can teach you some things, but surfing isn't one of them. Like... how to take a joke."

I narrow my eyes at him, but then gently place my hand on top of his in an attempt to calm him. It seems to work, his body noticeably relaxing at my touch.

I sigh. These guys are all so complex. They're very different from anyone I've met before or will probably meet again. I'm enjoying getting to know them more. But maybe it doesn't matter if I'm going to be leaving them soon.

Before I get too deep into my dark thoughts, a waiter interrupts us and serves us a table full of large steaks with baked potatoes and some other sides, just like I'd requested.

As the server walks away, Rake waves him back over. "Get her some hot sauce, would you? And make it extra spicy."

"You remembered!" I'm impressed. He beams, and the other guys frown and shift in their seats, as if they wish they thought to do that themselves. I snort.

After the server returns with a ramekin of hot sauce that I pour liberally over the contents of my plate, I realize that I'm ravenously hungry. The guys look impressed as I pack away my entire steak, a baked potato and a generous helping of the other sides.

"How was the hot sauce? Because you had a *lot*." Dom's eyes widen, and I can almost see steam coming out of his ears as he processes how many chili peppers I just consumed like it was nothing.

"It was no Carolina reaper, but it was pretty delicious. Thank you again, Rake, for being so thoughtful." I smile at him.

Rake beams at me, and once again the other guys look peeved.

I'm having fun with this little competitive streak that I've untangled, each of them finding little ways to impress me and show that they care. I'm interested in continuing to unpack this dynamic and figure out what makes them tick. I just wish I had more time.

"How did you get to know each other, anyway?" I'm curious how this gang of hotness found each other. I know little bits and pieces of how they came to be so close, but not the full picture.

This dinner is almost like a reset moment. I feel close to them, but as I think about it, I realize there's just so much about them I don't know.

"We grew up together, here on the island," says Zeke. "All of us were born here, except for Dom, but he moved here when he was really young. None of us had the most amazing home lives, and we each spent various times on the streets, sometimes together and sometimes one or two of us at a time. It could get rough, and I guess we ended up having each other's backs when things weren't so great."

This is illuminating. No wonder they're so close.

"At some point," Zeke says, "we ended up getting a place to stay together and naturally inherited the role of protecting the island, like Sky's dad before him. It's in our blood. Could never imagine doing anything else."

"Who's the leader, then?" I ask him. "I can't figure out if it's you or Sky, but everyone seems to look to you two to make decisions."

"Zeke's always been the responsible one," Dom grins. "Skyler's pretty responsible too, but he slacks off to go surfing more than anyone else.".

"I don't slack off!" Skyler narrows his eyes at Dom. "I make money and get information that helps us protect the island, bro!"

Dom smirks. "Mmhmm."

"And I find us pretty girls." Skyler winks at me.

I feel a twinge of jealousy smack me in the gut. "Girls, plural?"

"Girl, just the one. Clearly." He puts his hand out in a gesture of peace, and grins. "Easy, Dev." He glances at my steak knife and we all laugh.

"Whatever," I say, crossing my arms over my chest. "I found you, not the other way around. And then I got dropped off at your house because my father's a piece of shit that owes bad people money. That had nothing to do with you finding me."

Skyler does not get to take credit for how we met the first time. But now that's reminding me how I ended up at their house. I try to shove the thoughts down. I need tonight to be easy.

"Oh, I would have found you. I would have tracked you down," he winks again. "I had a plan in the works already before the universe forced its hand."

A little frisson of warmth fires up in me, generating heat in my chest and between my legs. He's either full of shit, just a good flirt, or maybe he really does like me. It's hard to pinpoint this man's motives. Either way, his attention temporarily makes me feel good.

"I'm the brilliant one," says Rake, and everyone laughs.

"Yeah, you're the class clown though, aren't you, Rake?" Skyler lobs a bread roll at Rake this time, and I snort as he catches it and throws it back as a restaurant manager glares at their antics from the corner.

For fully grown tough guys, they're pretty ridiculous.

"Be careful. Keep doing that and I won't be scared of you anymore."

"Maybe we're not scary to you because we all like you. I don't think I'm scary," says Dom.

I snort, because he would literally be one of the most terrifying guys you could run into in a dark alley. His tough exterior completely hides the fact he's gentle and sensitive on the inside.

"Says the scariest guy! You legit beat the shit out of people all the time, Dom!" Rake laughs, his eyes twinkling with delight.

I don't doubt for a moment that Dom has the ability to cause grievous bodily harm with his large, tattooed fists. I've seen his scars. He must be nearly all muscle, and he knows how to fight.

"You have to promise us something though, Dev," says Zeke, his eyes darkening. "You have to promise that you won't run away again. It truly could be dangerous. Tane's men aren't good news. And neither are the Brixtons. They've no doubt heard you're with us now. Maybe they've even seen us all together, and it means you have a target on your back."

"I can take care of myself," I sniff, tilting my chin proudly.

"Well, it seems like you couldn't the other night. And that's the kind of shit they pull," adds Zeke, his voice stern. "They put shit in girls' drinks, they kidnap women and do bad things to them."

"And you don't? How did I meet you guys?"

"Think of us as the nicest kidnappers you'll ever meet, Devon." Skyler winks, his eyes twinkling.

"You made me fuck myself with a cucumber."

"That was your idea if I recall," clarifies Zeke, smirking. "And from what I could tell, you were enjoying every moment of it."

The other guys nod. They have a point. That was all raw sexuality, empowerment, me putting on a performance, and four hot men with their eyes glued to me. Captivated. Me, a captive. An ironic dynamic, but I enjoyed every moment of it. I'd even consider doing it again if they asked nicely.

As our meal comes to an end and we vacate our booth, I shiver as my mind snaps back to what's meant to happen if my father doesn't pay his debt in a few more days.

This moment almost feels like a vacation, although an unusual one. A sexy, dangerous vacation before being auctioned off. Before I die. Or maybe worse, before I live.

CHAPTER THIRTY-NINE

Rake

"Devo, come with me." I grab her by the hand and pull her down the hallway to my room. "I want to show you something."

She laughs and lets me pull her along until we reach our room. "What do you want to show me, Rake?"

"It's a surprise!" I grin and bounce on the balls of my feet, almost skipping. I'm quite aware it looks quite ridiculous given my large frame. My head almost hits the ceiling on the upward jumps.

"I don't like surprises," she laughs again, as I pull her onto the bed. I wrap my arms around her tightly. "What are you doing? What's the surprise?" she asks.

"The surprise is that I'm good at snuggling, and I'm going to snuggle with you all through the night tonight."

"Haha, what? You're not going to shut me in my room of captivity?"

"No, my sweet Devo, you're going to sleep in here with me. I'll keep you safe so that you don't need to battle your nightmares alone. But also so that you can't escape."

"That's... kind of a sweet way to keep someone captive." She cranes her head to face me, and eyes me suspiciously. "You're not going to try to get up to any funny business while I'm asleep, are you?"

"No, I've told you before. I would never do anything like that."

"Alright then. This is more comfortable than sleeping on the floor in the other room. And you are quite good at snuggling. I'll give you that."

"What rating would you give me?"

"On what scale?"

"Like school grades." I grin at her.

"Like a B+, maybe an A-."

"That's the highest grade I think I ever got."

She laughs and smacks me with a pillow. "Somehow, I doubt that about you."

"It's true," I say, cracking up laughing. It's like she sees me, doesn't fall for my act.

She snuggles closer into me, and a little piece of me melts inside. I brush a strand of hair away from her forehead.

"Why do you have nightmares, Devo?"

"I don't like talking about it anymore." She looks down at the bed. For someone so outspoken, she appears to have a few topics that are off-limits.

"Why don't you?" I'm genuinely curious, trying to figure her out. People think I'm just a joker, but I'm fascinated by what makes people tick, what they share and what they choose not to.

"At some point I stopped trying to talk about it with anyone. There's just been so much, layer upon layer of pain. People got uncomfortable whenever I'd try to open up about it, and they'd change the subject. Once, I told someone I thought I was close to, and they replied, 'we all have our things' as if I was talking about having the type of bad day where the worst thing that happens is you stubbing your toe. You know? No empathy, and definitely no understanding. It always ends up hurting more, because hardly anybody ever responds the way you want them to, the way you need. I'd rather keep it inside, shove it down, maintain the numbness."

"Exulansis."

"Um... bless you?" She cranes her neck again and scrunches her face up at me. I love it when she does that, so cute. They're not super obvious, but she has a smattering of freckles that subtly run across her nose and cheeks and I barely notice them unless she's making this face. She's adorable, so fucking sexy. She drives me wild. "Was that a sneeze?"

I can't help but laugh. "No, no. Exulansis. It's the tendency to give up trying to talk about an experience because people are unable to relate to it."

She eyes me skeptically. "Seriously? I've never heard of it. Sounds like a wizard's spell."

"Yep," I laugh again. "It does sound like that, but it's actually a thing. Basically, people tend to respond in a way that says more about themselves than what you actually shared."

"Wow." She looks up at me, still twisting her neck, like she's never really seen me before.

"Wow, what?"

"I just didn't expect..." Her voice trails off, and she looks down.

"What? You didn't expect me to know a big word?" Story of my life.

She looks down as if I caught her in a lie. "No, I—." Her words trail off.

"It's okay, Devo. I know I don't come across as smart. I'm not offended."

"But I'm seeing that you are very smart. You just hide it under your goofball antics." She looks me dead in the eye. "Why would you do that? Why wouldn't you show the world how smart you are?"

"You think I'm smart just because I know the meaning of one word with multiple syllables? That's not how I define intelligence. I think intelligence has many facets to it, and linguistic capability is only one of them."

"Good god, who are you and where did you hide Rake?"

It's like she can't believe what is coming out of my mouth. Until now, I just wanted her to see me as quirky, wild, and sexy of course.

"What do you mean?" I play dumb.

"There was something about you I couldn't quite pinpoint. And here it is!" She grins at me. "You're an onion! With many, many layers that I look forward to unpeeling one by one."

"It sounds like you want to flay my skin from my body when you put it like that." I pull a mock scared face.

She snorts. "Seriously, though. Why would you hide who you are? It's like I just saw you peek out from under a mask."

"Don't we all to some degree?" I shrug. "Besides, it's just easier this way."

"But I like what I saw under there. I want to see more." Her voice is gentle.

I pull her closer to me, snuggling her tightly.

"I've been meaning to ask you again," she whispers. "How did you get your scar?"

"I told you, it was a shark bite."

"I don't believe you." She says it with no judgement.

"I'm not ready to tell you." I just can't go there yet. I can't.

She tilts her neck up and touches her lips to mine, kissing me gently. "That's okay," she whispers. "I'll figure you out one day. Goodnight, Rake." She turns back around and snuggles into me further, molding perfectly to my chest. My heart melts a little bit more.

I kiss her on the top of her head. "Goodnight, Devo," I whisper, quietly. If only every night could be like this.

CHAPTER FORTY

Devon

"Oh, you two spent the night together?" Dom looks up as Rake and I walk into the kitchen, our hands entwined. He has a strange expression on his face.

"Yep, we sure did," grins Rake. "Tell him who you got to meet, Devo!"

"Oh god, are you still calling your penis by a nickname?" Zeke scrunches up his face in disgust and rolls his eyes. "What was it again? Elvis?"

"Haha no," I laugh. "I met Rake the Snuggle Monster."

Dom snorts. "Best snuggler on the island, apparently. All the ladies rave about him."

I feel a twinge in my stomach. "Who else do you snuggle with?" I peer at him.

"Just you these days, baby," he says, squeezing my shoulder. "Just you, I promise. You can be my Mrs. Snuggle Monster."

I snort, and feel the knot in my stomach unravel just a little. "Where's Sky?" I ask. It's strange only seeing three of them.

"He had a surfing lesson this morning," says Zeke.

I feel another twinge. "With a girl?"

"Maybe. It's one of the likely options. Why? You jealous?"

Dom peers at me, and I try to keep my expression neutral but my mouth twitches involuntarily. "Oh, my gosh! You are. You're jealous!"

"Stop! I am not." I frown at him and plop myself down on an empty chair.

I grab a piece of toast from the pile in the middle of the table and spread some butter on it.

"Can I have a coffee, please, Rake?"

Rake nods, grabs a mug of coffee and hands it to me. This time, it's steaming hot, like they now trust me not to throw it in their faces. Strangely, I don't have the urge to do that today.

"So you are jealous?" Zeke asks, looking up from his laptop.

"Maybe I like having you all to myself." I try to say it lightheartedly, but I mean it. These guys are really growing on me, and very quickly. I'm becoming a little obsessed with each of them in their own way.

"Listen, Skyler could have five supermodels stacked on a surfboard in front of him and I think he'd still be thinking about you, from what I've seen," says Rake. The other two guys nod.

"What?" I feel a flush creeping up my neck and onto my face. I'm sure I look like a tomato.

"Yep, Skyler likes you," says Zeke.

Dom nods. "He's just really bad at showing his feelings."

The twinge in my stomach stops and is immediately replaced by a school of butterflies.

I have a feeling that things are about to get more interesting than they already are.

———

A couple of hours later

"I'm sorry I stabbed you the other day, by the way."

Dom and I are sitting in the living room, playing one of his violent video games. He's teaching me some combos that cause extra gigantic explosions to go off, killing more people at once. It's kinda fun, and it's cute seeing how much enjoyment he gets out of it.

Rake and Skyler are out doing a job, and Zeke's in the kitchen working on his laptop as usual.

As I use a plethora of weapons to cause grievous bodily harm to non-player characters in the game we're playing, I feel compelled to apologize for slashing at him in real life.

"It's okay. It was kind of hot." He turns away from the TV for a moment to wink at me.

I laugh and shake my head. "You're a real weirdo, you know?"

We play the game for a few more minutes.

"Want to make a bet about something?"

He pauses the game and looks over.

"You're getting pretty good at this game, so it wouldn't be completely unfair."

"A bet? Like what?"

"If I win this next level first, I get to pick something, and if you win, you get to."

"What will you pick?"

"You tell me first," he says, grinning.

I have a feeling he has something up his sleeve. From the way his eyes trail down my body, I have an inkling it could be something sexy.

"Hmm." I think for a moment, and then a grin spreads across my face. "If I win, I'm going to make you taste each of the hot sauces that are in the fridge, from mildest to hottest. And you're not allowed water or milk."

The color momentarily drains from his face. "You wouldn't!"

"Oh yes, I would." I grin.

"You *are* a monster! I knew it!"

I laugh. "Alright then, Dom, your turn. If you win, what will you pick?" He pauses for a moment, as if not sure if he should say what's on his mind. "Go on, tell me," I prompt him.

"If I win, I get you. All of you to myself, in my room, for an hour. Naked."

I feel a twinge between my legs as his gaze glides over my body. My eyes roam over him, observing his tattooed, muscular figure.

"I could be down for that," I say, maintaining eye contact, my voice growing husky.

"Oh, really?" He bites his bottom lip, as his eyes descend to my chest.

"Yeah, really. I might even let you win, just to ensure that happens."

His gaze meets mine, and it makes me feel tingly, heat generating between my legs.

A lightbulb flashes in my head. "What if we just say we've both won, and we have to follow through on what I picked *and* what you picked?"

I touch his thigh, keeping eye contact. My heart rate increases, and I can feel his pants grow tighter under my touch.

it"But I recommend we do yours first. Your mouth is going to be on fire after you finish my challenge, and depending on what you have in mind you might need it."

He groans. "Oh god, just come with me right now." He stands up and pulls me to my feet, and I happily follow him to his room as a dull throb starts in my core. Bet be damned, I want this man and I'm not afraid to say it.

He pushes me down onto his bed and presses his lips to mine. I kiss him back. He swipes his lips over mine and our tongues explore each other hungrily.

"God, you're sexy," he growls. "I've been wanting this ever since I first saw you."

"You're not so bad yourself," I wink at him, and trail a finger down his tattooed chest. "You're very sexy, in fact, my rectangle man." I grin, and he laughs back.

He gazes into my eyes and cups one of my breasts, his face close to mine.

"So, you want me? You want to spend an hour in here learning all about each other?" He kisses me on my neck, little butterflies that make me tingle.

"I could take it or leave it. It was a choice between this or stamp collecting and I found it hard to decide. Both were equally attractive."

"Hey!" he pouts.

"You narrowly won out, so stop complaining." I playfully punch him in the chest, grin mischievously and wiggle my eyebrows. He laughs again.

He leans down and takes one of my nipples in his mouth, nibbling at it roughly and then applying suction. A little frisson of pleasure goes directly from my nipple down to my pussy. I moan, and my back arches in response.

I'm not surprised that he's good at this, my brutish, gentle giant. He makes his way down my body, leaving a trail of kisses and gentle nibbles.

"My, my," he smirks, admiring my pussy from inches away. "It looks like someone's a lot more turned on than they led me to believe. I don't think the thought of stamp collecting would have got you this wet."

Once again, my vagina betrays me. My soaking wet, want-to-ride-his-face-and-his-cock-so-badly, vagina of betrayal.

He reaches out a finger and flicks at my clit, and then slides two of his fingers inside of me. My pussy clenches around them.

"Oh, and you're very tight, too. I had a feeling you would be," he says, slowly sliding his fingers in and out of me as my wetness intensifies.

Removing his fingers which are now slick with my arousal, he puts one into his mouth, licking it clean. "Mmm, you taste amazing. Taste yourself," he says, extending his other finger to my lips.

I make eye contact with him as I obediently lick his finger, taking the length of it into my mouth and slowly releasing it. When it's halfway out of my mouth, I can't resist and I bite down on his finger. Hard.

He pulls it out of my mouth and narrows his eyes, and I worry for a moment that he might hit me. But instead, he smirks.

"Oh, you like to bite? So do I."

With that, he leans forward and kisses my inner thigh.

"Ouch!" I can't help but cry out as he sinks his teeth into my flesh. They feel sharp against my delicate skin. My pussy clenches in response to the pain.

That's the thing about me. I adore pain. I've enjoyed every tattoo I've ever gotten. Riding that knife edge between pleasure and agony.

I feel suction against my thigh and realize that he's giving me a hickey, marking me as his.

I moan as he dives headfirst inside between my legs and starts licking me hungrily. He holds me down on the bed as he proceeds to feast on me.

I've spent days trying to get away from this man, even stabbed him in the chest, and now he's eating my pussy so ravenously. He's so goddamn hot. I feel my arousal seeping from my core.

As he slides three fingers inside me and starts finger fucking me, he increases the pressure of his tongue and its pace on my engorged clit.

As his tongue flickers over me, his eyes meet mine, and he sucks his clit into my mouth. I gasp as he continues to pump me with his fingers, stretching me and sliding through my arousal.

A coil forms within me, growing tighter as he continues to lap at my clit. He rams his fingers into me, and I moan as I think about how much pain his hands have caused, and how much pleasure they're bringing me. My pussy clenches around his fingers at the thought and he groans, his mouth humming against my clit.

My back arches as an intense orgasm rips through my body. "Dom!" I cry out as my hips buck crazily, but he doesn't stop, and I squirm under the spell of his tongue and fingers, electric shocks radiating through my limbs.

As he continues to swirl his tongue around my clit, I pull his face into me, crushing it against my pussy. I wrap my legs around his head as my body erupts in one final shudder.

"That's my girl," he says, reaching out his tongue again to lap lazily at my now extremely sensitive swollen bud, and I writhe in pleasure.

He pushes himself up and leans over me as he brings his mouth back to mine. As he swipes his tongue through my lips again, I'm turned on by him tasting like me.

This recent enemy of mine, who I stabbed with a piece of broken guitar, just ate me out like a pro. But I don't know what any of this means. Maybe it's just a one-time thing. He's still one of my captors, after all. Maybe this is just about control for him.

I push him off me, and I feel a bit angry at myself for letting him make me come.

"We're not finished, Dev," he says. "I want my cock inside you, to fill you up." He licks his lips as he looks down at me, my breasts and pussy fully exposed under his primal gaze. "You're not done finishing my challenge."

"Another time, maybe." I try to sound nonchalant, but I grin. My pussy is ready for his cock to fill it up. Very ready. Craving him inside me, clenching in anticipation.

"Hey! I make the rules," he says, grabbing my wrist firmly. "And we're not done with my challenge." He brings my hand to rest on his cock through his pants, and oh my god he's massive. Thick like a beer can and rock hard, hungry for me.

"Oh god, you're huge," I moan.

He smiles and rubs my hand against him. "You want me to fuck you with my huge cock, baby?"

I shouldn't fuck him. He's dangerous and unpredictable. And definitely very capable of hurting me. But he's so fucking hot, and he wants me. My body throbs at the thought of him dominating me, of being on top of me and inside me.

He strokes at his erect cock while I watch, my pussy making it clear that I need this man immediately. Throbbing intensely, I can't help but watch as he strokes his length. I may have just orgasmed but I need more of this man.

I decide to come clean. "Oh my god, yes I want you, Dom. I've been wanting you inside me ever since you first picked me up and threw me over your shoulder."

He growls. "I wanted you before that."

Without needing a further invitation, he flips me over and pulls me towards him ass-first by my hips. He lines his cock up against my asshole and then shoves it roughly into my pussy.

My head grinds into the pillow as he thrusts, his length filling me up, and I cry out each time he slams into me, right to his hilt.

He slaps my ass firmly, and it makes a resounding smack. I cry out again, this time from the pleasure of the sting. I know he's going to leave a red mark, welts even, but I don't care. In fact, I savor it.

As he pounds me from behind, I reach for one of my nipples and roll it between my thumb and forefinger, pinching it myself to create even more pleasureful pain.

I gasp as he continues to pull me onto his cock, my pussy seizing around him, barely containing him, his powerful hands navigating me by my waist. Holy shit, this man can fuck.

My breasts bounce back and forth as he continues to pierce me from behind, rocking into my body with his hardness.

He reaches forward and once again strokes my clit as he continues to pound his cock into me. I moan and realize that another orgasm is building inside me. How can someone who is holding me captive now make me feel this much pleasure?

"Tell me you want it." He lets out a primal growl in my ear as he continues to thrust in and out of me. My pussy clamps down on his hardness and he groans, his thrusts becoming even harder.

"I want it. I want you bad, baby." He slaps me again, and this time it's too much. I writhe around in ecstasy as he continues to slam into me and my pussy clenches even more firmly on his cock.

I shudder around him, squeezing and bucking as I orgasm on his cock. "Fuck!" He growls as the friction sends him over the edge, and I feel his body stiffen. He growls as his hips buck forward, and he pulls me as far onto his cock as humanly possible, groaning as he releases inside me. When he slowly slides out of me, I fall forward, panting, onto the bed. He leans forward and, just for one moment, cradles me in his arms, and kisses me on my back. Then, just as quickly, he releases me.

I look over towards the door and notice it's still open. Skyler is standing there, silently. He slowly claps and walks off.

"That was weird. Does he always watch you fuck?"

"Sometimes," shrugs Dom, as if it's the most normal thing in the world. I'm always learning something new about these guys.

CHAPTER FORTY-ONE

Skyler

The image of Dom fucking Devon is burned into my mind, to watch on repeat as I please. I've already jerked off twice today at the thought, the way he rammed into her while she played with her nipple. She was pinching and tugging on it pretty hard.

I'm coming to learn that she seems to enjoy straddling the fine line between pain and pleasure just as much as I do. And I very much plan on subjecting her to a good amount of both. I grow hard as I think about my teeth scraping along her clit, making her cry out.

She seems to be having this effect on all of us. Clearly, Dom is taken with her and he'd be an idiot if that little interaction of theirs didn't leave him wanting more. I certainly want more of her. And I've seen the way both Rake and Zeke look at her, like love-struck, horny teenagers.

I desperately hope that we get to keep her around longer than expected. A plaything has its uses, but if I'm honest, she's quickly become way more than that. I don't know how we'll pull it off, but I think we're all desperate to find a way at this point. Even if it risks everything we've ever worked for.

For whatever reason, she seems to think that I have some sort of leadership role in this group. She seems to find that sexy. When she mentioned it at the restaurant, I was kind of thrown. I don't know that she'd think so highly of me if she knew I wasn't.

My father clearly didn't think so, and his words are forever imprinted on my brain. My brother died doing the type of sketchy shit my dad used to, the things our group has refused to do. I could never measure up to him or Zeke.

I'm sure she'll see that in me at some point, see I'm just a nobody, not the leader she seems to think I am. Nobody ever loved someone just because they were the best at surfing, and that's really all I have to hang my hat on.

But it doesn't stop me from wanting her body and her love. And I'll do anything to get it, even if it kills me.

Later that day

"I have a question for you, Skyler." Devon looks at me with an eyebrow raised and a hand on her hips. She's sexy when she's serious. We're trying to figure out what to watch on TV, and I'm finding it hard to pick something. I'm trying to get Zeke to choose. He's good with decisions.

"What?"

"Why are you always deferring to the other guys? Well, Zeke mainly." She may as well have slapped me squarely in the face. Of all the things she could have said. It's like she can read my mind.

"Because I can't pick a TV show?"

"It's more than that. This is just one example." Jesus. She really doesn't miss a thing.

"He makes better decisions than me. I'm better at executing on other people's ideas." I don't know why she doesn't get it.

"You don't see yourself the way I do. Clearly. Who do you think controls this group? Zeke? You defer to him on things you know the answer to. I can see that you love him. I can see that you trust him. That doesn't mean you don't know the right path to take. It's like you stutter at the moment they most need you. And it's not because you don't know what you're doing, it's like you doubt yourself."

She gestures at the TV. "Even about things like what to watch on TV. It's pervasive."

This is authentic Devin, speaking to me directly, with a rawness I'm not used to. Just like she always does. She's forthright and doesn't beat around the bush.

Fuck. It's like she sees into my soul in a way that nobody else ever has. Including myself. She's a witch. A beautiful, intoxicating witch. Who I can never get enough of. How does she see me in a way that I can only dream of?

"I can see you thinking. You're processing what I'm saying. Just accept it, Sky. You're a true leader. You just have to give yourself some credit."

"Yeah? Tell that to my dad. He would have told you that my brother and Zeke are much more than I am."

"And where did that get him? Zeke is a leader, too. But he's different from you. You're innately powerful, and it radiates from you. It's something you're born with. As for your brother, I can't comment. But he lived his life, it doesn't seem to have done him any favors."

"Be careful." I don't mean to growl, but there's a certain sensitivity toward criticizing my father or my brother. They weren't my favorite humans, and I didn't agree with the way they operated, but they're still my blood. Loyalty is my biggest strength and sometimes it's the opposite.

"I'm not meaning to be insensitive. You just need to realize how amazing you are. Casting aside the fact you're fucking hot, you're an incredible leader, the best surfer, entrepreneurial and funny and so fucking perceptive it's actually annoying. You can read minds, too, I swear."

She smiles, her eyes earnest and kind. She's observing me, and I can tell she doesn't know how I'm going to react, but she's going all out no matter what. Which is brave given how I've been so erratic with her since she got to the house.

Ugh, she's melting me piece by piece. It's infuriating, but also sweet. I'm not used to feeling so seen, although I guess? the guys have tried to give me similar feedback before.

"People just aren't that hard to read." I glance at her, my arms crossed tightly across my chest.

"No, they're not. When you're you." She smirks, crossing her arms in a copycat move. Wow, I think I may have finally met my match.

CHAPTER FORTY-TWO

Devon

Later that day

I'm still in a pleasantly hazy afterglow following my time with Dom earlier. My pussy is sore after being pounded by his giant cock. That guy can fuck, and god, he's only grown sexier in my mind. Who knew someone so big and brutish could be so gentle and so rough in all the right places? He's incredibly talented with his hands and his tongue. I hope there's a round two later. But then there are the other guys as well. I worry that this will change our dynamic, especially seeing Skyler was watching at least some of it. Maybe the other guys were too, and I just didn't notice them. I guess I'll find out soon enough. In the meantime, Dom owes me.

An evil grin spreads across my face. "Dom!" I call out to him from the kitchen. "You're needed in here, please. Come here!"

A groan emanates from the living room. "Do I really have to do this?"

"Yep! I followed through on my part of the deal. Now it's your turn!"

I hear Dom get up and his footsteps fall heavily as he slowly makes his way to the kitchen. Rake bounds in excitedly after him. "I have to see this!"

Zeke smirks from the kitchen table where he's been typing away on his laptop. Skyler's nowhere to be seen.

"Alright," I say, pulling out the hot sauce bottles from the fridge and grabbing four spoons from the drawer. "We're starting mildest to hottest."

Dom looks at the bottles warily. "Ugh, fine."

I smirk at him. "Okay, here's the first one." I take the mildest hot sauce and place a few drops on a spoon and feed it to him. He swallows, and his eyes grow large. "Fuck! This is *mild*? Jesus fucking christ!"

I laugh. "Yes, that's like a two out of five on the scale. Now let's move onto the next one, which is more like a three out of five."

Dom frowns, and he visibly steels himself. "Hit me," he says, and I spoon a few drops from the second bottle into his mouth.

Rake claps his hands with glee as Dom winces, his shoulders shooting up high as he braces for the heat. "Oh my fucking god! And you people eat this voluntarily? What is wrong with you?! My mouth is on fucking fire!" I grin at him as he yells.

"Still two more to go, Dom, and it's only going to get hotter from here. Pace yourself." I wink at him, and his eyes narrow. "Here's the third one," I say, spooning it into his mouth.

He swallows, sweat forming on his brow and the pace of his breath increasing. "Oh my god, I need water. Or milk. Or something. Fucking hell!" He fans his mouth with his hands, and begins panting. His eyes water uncontrollably. "I can't!".

"Dude, you still have one more to go, and that one wasn't even that hot!" I look at Rake and we crack up laughing. Zeke snorts from his chair.

"It's not funny!" Dom yells, which only makes us laugh even more.

I get the fourth spoonful ready and extend it toward him. He puts his hands up in front of his face, blocking the spoon from getting near his mouth. "No, no, no. I can't. No more," he says. "Too hot. I give up."

"We had a deal, Dom. I followed through on your part."

"I'll do anything, anything at all. Just please, please don't make me eat that. I can't do it. I just can't." His eyes are large, and the panic is emanating off him.

"Fair's fair." I cross my arms over my chest, still holding onto the fourth spoon.

"But you enjoyed my part of the deal, Dev. I'm not enjoying this at all."

"Okay, okay," I laugh, feeling a twinge between my legs as he reminds me of the fun we had earlier. "You have a point."

"So I don't have to do it?"

"I'll let you off the hook this time," I laugh.

Dom takes a deep breath and his shoulders move back to their regular position, as if a monumental weight has just lifted off his shoulders.

Rake grabs the spoon from me and eats the remaining hot sauce. "Delicious!" He winks at Dom, smacking his lips.

Dom rolls his eyes, and Zeke and I look at each other and smirk.

Later that afternoon

Zeke and Rake head outside with some food items. "Want to come help us grill? We're having an early dinner," asks Zeke.

"Are you sure you feel comfortable with me outside and around flames?" I shrug, surprised they'd even consider granting me this type of freedom. "Don't think I'll try to run away or set you on fire?"

"I can only hope you try, so we get to punish you in return," grins Rake. "Because next time it won't just be a kiss." He wiggles his eyebrows at me, and I laugh.

I stand outside with them while they grill burger patties and chicken breasts. The smell makes me salivate, and I swig from a beer they gave me as I watch them cook. It's fun spending time with them, just being around them.

When the meat's almost done, I head inside and root around in the cupboards and fridge. I find hamburger buns, lettuce, tomatoes, onions, mayo, mustard and ketchup.

Locating a chopping board and a knife, I slice thin rings of onion and slices of tomato. Pulling out five plates, silverware for five, and some napkins, I set the table.

I also take some tomatoes and lettuce, and prepare a simple salad dressing using garlic, olive oil and balsamic vinegar, all of which I'm quite surprised to see in their pantry. I place the salad bowl on the table, as well as salt and pepper.

The guys come in as I'm washing up. Dom and Skyler are with them, and Rake lets out a low whistle. I happen to be rinsing off the chopping board and knife, and the knife is in my hand. Dom glances at me sideways and puts his hands up in mock surrender. I laugh and put the knife down. "Too soon?"

He snorts. "Nah, you're fine."

"Wow," says Zeke, checking out the table. "This is the first time I think anyone's ever set this table. This looks amazing."

"I figured it would be nice to sit down and eat. All of us together."

Skyler beams at me. "This was really nice of you." He walks over and wraps an arm around me, and kisses me on top of my head.

Rake places the meat in the center of the table, and Zeke brings over the burger buns and other ingredients I got ready.

As we chat and eat, it feels so natural being around them, like I've lived here for ages and by choice. The conversation is funny and light, and I enjoy hearing stories about mischief they got up to while growing up. They naturally draw me into the conversation, like I was part of those stories too, asking me what I think and sharing extra detail so I don't feel left out. It's like I'm part of their group, like I've known them for years.

After dinner, they refuse to let me wash up and make me sit down and have a beer while they clean. With the four of them focused on getting dishes cleaned and put away, it takes barely any time. They're an efficient machine, and I enjoy watching how synchronized they are, communicating without needing to speak.

"We have a surprise for you, Devon," says Skyler, after they're done. "We'd like to take you out surfing as a thank you for spending this amazing evening with us."

"And for not stabbing us!" Dom calls out from the other side of the kitchen, making everyone snort, including me.

The guys load up the surfboards, including a spare one for me, and we all hop in the car and head off to a quiet beach where it's just us.

The waves are fairly calm today, maybe even more calm than my first lesson with Skyler, and perfect for learning. All four of them are patient as they teach me a few different tricks, and I can tell they're definitely showing off as they surf, sitting down, backwards, and all sorts of tomfoolery. I laugh deep belly laughs as they entertain me, and even manage to catch a few smaller waves of my own.

As the sun sets, we sit out in the water and just relax together. I watch in awe as the sky changes color, beautiful pinks and golds, until it finally disappears into the horizon and we make our way back to shore. If only life could always be this good.

CHAPTER FORTY-THREE

Zeke

Skyler picks a channel as we all sit down, strewn across the couch and the floor and the armchair, pleasantly tired from our earlier surfing session. Well, technically, watching a movie was the plan and there is one on the TV. It seems to be some type of action movie, judging by the fighting and the blood.

Normally I'd be fixated on the screen like everybody else, but I can't keep my eyes off Devon. She's sitting next to me and our legs are touching, her thigh pressed against mine. I see each of the other guys steal a glance now and then. They're hardly subtle, but I'm the one who gets to sit beside her, touching her.

This is a far cry from when we first met. I've sensed her attraction to me since the first time I brought her a cup of water. But it was tinged by fear. And that was back when I tried to avoid her, to push her out of my mind and think of her like she was just any other female. Disposable. It was impossible to keep that up. She's far too distracting, invading my mind constantly. There's no way to keep her out. She's the one I should be afraid of. The one who could rip our group apart. But I can't stay away.

I can feel the heat emanating from her. She seems comfortable, like she's used to being near me. She presses back against me, like she enjoys the slight friction between my shorts and her leg.

I grab a blanket and throw it over us. It's not cold, but I have a plan in mind. The other guys don't seem to notice. I casually reach out a hand and place it on her thigh.

She glances sideways at me, at first glancing with surprise, but then a little smile curls at the corner of her lips. I take that as an invitation, and my cock twitches aggressively in my pants in response. I slide my hand further up her creamy thigh and can feel the heat emanating from her core as I slip it between her legs.

What a dirty girl, pretending to casually watch the movie while clearly her pussy is focused on other things. Well, it's mutual. My cock twitches again as I slide one of my fingers so that it hooks inside of her panties and grazes against her folds.

Her mouth opens in a silent gasp as I move my entire hand into her panties and glide my fingers across her slit, sliding two fingers inside her. She's soaking wet, and I savor the feeling of her slick walls, wondering what they'd feel like being stretched out by my cock. She clenches her pussy, and it wraps around my finger. God, she's so tight. The things I want to do to her.

My cock is rock hard, and sitting next to her and fingering her is getting me close. I feel like I might come in my pants just from touching her. I'd be okay with that but would prefer it if I came at the touch of her hand. Getting a handy in secret while we watch the movie in a room full of people, now that's my style.

As if she reads my mind, and very much to my surprise, she reaches out her hand and touches my thigh. My cock jerks again as she moves her hand over my hardness. She begins to stroke it through my pants. Pausing, she removes her hand. For a moment, I think she's stopping, that she just wanted to tease me. But then I realize that she's wriggling out of her underwear underneath the blanket. She winks at me and places her hand back on my cock. The dirty little slut. I grow harder. She wants me to have easier access to her soaking pussy.

I continue to finger her while she rubs against me through the material of my shorts. I can see her chest heaving a little, but she's doing a good job of keeping quiet. So far. But I might try to change that shortly.

Her eyes meet mine in a brief glance as she slides her hand up over my waistband and down into my shorts. I intake a sharp but fairly silent breath as I feel her palm now directly on my shaft, her fingers wrapping around and beginning to stroke my bare cock. Good god, she feels good. The combination of her hands on me and my fingers inside her, sliding in and out, is getting me extremely close.

I swap the attention of my finger to her clit and rub it gently, using the cream from her entrance to create a slippery surface. Keeping my finger strokes long and languid, I watch her close her eyes in pleasure, tilting her head back slightly, and she gently rocks her hips, arching them toward my hand. Her mouth is open now, and she lets out an almost imperceptible moan. She snaps her mouth closed, trying not to gasp I plunge my fingers inside her.

Her hand increases the pace at which it strokes my throbbing cock. Her breath gets faster now, and her hips buck more obviously.

I notice by now the other eyes in the room have shifted their attention from the movie to the two of us. I guess we haven't been as quiet as I thought. But I don't care. It's not the first time these guys have seen me doing something like this, and I'm fairly certain it won't be the last, especially now that we've met Devon. They can look all they want. I'm the one with my fingers in her cunt and her hand on my dick. I smirk smugly.

She notices and follows my gaze, seeing them all watching her. I figure she's likely to stop and I watch for her queue, but she looks around the room, making eye contact with each one of them, and then back to me.

She strokes my cock faster now, and I reciprocate with my attention on her clit. I swirl my finger against it and she arches her neck back, throwing her eyes to the ceiling in pleasure. Her hips start to buck more wildly and the skin of her cheeks is flushed and becoming slick with sweat, a combination of her pleasure and the exertion of jerking me off under the blanket.

"Are you almost ready to come, baby?" she asks, smiling at me as the others look on. "Because I am. Let's give them a real show." I nod.

She rips off the blanket, exposing my hard cock as her hand strokes it up and down, milking it. Exposing her soaking pussy to the group.

The other men look on with envy as they watch her work me, and see the pleasure on her face as I stroke her engorged clit. I plunge two fingers inside her and she moans as I fuck her with them, the pace of her hand increasing in rhythm with mine. She's so wet we can all hear the sound as my fingers slide in and out of her.

Dom licks his lips, and I see his pants have become incredibly tight.

Rake removes his cock from his pants and strokes himself, not caring who else is in the room.

Skyler's pants are also obviously bulging.

Their eyes on us, full of desire, knowing that she's all mine right now, are enough to take me over the edge.

I shoot my load and it sprays over the edge of the couch, but I don't care. I'll clean it up later, or maybe I'll make her do it for being such a dirty girl.

Right now, all I can care about is the pleasure of my orgasm ripping through my body, and making her come in front of them. Showing them all what power I have over her body.

Rubbing her clit with my thumb, she thrusts her hips against me wildly, trying to ride my hand. She cries out as I plunge three fingers inside of her. I pinch her clit, and it's enough to end her.

She gasps as her hips buck one last time before she flings her head back, exposing her delicate throat, arching her back and crying out as her own orgasm shreds through her. If I hadn't just come, seeing her crest the wave of pleasure would have been enough to set me off. I continue to finger fuck her while her body writhes against me. She tries to pull away, but I keep going until her body finally stops bucking.

I slide my fingers out of her gorgeous pussy. They're slick with her juices, and I lick them clean. She looks at me, and then at the other guys. Her beautiful face, flushed with arousal, wears a combination of embarrassment and excitement and satisfaction.

What a sexy, beautiful creature we've found. We can't lose her now.

CHAPTER FORTY-FOUR

Devon

I t was extremely arousing, having Zeke make me come in front of the other guys. How their eyes were ravenous, unsure of whether to focus on my pussy, or my face, or even my hand as it stroked Zeke's cock to orgasm.

I've never felt so desired, so powerful.

I could never have imagined myself in this situation before, didn't know it was a thing, but I feel wild and free and sexy and amazing.

And apparently, this playtime session isn't over.

As I come down from my orgasm, Rake gets on his knees and approaches me.

"It's my turn now," he says, his voice husky. "I want to taste you. Dom told me you were delicious, and I want to see for myself."

He spreads my lips apart while he's at eye level, and he begins to devour me with his tongue. He licks and swirls, his tongue exploring my clit and my lips. He sucks on my clit and I moan as little sparks of pleasure start radiating through my body. He extends his tongue inside me now, licking and tasting and exploring and devouring, and it's like he can't get enough. He removes his cock from his shorts again and begins to stroke it while he licks my pussy and sucks my clit into his mouth.

Dom approaches me now, too. He obviously isn't done with me today.

"Open your mouth and suck my cock," he growls, pulling his pants down to reveal his rock-hard girth. "My cock wants you again."

I see a glistening bead of pre-cum on the end as he brings it towards me and I lick it off, greedily, enjoying the salty taste. He presses his cock to my lips and I extend my tongue and swirl it around, exploring the tip. I open my mouth as he presses himself inside it and I begin to use my tongue and lips, applying suction as he begins to thrust in and out of me.

I enjoy the sensation as Rake eats me out while I suck his chosen brother's cock.

Dom pulls my mouth back and forth along the length of his shaft, face fucking me. I like the roughness, of feeling his cock as it goes a little past my gag reflex and then is rapidly pulled back out, causing gushes of saliva to pour out of my mouth.

"That's my girl," he says, smiling down at me. "A nice sloppy blowjob while you get your cunt licked."

Zeke continues to look on, getting hard again while he watches two of my holes get attended to by his brothers, and he begins to stroke himself.

Dom's pace increases as he continues to fuck my mouth, and I feel his body tense up. He lets out a groan as he withdraws his cock from my mouth and releases his cum all over my chest, marking me with his stain. I reach down and dip my index finger into the mess he made, and bring it to my lips, licking it clean.

He smiles back at me, seeming to be impressed by this. "Good girl," he says, nodding as I savor his release.

By now, Rake's tongue is having a field day with my clit, and he inserts three fingers inside of my slick wetness. I pull his face to my pussy, grinding him into me as the pace of his tongue and fingers intensifies, and he nibbles on my clit, applying suction. He's stroking himself more quickly now, and I sense that he's not far off reaching his peak.

I cry out as an orgasm tears through my body like a freight train, the second orgasm even more intense than the first. I buck and grind against his face as wave after wave of pleasures shoots between pleasure points throughout my body.

The sensation of having his face jammed into my pussy is enough to take him over the edge, and he groans but keeps lapping at me as he comes himself.

Finally, the powerful rush subsides and I release his head from my grip. He slides his fingers out of me and makes eye contact as he licks them clean.

"Mmm, Dom was right. You are truly delicious," he says.

I sit back on the couch, sated and exhausted, when I notice Skyler approaching me, a bulge still prominent in his pants. "Don't forget about me," he says, winking at me. "I get the grand finale."

"I would never forget about you," I smile back. "What can I do for you today, baby?"

"Sit on my cock on the couch, in reverse. I want everyone to see you while I fuck you."

He sits down and I marvel at his beautiful, pierced cock that stands proudly before me. Oh god, it's pierced. My other weakness. I can't wait to feel his Prince Albert grazing against my walls and making them tingle as I raise and lower myself on his girth.

Obediently, I straddle him in reverse, and the other guys look on, tired but also very interested, as I line him up with my pussy and slowly lower myself onto his cock. I moan as I feel him fill me up, and despite my extreme levels of wetness, I feel the smooth coldness of metal from his piercing as I slide onto him.

"That's my girl," he says, reaching around to cup my breasts, my nipples hard as rocks underneath my shirt and bra. "Bounce on me. Ride me hard."

As the others look on, I begin to slide up and down on his cock like it's a pogo stick inside me. My ass slaps down onto his legs with a satisfying smacking sound each time I descend. I cry out as he impales me with his length.

Jesus, his cock feels amazing. My breasts bounce wildly as I rise and fall on him, letting him pierce me over and over again. He holds me by my hips, helping me to slam down even more forcefully.

He's clearly not afraid of me breaking his dick, even though I've heard horror stories about this position. It's like this man fears nothing, and it's so sexy.

I hear his breath increase and know he must be close. He reaches around and rubs my extremely sensitive clit, causing my pussy to clench even tighter, and I hear him let out a loud groan as he releases inside me. He pulls me down hard onto him, to his hilt, as his cock throbs wildly. I clench my pussy even more tightly around him as his cock continues to jerk, and he groans.

After his orgasm subsides, I slowly rise back up off him, enjoying the feeling of his piercing for one last stroke, and sit beside him.

I look around, and all four men have their eyes on me, and are in various stages of post-orgasm. Happy, tired, maybe still a little bit horny, a series of emotions in their eyes. The room reeks of sex and sweat.

Smiling at each of them, I announce, "I don't know about you guys, but I'm going to go take a nap." They watch me as I exit the room, leaving them there, strewn across the couch and the floor.

Their release mixes with my own, but I don't even bother to shower. I can do that later. I really am exhausted, and very, very satisfied. Reveling in the pleasure that I just enjoyed with each of them. So a nap I will have, while my mind is full of positive thoughts that I hope make their way into my dreams.

I climb into Rake's bed because the door's unlocked, and I snuggle into his comfy, soft blankets.

Chapter Forty-Five

Devon

The weather is gorgeous today, sunny with not a cloud in the sky, and the guys have brought me surfing again as a treat. They've picked a secluded beach near their house, a little busier than the one yesterday, but still much more private than the chaotic tourist area where I first met Skyler.

Apparently, I deserve it because I haven't tried to stab any of them in the last 24 hours or so, and I'm sure our group playtime didn't hurt, either. But today the waves are pretty big, definitely not for beginners. So I'm just going to relax and observe from the shore.

I watch as they control the waves, slicing through the water in a beautiful water dance, each so capable of dominating the powerful ocean. It bends to their will as they slice through it, letting them ride it through its peaks and valleys and tunnels in an elaborate dance. And at the same time, I can tell that they respect it deeply, understanding that it has its own endless power and that it could most certainly hurt them if they didn't treat it right.

I laugh as I watch Zeke purposefully fly in front of Rake, who manages to dodge and swerve to avoid wiping out. Dom follows Skyler along a swell and they surf side by side, one goofy-stance and the other regular so that they can talk while they slice through the water as if it's the most natural place to hold a conversation. As if they've done this all their lives.

Every now and then they wave at me, grins on their faces, and I can tell they're enjoying showing off for me. I don't mind that I'm not in the water with them. It's so much fun to watch from the shore, and I know the waves are too big for me. At least for now. I hope they continue to teach me so that I get half as good as them.

A hand grips my shoulder roughly, and I immediately turn around. In addition to the man who has me in his grip, two others are standing beside him, smirking at me. I don't recognize them, and they're dressed casually, not like Tane's men that brought me to my guys. Ripped tank tops and baggy shorts. They must be local here.

"Hey there, love," winks one of the men. He smiles as his gaze trails down my body, spending extra time hovering on my tits before continuing their journey downward. "Want to have a party with us?"

"No thanks," I glare at them. "Get your fucking hands off me."

"I was being polite asking the question. Wasn't I?" He glances at his two buddies and they nod, also grinning and looking at me in a way that, sadly, I'm more than used to. They don't see me as a person, they see me as a pussy that they can fuck. A body that they can ravage at their will.

"Get the fuck away from me," I say, trying to shrug the first man's hand away from me, but he's clamped it down strongly and I can't wriggle free.

"Oh, you like to fight, do you, sweetheart? That's going to make this a whole lot more fun. We like it when bitches fight. Makes it more exciting. Ever been gang banged before?"

He's surprisingly strong and increases his grip on me, lifting me to my feet. He turns me towards the parking lot, which is surrounded by rows of trees and brush, pulling me along until the sand beneath my feet transitions into hard concrete. Fuck, they're either going to try to get me into a vehicle or just take me right there in the bushes.

I turn my neck and try to look over my shoulder, but the guys are far out in the surf and they wouldn't hear me if I yelled. Jesus, these guys are trying to take me captive when I'm already captive on behalf of being owned by some gang boss. Like a Russian doll of captivity, the common thread being men wanting me for sex. This is actually fucking enraging. So much for bodily autonomy.

My heart pounds in my chest. Blood rushes to my temples and pounds in my ears. I've had enough of men deciding my fate. I might die trying, but I'd rather go down fighting than let these fuckers rape me. I don't care how big they are.

I take a deep breath and spin on the ball of my foot, ducking. The man who is holding me is thrown off by this, and he loosens his grip, just a little.

I take the opportunity to lower myself into a crouch, the way Skyler taught me to surf. Side-on, my center of gravity low. The men turn to face me in surprise. One of them snickers, a cruel smile playing on his face.

"Oh, you really do have some fight in you, don't you, you little bitch? We'll see how much fight you have when you have our three dicks inside you. We'll see how you like that."

The other two guys nod and they all begin advancing on me, the hunger growing in their eyes. As much as they want to conquer me sexually, I can tell that this is about power, about control.

"You must have small ones, having to pluck women off the beach to get pussy," I cackle at them, attempting to make myself seem unhinged. If only they knew.

The one who had grabbed me growls, "Get her!"

"Clearly I've struck a nerve. Sorry about your small pee-pee."

I don't wait around to see how they react to that comment, and I duck and weave and sprint off towards the shore. There's no need to turn back and see if they're following me because I hear their yells and their footsteps thudding on the asphalt of the parking lot.

I run as fast as I can, but I'm barefoot and I can tell by the sounds that they're advancing on me. I make it to the sand and keep running toward the ocean. It's instinct, but it's dangerous. I can swim, but the currents are strong here and the waves are big.

As I reach the water's edge, the first of the men catches up to me and tackles me to the ground. I fall into the firm, wet sand. He slaps me on the side of the face, hard. It stings, blurring my vision on the side that he hit, and I put my hands out to stop him, but he grabs them and pins me down.

"You fucking little slut, trying to play hard to get."

I try to wrestle my way out of his grip, but he's holding me down firmly and I can't get up. "We're going to take what we want from you. There's no way out," he growls.

I squirm and I try to use my feet as leverage, but they sink into the sand instead. Fuck.

His two buddies stand on either side of them and start undoing the drawstrings on their shorts. One pulls his pants off completely, and he's rock hard, clearly ready to stick it inside me.

I can't resist. "I was right. You do have a small dick. What's that, three inches hard?" The man snarls at me and starts moving toward me.

"What about you, ugly? Does yours match your buddy's, or is it even smaller?" I call out to the other man who's about to pull down his shorts. "Give us a look!"

The man holding my arms down pulls one of his arms away to start removing his own shorts. I use the opportunity to try to throw him off balance.

Bending my feet, I kick up towards his chest, trying to catapult him off me. He lifts in the air slightly, but not enough for me to break free of his arm that's still holding me down. He rears his fist back and, in what seems like slow motion, I see it descend, smashing into my face. Little flashes of light explode in my head, and my mouth immediately tastes of blood and sand.

He laughs, spittle flying from his mouth to my face, and goes back to removing his shorts. "You stupid little bitch. You're going to get it now."

I try to swing at him as he pulls his mottled, gnarled cock from his pants and starts leaning in towards me, but his head is too far away. He wised up after the first time I tried to kick him off and is leaning heavily on my legs, rendering me helpless.

Flashbacks rush into my head of the times that this and similar things have happened to me before. Despite my rage and my fear and my panic, I can't get him off me, and a slow-motion déjà vu feeling of resignation and numbness starts to settle into my body.

"Yeah, get her! Stick it in the stupid cunt!"

"Tell us how she feels on the inside, boss!" The yells of his friends start to blur in my head in a chorus.

I want to keep fighting, but perhaps it's just easier if I let it happen. Maybe they'll even kill me in the end, if I'm lucky. I don't think I can do this anymore.

I lay there, waiting for the inevitable, still trying to move but rendered immobile. He grabs his cock, and I know he's about to put it inside me when suddenly there's a giant crack and the guy flies off me.

Disoriented, I try to scramble to my feet but fall backwards, and feel arms under my shoulders, lifting me.

"It's okay, it's okay, I got you, Dev." It sounds like Skyler. I look over to where the man flew, and see Dom on top of him, pounding his face so that the back of his head sinks into the sand.

The man's face is unrecognizable as Dom beats it to a bloody pulp, growling like an animal, his own face distorted with rage.

I look to my left as Rake cracks one of the other men over the back of the head with a surfboard, knocking him to the ground, unconscious. Rake shows no mercy, walking over to him and stomping on his head. Zeke calmly places his own surfboard down and approaches the third man.

Seeing the deathly, chilling stare in Zeke's eyes, the man tries to run, but he doesn't get far before Zeke spins him around in the sand and punches him in the face. Blood spurts from his nose and mouth. Zeke punches him again and his legs crumple beneath him.

As Skyler holds me up, an orchestra of my guys stomping and smashing and pulverizing the men who tried to hurt me plays out before me.

The faces of the men who attacked me become increasingly unrecognizable, as sounds ring out of bone being crushed by rage-filled fists. Skyler spins me around gently to face him, and I bury my face in his chest while he wraps me in his strong arms. My chest heaves as I erupt into wracking sobs, and he pulls me even closer.

"It's okay, sweet Dev. You're okay now. You're safe. We've got you."

Eventually, the sound of breaking bones ceases, and the other guys run to me.

"Is she okay?" I turn from Skyler, who leaves one arm wrapped firmly around me for support, and they all stare at me with deep concern in their eyes.

"Nothing that hasn't happened to me several times before," I sniff, trying to be brave, trying to control my tears.

"Well, it's never ever going to happen to you again. We can promise you that," says Dom, a combination of deep anger and softness in his eyes. Hatred for the men who tried to do what they just did and the ones who did it before, and caring tenderness toward me.

The rest of them nod.

While I stay in Skyler's supportive grip, the three others drag the would-be rapists to the water's edge and leave them there. I'm not sure if they're alive or dead at this point.

Rake spits on the one he disposed of.

"Come on," says Skyler, squeezing my arm, his voice soft. "Let's get you home so we can take care of you some more."

CHAPTER FORTY-SIX

Skyler

E ven though I drove on the way here, there's no way I'm letting Devon out of my arms.

I throw Zeke the keys as the others load the surfboards onto the top of the truck, hop into the back seat, and gently place her in the middle.

Dom hops in on the other side of the truck, and he helps lift her up so she's half-sitting, half-laying across both of us.

She curls up with her head against me and her legs on Dom, who places his hand protectively on her lower back.

Rake hops into the passenger seat, and we quietly leave the parking lot, the loose asphalt and sand crackling under the tires.

Before we're even out on the highway, Dev falls asleep against me and I can hear her gentle breaths. She must be exhausted after those fuckers tried to rape her. She put up a good fight, but they were big guys and they were hellbent on attacking her.

I feel so guilty for taking her to that beach and letting those pieces of shit almost...goddammit. That was far too close for comfort.

I punch the car door and see Zeke eye me in the rear-view mirror, but thankfully, it doesn't wake her. I don't know if I'll ever forgive myself for letting things get that close.

From the silence of everyone else in the car, I'm fairly certain they're feeling the same way.

We had one precious queen to protect, and we almost let... god, she'll probably never want to talk to us ever again when she wakes up. I know we saved her, but we never should have let it happen in the first place.

We had one job to do, to keep her safe, and we almost fucked it up. We're about to lose her, for good this time, unless we come up with a plan.

And now I know I'm not just falling for her. I've fallen.

CHAPTER FORTY-SEVEN

Devon

I wake as the car pulls into the driveway. I've fallen asleep wrapped in Skyler's arms with my legs curled up on Dom's lap. As the car stops and Zeke turns off the ignition, all four of them turn to look at me with deep concern in their eyes.

"What?" I say, in a feeble attempt at bravery, defied by the shaking in my voice. "I didn't die."

Dom says, "Come here," and Skyler lets me untangle from his arms.

I wouldn't have let go of him, but Dom is equally protective, and he lifts me gently into his muscular arms and carries me from the car.

As we make our way back to the house, the exhaustion crashes over me in violent waves. I guess I was all hopped up on adrenalin earlier, but those feelings are subsiding and I'm realizing how tired I am.

When we get into the house, Dom carries me over to the couch and gently places me on my back. It's very different from the first time I arrived here. No hog-tying, no locking me in captivity. Just deep care and concern and gentleness.

They all come and sit, Dom at my feet, Zeke next to me with Rake beside him, and Skyler perched on the arm of the armchair beside us.

"What can we get for you?" asks Rake, his eyes full of worry.

"We'll get you absolutely anything you want, babydoll. Anything that will make you feel better, anything at all," says Zeke, his voice gentle. The others nod.

"I don't need anything more than I have right here," I reply, smiling weakly.

Anger sparks in Skyler's eyes. It's like cogs are turning in his brain. They're almost visible. "Back there, you said... you said that what happened back there has happened to you before. More than once."

I look down, emotion suddenly flooding me. Flashbacks flood my brain and I wince.

"I'm sorry, I shouldn't have said that," Skyler says quickly. "This isn't the time."

"No, it's fine." I sigh and meet his concerned gaze. "I just—it's been a long day, that's all. And yes, it has happened before."

"Well, when it's the right time, you're going to give us a list of every man that ever hurt you—hell, every human that ever hurt you. If a dog bit you, add it," says Zeke, frowning. "And we are going to go after them, one by one, until nobody on that list exists. We will kill them all. Nobody messes with our queen."

The other men are getting equally worked up. I can tell by the way their breathing has intensified, each of their eyes clouding with rage and thoughts of revenge.

"Please, guys," I say. "You saved me. Nobody has ever done that for me before. Thank you for making me feel safe, and for protecting me in a way that nobody else ever has."

As the words leave my lips, I realize that for once, maybe for the only time in my entire life, and despite all that has happened today, I truly do feel safe. It's just a shame that this can't last, and this moment in time where I finally get to feel safe is about to end as abruptly as it began.

Chapter Forty-Eight

Dom

I glance into the living room. Thankfully, she's not shooting up where my brother and sister are playing like she did last time.

Walking down the hallway, I see she made it to her room to engage in her favorite pastime. She's lying there, passed out, a needle in her arm like usual.

My sister is crying while she plays because she's hungry. My little brother is trying to distract her from her hunger with toys and made-up games. He's a good kid. They both are. They both deserve so much better than this.

I head to the kitchen and open the cupboards and the fridge, but they're basically empty. Just one sad and lonely bottle of beer in the fridge. I'm kind of surprised she didn't finish that before she passed out. It's unlike her to leave booze unopened. A sigh escapes my lips.

Reaching into my shorts, I pull out the crinkled dollar bills I took from her purse when she wasn't looking. This should be enough to get some ramen noodles for the younger kids. I won't eat tonight, but I'd rather go without and make sure they're fed. I'll figure myself out tomorrow.

Heading out the door, I call out to my siblings to be good and tell them I'll be back soon. They wave and call out that they love me. I say the same back.

At the store, I grab a few items that I can cook as soon as I get home. Noodles and a couple of vegetables, because they deserve something fresh. I'm a dollar short and have to put one of the items back, but I'll make do. At least my brother and sister will eat tonight.

Walking back to the house, I try to hurry. It hurt to see my sister cry and I know her stomach aches with hunger, the way mine does too but that I've learned to ignore.

As I hurry along the street, I hear sirens off in the distance, not uncommon in this neighborhood. It's a haven for domestic disturbances and gang activity. A fire truck goes by me and I see a plume of smoke billowing into the air in the direction I'm walking. A second truck goes by and I see flames shooting up where they're headed.

As I round the corner onto our street, a nauseating knot occupies my stomach as I realize they're headed towards my house. My house is on fire.

I break into a run and when I get to the house. The firefighters are valiantly attempting to put out the flames that burst from the foundations and aggressively lick at the walls and the roof. I try to run in and save everyone, but the rescue workers hold me back. Their voices are blurry as I scream for them to let me in, to let me save my brother and my sister. But they won't let me. The damage has been done.

As they try to put out the fire, other men in firefighter uniforms emerge from the home. Their facial expressions say it all. Frowns and somber

expressions that can only mean one thing. They're dead. Everyone is
dead. My entire family. My innocent brother and sister didn't even
get to eat dinner. They were starving while my mother lay passed out
in her room, indulging her dark demons, and now they are all dead.

And it is all my fault.

I wake up screaming. This is why I barely sleep. The reason I
have night terrors where I wake up thrashing and crying in agony.
Because every time it's the same. Reliving that night. I wish I could
have died with them.

"Dom." I hear Dev's voice and feel her touch my shoulder gently. "It's okay, it's okay. Come back to me."

I turn and she hops onto my bed and lays next to me, wrapping
her arm around me.

"I heard you screaming. You were having a nightmare. I didn't
want to scare you in your sleep."

"Yeah, you're lucky you didn't. I've knocked people out before
when they've tried to wake me up."

"Why do you scream?" As usual, there's no judgment in her
voice. Just concern. "What are you remembering when you cry out
at night?"

"The way my family died." I've never told anyone this story
before, except for the guys. The pain is still too raw, even though
it feels like a lifetime ago when I lost everyone I ever cared about.

I look down as their faces flash into my mind. My sister with her
bright eyes, and my brother with his cheeky grin. Even my mother,
the way she was when she was younger. Before the demons consumed her soul.

Turning over on the bed, I face her. "They all died that night.
My brother and my sister, so young and innocent. And my mother, strung out of her mind."

I tell her everything. About my mother, who took me to doctor after doctor to get prescription pills, which she then sold on the street for drug money. The mother who made it clear that once my sister reached a certain age, she intended to sell her.

The abusive 'stepfathers' that she'd bring home, who she'd leave me alone with while she was out making money or passed out and oblivious to the pain and sick acts I endured at their hands.

I tell her about how I protected my brother and my sister and took every punishment she dished out as a means of saving them.

"I couldn't save them in the end, though. A piece of me died that night, too."

"I'm so sorry, Dom. That is awful, and I'm sure incredibly painful. But why do you blame yourself?"

I sigh. "When I went and checked on my mother, I saw the needle in her arm, and I was so disgusted I turned around and left the room. I didn't stay to look any closer. I just wanted to get out of there and get my sister and brother some food."

I pause. It's so hard to get the words out. They've been buried for so long.

She squeezes her hand on my shoulder.

"Every day I wish I had looked, because I should have, Devon. I didn't notice that she'd passed out with a cigarette in her hand. It kept burning when I was on my way to the store, and that's how the fire started. I should have looked."

"Oh, Dom, I'm so sorry. But there's no way that's your fault. The adults in your life put you in an awful situation that no child should have to bear."

For the first time in what feels like forever, lying in her arms, I allow myself to cry. Cathartic sobs that wrack my entire body while she holds me.

She cries with me, her beautiful face streaming with tears. Like nobody else has ever been able to, Devon is helping me feel.

CHAPTER FORTY-NINE

Devon

This beautiful, giant human cries in my arms, and I pull him into me. We lay together, and my own tears flood from me. For him and his story, and for all of my dark experiences, both shared and unspoken.

I can tell this is cathartic for him, his body heaving as he releases emotions that have lain trapped, dormant within him for what must be more than a quarter of a century. But I don't view this as a weakness. What a burden to keep inside for so long, blaming himself for something that was most certainly not his fault.

Putting himself in harm's way to protect his siblings, taking care of them when no adults would. The abuse he endured at the hands of so many adults who were meant to protect him.

And holding that blame for something that was not at all his to bear.

"It's okay, baby." I stroke his back as the sobs wrack his muscular body. "It's going to be okay."

This incredible, gentle giant whose fists can pulverize another man's skull in seconds.

My sweet, loving, and sensitive Dom.

I'm not sure if I'm going to be okay, but I'll do everything I can to make sure he is. To make sure all of them are.

CHAPTER FIFTY

Rake

"You didn't run." I'm reflecting on what happened at the beach and I need to say something.

"What?" Devon looks at me sideways, her brow furrowed.

"You had the opportunity to run away from us, but you didn't. Why not? Yesterday, on the beach, I mean. Before those scumbags tried to hurt you. We were all in the water and so far away that you could have run away, and you didn't. You even had the car keys."

She shrugs. "I didn't want to."

"Why not? If I was being held against my will, I would have gotten the fuck out of there."

She shrugs again, and a little smile appears on her lips. Adorable. "I guess I didn't feel like it," she says. "Plus, you all looked kinda cute out there cutting each other off and doing your goofy tricks."

A big stupid grin spreads across my face. I can't help it. "Oh my god, you like us. You really like us! I thought you were just here because you have to be. And I know you were at first... but I think we've grown on you, and now you want to be here forever!"

She snorts at my childlike excitement. "You're this extremely hot, fully grown man, and you're cheesing so hard. I can't figure you out, Rake." She laughs.

I clap my hands and she laughs some more.

"You're like a school kid at a birthday party!"

"Guys, we have a very exciting development!" I call out loudly enough that everyone in the house comes into the living room.

"What's going on?" Dom raises an eyebrow.

"Our little Devo here didn't run away from us yesterday when she could have. And it's because she likes us and wanted to stick around and stay with us forever!"

"I didn't say that!" She places her hands on her hips and tries to act nonchalant, but her lip quivers and her eyes are sparkling.

"Yeah, you did, with your body language and your actions. You can't keep that pretty smile off your face!" I can't stop grinning.

The other guys grin, too.

"You've been found out!" says Zeke. "This *is* a very exciting development. What are we going to do about it?"

Just then, Skyler's phone rings. He glances at the caller ID and a dark cloud passes over his face.

He walks out of the room and beckons for me and the rest of the guys to follow him. We go into the soundproof room at the back of the house and pull the door closed, taking care not to lock it.

"Fuck, Tane's men are calling."

Skyler answers the phone and puts it on speaker.

"Bring the girl," says a clipped voice.

"What do you mean?"

"Time's up. The associate has not repaid his debt. Your assignment is now complete. You will hand over the girl tomorrow. We'll text you the instructions for drop-off." The call ends, and we all look at each other.

Shit. I can't believe her piece of shit father couldn't stump up the cash to set her free. What kind of father would do that? Especially to someone as amazing as Dev. I guess my father. And Dom's. And Skyler's. Okay, and Zeke's. Jesus, it's like we all won some paternal anti-lottery. Or maybe a lot of dads are just evil, lowlife pieces of shit that shouldn't have procreated. Probably a more realistic assumption.

"Guys, it's time," sighs Skyler. "We're meant to hand her over. Fuck."

"Do you think they'd just let us keep her?" The other guys glare at me like I'm an idiot.

"I don't think so, man. It sounds like there are a lot of offers on the table." Skyler bounces on the ball of one of his feet.

"I'd buy her." I don't even know why I say it, but I blurt it out.

Skyler rolls his eyes. "You don't have the cash, man. And don't you think we've thought about repaying the debt if we could?"

"We can't let them sell her to some pervert that rapes her, tortures her, or worse." They look at me. I'm stating the obvious.

"What are our alternatives? We can't cross Tane Brown." Zeke runs his hands through his hair and exhales loudly. "He controls everything. He'd run us off the island, and then where the fuck would we go? This is all we know, all we have. We'd be nothing elsewhere."

"We have to tell her," says Skyler. "We can't keep this from her."

"We can't," says Dom. "She might do something stupid."

"How would we explain dropping her off to Tane's goons, then?" Zeke frowns. I can see his brain working as he tries to think things through. "Oh, we're going surfing but first we need to drop you off with these nice men who will take good care of you? We can't do a bait-and-switch. She needs to know what's going on."

CHAPTER FIFTY-ONE

Devon

T ime is up. The guys have to hand me over to Tane's men to-morrow.

I've never seen them so distraught. It's clear they didn't want to tell me. Dom cried when Zeke broke the news, and then they all just held me. None of them wanted to let me go, and I didn't want them to, either.

I feel crushed. Not that loss, or getting the short end of the stick, is new to me. I'm resigned to it at this point, with literally every parental figure abandoning me, some more than once.

I complained about the yearly trips I used to take with my father, but I always held out a secret hope that they meant something to him, that I meant something to him and that his love for me didn't come with conditions. Yet here we are. I'm about to be sold to some sadistic man. Goodness even knows who the hell it is. It doesn't even matter who, really. Any contender is no doubt very evil and will almost certainly traffic me, rape and or kill me, and my good old father couldn't even hustle to come up with the funds to have me released. I wonder if he even tried at all.

Maybe he even thinks it's funny in his warped mind. That even now, as an adult, he can screw me over in the worst way. That I am the one that yet again has to bear the consequences of his poor decisions.

I guess I'm destined for this fate, and I was never worth fighting for, to begin with.

My mind races as I think of all the things that could be my fate in just a couple of short days.

I need a distraction, something to take my mind off the inevitable. Normally I'd just get drunk, but I need to be sharp for what I have planned.

Because there's one thing I'm certain of. I will not be sold to another human without putting up one hell of a fight.

CHAPTER FIFTY-TWO

Skyler

I'm in my room, contemplating our options, which are few. Full of nervous energy, I can't stop bouncing my feet and tapping my hands on my bed.

Not handing her over isn't an option. Tane is just going to keep sending men until we do. We can't cross him, because he's too powerful, and we'd all end up dead, including her. I wonder if there's a way that we could smuggle her out of the islands, but I know he has contacts at every air and shipping port. He controls this place with a vice-like grip, and if we could even do that, he would put a bounty on our backs. He'd definitely relinquish our control over this island, no question about that. I can hear my dad laughing at me from beyond the grave, like this situation amuses him. Asshole.

Devon walks in. Understandably, she's frowning and appears to be on the verge of tears. But then she looks up at me, her gorgeous blue eyes boring into me with an intensity I haven't seen before.

"Distract me. However you want." She bites her lower lip.

Her vulnerability is palpable, and it makes me melt a little inside. But she approaches me with confidence, and as she gazes deep into my eyes, she starts to remove her clothing. My cock twitches and I press my lips together. Jesus, she's distracting.

She unhooks her bra, and her gorgeous breasts fall free. I can see that her nipples are rock hard, pebbling under my gaze. She maintains eye contact as she removes her panties, her gorgeous pussy shaved and bare. Sucking her top lip into her mouth, she raises her hands and begins to massage her breasts.

I groan softly. She brings out the animal in me.

"Are you sure?"

"Yes, just take the pain of this situation away for a moment, with better pain."

My cock jerks more forcefully this time as her hand descends between her legs. She begins to rub herself, and I sit mesmerized as she strums her fingers along her slit.

She takes my hand and puts it over her pussy. I feel the heat coming from her core, and I'm rock hard, craving her.

"What do you want to do to me, Skyler? Because you can do whatever you want. I mean it. Anything at all. What do you want to do to me?"

She smiles at me, and I start to massage her clit with two of my fingers. Her mouth parts in a gentle moan.

Dirty thoughts flood my mind. There are so many things I want to do to her. To do for her.

"I've been wanting your hot little ass ever since you lay on that board. I want to taste you, and I want my cock inside your ass. What do you think about that? Would that be distracting enough? I'm sure it will hurt."

She moans softly as I cup her pussy in my hand, then turns and grinds her gorgeously curvy backside into my hard cock through my pants.

I groan, and can't help but run my hands over the enticing full curves of her ass. God, she's sexy.

"Would you like that, Dev?" I want to be sure. "Do you want me to make your ass burn with pleasure while I slide my cock in and out of you?"

"Yes. In fact, I demand it. I need your gigantic cock in my ass, and I want to feel your piercing dragging against my walls. I want you to pump your cum deep inside my hole."

A big grin spreads across my face and a groan bursts from my lips. Jesus. I don't think I've ever been so hard. I'm finally going to get to enjoy this part of her. Haven't met a part of her I haven't fallen for yet, and I have a feeling this is going to be a favorite. I feel like I'm about to come before I even get started.

"Happy to oblige."

I bend her over on the bed and spread her cheeks wide apart, admiring her. "God, your ass is beautiful, just like the rest of you."

I kneel behind her and lap my tongue at her little asshole, enjoying its smoothness, devouring her. She moans at my touch.

There's no part of Devon that I don't absolutely love, that I don't want to taste. I glide my tongue in and out, flicking around the entrance and slotting it into her over and over again. I tongue fuck her asshole, trailing my tongue down to her pussy and back to her ass, teasing her while she lets out small, husky moans.

She gasps at the flutters my tongue makes inside and around, and rears back, mashing her ass against my face. A growl breaks free from deep within me.

"Good girl, Devon. Do you like your tight little asshole being licked? Do you enjoy it when I tongue fuck you?"

She moans as I reach around and flick at her clit with my finger. Using some of the wetness from her glistening pussy, I slowly slide a finger inside her asshole, and she gasps.

"You like that, you little slut?"

"Mmhmm," she moans, grinding against my finger. "More!"

"I'll give you fucking more!"

I open my bedside drawer and grab a bottle of lube, snapping it open and squirting it so that it drizzles down her ass. She gasps as the cold goo caresses her hole.

I slip a finger inside her again, gliding it in and out. She's incredibly tight, but I feel her slowly opening up for me as I work her with my finger.

"Relax, baby," I say. "It's going to hurt in a good way."

I add a second finger and she moans. It's guttural, and my cock clenches again. She leans back, gently rolling her hips, and I almost lose my mind.

I dip my cock into her soaking cunt, and then line the tip up with the entrance to her asshole, and slowly work my way in. I want to hurt her, but just the right amount.

After inching my way in and slowly pulling my cock out each time, I work my entire length into her tight little hole and start to slide in and out, gently at first.

She gasps as I slide my entire cock into her ass, right to the hilt. A growl bursts from me as I grip her hips. I thrust in and out of her, making sure she feels every single inch of me.

She moans as I reach around with one hand and plays with her clit, letting me impale her asshole with my hardness. The sight of my cock sliding in and out of her tight little ass is nearly too much for me, and I try to slow things down slightly, but she's not having it.

"More! Faster!" She screams, arching her hips back, attempting to take more of me inside her.

I increase my pace, and she bucks her hips against me, screaming as I fuck her.

"Fuck my ass, Sky. Fuck me harder!"

I continue to pierce her with my cock and she cries out each time I thrust all the way into her.

She clenches her walls even more tightly around me, and I growl. I didn't think it was possible for her to get any tighter. I struggle to thrust as she seizes against me.

"Jesus, you're just so fucking tight! I can barely move inside you."

Sweat pours down her back, and she's being brave, taking all of me deep inside her, bucking her hips so that I can get even deeper.

I groan as I realize I'm about to let go, and I bite her on her shoulder while I reach around and play with her clit. I rub it in rhythm with my thrusts and she moans. "Yes, more!"

I continue to stroke her clit as I glide in and out of her tight little hole. I thrust faster and harder and she gasps.

"Fuck! You're breaking my asshole!" she screams at me, and I know she's getting close.

She cries out as her orgasm rips through her, her hips bucking wildly, and I feel her already insanely tight ass clench even more closely around my engorged cock. As she squeezes around me, I feel like it's about to break off. This feisty bitch is going to sever my cock from my body with her gorgeous ass.

I can barely move and the intensity of her pulsating asshole is enough to send me over the edge, releasing into her. White stars pop in my peripheral vision as I pump her with my seed. Panting, I put my arms around her, still inside her, and kiss her on the back.

"Was that what you needed, my sweet Dev?"

"Yes, that's exactly what I needed." She half-giggles and half-moans, reminding me of how she acted back during her first surfing lesson.

I fantasized about her ass that day, and now it's mine. The thought of seeing her ass on the surfboard makes me grow a little hard again, even though she just milked it with her life-changing ass.

"Oh god, I love making you laugh baby. But not as much as I enjoy making you scream. With pleasure and a bit of pain."

"Thank you for making me feel again. Something. Anything."

I slowly pull out of her and my cum slides down her thighs, but she doesn't seem to care.

"Are you going to sleep now?" she asks me. Her eyes cloud with fear, and I know she doesn't want to be alone with her thoughts.

"Not yet, my queen." I brush her hair away from her face. 'I want to make you come again." My teeth rake over my lower lip. I want more of her. I want to devour her. And she needs more distraction.

I reach down and gently nibble and lick on one of her hard nipples. She shudders and lets out a soft moan. I reach down and massage her clit, and she arches her hips toward my hand. She gasps as I bite down on her nipple, clamping my teeth around it and then sucking it into my mouth. I roll her other nipple between my forefinger and thumb, the way I saw her do when Dom railed her from behind, and she moans.

Leaving a trail of kisses down her body, I reach her slick folds and kiss my way along her slit. Using the flat of my tongue, I lick her from her ass up to her clit. She bucks on my tongue and I plunge it into her soaking entrance.

"Jesus, you're so fucking wet!"

I feast on her, sucking her delicious juices. She tastes sweet and I can't get enough. I hold her hips in place to still her wild bucking as I suck her swollen bud into my mouth.

Slipping a finger inside her, she clenches her pussy and rolls her hips in rhythm with my licks. She comes for me, crying out and arching her back, her tits jerking toward the ceiling as I lap at her. Her body shudders and I feel her pulsating around my finger, seizing around it as the orgasm rips through her. As she comes down from her peak, I continue to nibble and suck on her clit.

Gasping, she tries to thrash against my face, but I hold her still and quicken my pace. She writhes around and I feel her body tense. She cries out again, this time wet heat gushing from her cunt and splashing my face.

"Baby, did I just make you squirt?" I grin at her.

She laughs. "First time that's happened."

I kiss her pussy and move up on the bed to face her, curling my arm around her. I kiss her softly on her gorgeous, full lips. She returns my kiss and swipes her tongue through my lips, tasting herself on me.

"Can I just lay with you for a bit?" she asks, sleepily. "I just want to be in your arms tonight. I don't want to think about tomorrow until then."

"Of course you can, sweet one." We get under the covers and she entangles her limbs with mine, dozing off within minutes.

It would be unrealistic to think I could sleep right now. Instead, I hold her close and watch her chest rise and fall as she sleeps.

I would do anything for this woman. And I have one last idea, one tiny sliver of hope. I would normally run this past the other guys, but I'm the only one who can make this happen.

I slip silently out of the bed and make a call.

CHAPTER FIFTY-THREE

Devon

I wake in the middle of the night, and Skyler's arm is around me. He seems to have finally fallen asleep. I gently remove his arm and he doesn't wake.

I tiptoe to the room at the back of the house where I know they keep their weapons. It wasn't too hard to see Rake punching in the code a couple of times, and I kept it etched in my memory, figuring it might come in useful at some stage. I press the same sequence of buttons, and thankfully the keypad doesn't beep. I hear a latch unlock and I quietly open the door.

Inside, I grab two holsters and attach them around my waist and ankle. I slip a knife into my belt and a smaller blade into my pocket. I grab a sawn-off shotgun from a shelf and load two handguns, which I add to the holsters.

Thinking back to my times at the shooting range with my father, I feel grateful that for once something he did seems to be proving useful. I'm actually a fairly decent shot.

Realizing the shotgun is probably overkill and will only get in my way, I place it back on the shelf and instead grab a box of extra bullets for the handguns.

If Tane's men are going to try to take me and sell me, I'm not going to just let them do it. I'm sick and tired of men deciding what to do with me, with my body. I don't want to be sold to some pervert who wants to sex-traffic me or snuff me on a yacht somewhere. I'd rather go out in a blaze of glory and take Tane and his evil goons down with me.

A chill travels down my spine as I think about the plans the bidders might have for me. But I shove the fear down and decide to let it fuel me, to steel myself as I take back control of my situation.

Quietly shutting the door and heading out into the living room, I jump as I see Dom standing in front of the front door. Zeke and Skyler flank me on either side. Hearing footsteps from behind, I don't need to look to know that it's Rake. Fuck. I was really quiet, too.

"I thought you were all asleep," I say, sheepishly.

The guys eye the weapons holstered to my body.

Zeke, his arms folded tightly in front of him, says, "We have alerts on our phone when people access our armory, Dev. What did you expect?"

"Nothing less from you." My eyes narrow at him.

They can't stop me. I have to keep going with my plan. Even though something terrible might be about to happen, it can't be as bad as what might happen if I don't do this.

I swivel so that Rake can't grab me from behind and so that they're all in my line of sight. I pull a gun out of each holster and point them at Dom and Skyler. The safety isn't on, and I'm ready to shoot.

"I've shot many guns before, and I rarely miss," I say, my voice low. "I'll shoot you if I need to." Gesturing at Dom with the firearm in my left hand, I say, "Open the door and get out of my way."

"No, I'm not letting you out of here like that, Dev." He stands still, refusing to move.

"Let. Me. Out." I speak through gritted teeth. "I don't want to shoot you, but I will."

"Where are you going?" Zeke asks calmly.

"Where do you think I'm going? To the drop-off point to pretend to surrender. I will not be a victim again. I'm tired of it. And I will not let Tane *fucking* Brown sell me to some rich fucking sadist. It's not going to happen! So let me out of the fucking door, or I will shoot all four of you square between the eyes."

"We're going to help you. We'll figure this out." Skyler's voice is calm, but his eyes are dark and the twinkle is gone.

"Only I can help myself now. There's nothing you can do to save me this time."

Dom refuses to budge from the front door, leaving me with no choice.

I shoot at his foot, which makes him jump to the side in surprise. He cries out in pain as the bullet makes contact. I waste no time and shoot at the locks beside him.

As he grabs at his leg, I charge at the door and run out.

The guys didn't hear me grab the car keys earlier or notice them missing, and I have them in my pocket, ready to go. I run to the driver's seat and hop in, locking the door and placing the handguns on the seat beside me as I start the ignition and take off down the driveway. As I screech down the path, I glance in the rear-view mirror. Rake, Zeke and Skyler are running down the driveway, and Dom's silhouette is in the doorframe, standing on one leg. I'll have to make it up to him later if I make it out of this situation alive.

The tires screech as I turn out onto the main road. As I drive away, I type in the address for the drop-off point into the truck's GPS. I fumble because my hands are shaking and it's hard to get the letters right. I pull over when I'm several blocks away from the house and manage to get the right address to show up. Trying to slow my breath, I pull back out into the road and start following the directions.

The drop-off point is an hour away. An hour to decide how I'm going to end things. This wild animal is not okay with being caged.

CHAPTER FIFTY-FOUR

Zeke

"F uck. *Fuck*!!!" Dom punches the door frame, his meaty hand splintering the wood. He pulls away his bloody knuckles and punches it repeatedly.

"Stop, Dom," says Skyler, his voice calm but peppered with worry. "I understand, but we can't save her by doing that."

"Are you okay?" Rake points at Dom's leg.

"Yeah, just a graze," Dom says dismissively. "I'll worry about it later."

"You sure?" asks Skyler. "We can't save her if you bleed out because of it."

"I told you I'm fine. I've had much worse." We all know he's right, and we don't have time for unnecessary first aid right now, so we run a block away, Dom limping behind us. We locate our backup vehicle, covered under branches and leaves. Devon didn't know about this car, thankfully.

We jump into the car, and I turn the key in the ignition. Despite not being used for several months, it thankfully starts on the first try. It's not the newest car, but it's fast and that's what we need right now. It also has a full tank of gas.

Tires screeching, I pull out of the hiding place and start racing in the general direction of the drop-off point while Rake, from the passenger seat, keys the address into the GPS.

As we race to catch up to her, Skyler tells us about the call he made in the middle of the night.

I glance over at him. "Jesus. That's pretty ballsy, Skyler. It's going to be hard to come back from, but we just might be able to save her."

After what seems like forever, but has probably only been 20 minutes, we spot her truck. Well, our truck, technically, that she stole. Home court advantage is paying off, and enabled us to catch up with her.

This brave little woman armed herself with guns and, knowing her, also knives and maybe other things. Then she stole a truck and drove off alone to confront a mafia boss and his goons. What the fuck was she thinking? But then again, if I thought I was going to be sold off to a rich deviant sadist who probably wanted to rape and kill me, I might go on a rampage as well. But we can't let her do that. She could never take them down by herself. And there's no way we can lose her.

"Listen, we need to approach this carefully. We have to intercept her before she gets there."

We all know that if she gets there by herself, she'll die. If we get there with her, we might save her and we can likely take down all Tane's goons, but then Tane will never let her or us out of this debt. I really don't know how this will end.

As we pass her, everyone but me ducks down. She doesn't know the vehicle and wouldn't be looking out for one guy traveling alone.

I slow the car so that she, too, has to decelerate. I see her in the rear-view mirror waving her hands in frustration, cursing, and giving me the finger. Of course, she would have feisty road rage.

Using a move that I've never tried in real life but have in many a video game, I mentally cross my fingers and wrench the steering wheel, slamming on the brakes so that the car turns in front of her. Because we're moving slowly, she's able to stop just in time, screeching to a halt within inches of us.

She gets out of her car, scowling, clearly angry as fuck, gun pointed toward me as I hop out in front of her.

"Hello, stranger," I say.

She frowns in the car's direction, trying to figure out what's going on. The other guys hop out as well. She keeps the gun pointed at me, but her mouth drops open and her eyes flash with anger as she realizes we've all followed her here.

"What the fuck are you doing here? Get out of my way! You shouldn't be here!"

"This is the only place we should be. With you," growls Dom.

CHAPTER FIFTY-FIVE

Devon

"Drop the gun, Devon!" Skyler yells at me, his eyes pleading. Even from here, I can tell the normal twinkle is still gone. "Please!"

"We care about you!" yells Zeke. "More than anything in the world."

"The fuck you do!" I call back, trying to project my voice confidently, but I can hear it quivering, betraying my fear.

"Be careful!" calls Dom, his own voice shaking. "We'll come and get you! We're here to help you."

"No! I refuse to be sold. I'd rather die!"

"Devon, please." It's Rake, and he's edging to the side, separating himself from the other three guys. "Please put the guns down. We need you. We all need you, love."

"Nobody needs me. Everybody leaves me."

I turn a gun on myself, and despite their deep tans, all four of their faces visibly blanch.

"That's their loss, Devon. But we see you. Please don't hurt yourself," pleads Zeke. "We want you and we love you. And we will never, ever leave you."

"I'm nothing special, Zeke."

"You're the most special person any of us has ever met. Can't you see how unique and amazing we think you are? And you're one of us. We're nothing without you. We can't go back to who we were before. You've made us better."

Distracted by Rake's movement, I didn't see Skyler as he apparently edged to the other side. Now they are way too far apart for me to shoot them all, even if I'm quick. Fuck.

"You haven't known me for long enough to know that," I say, pointing my gun at Dom and then at Rake.

My eyes narrow as I try to see through their bullshit.

"When you find out the real me, when you spend a longer amount of time with me, you'll get bored and cast me aside. Abandon me, like all the rest."

"You're underestimating our loyalty, princess," Skyler yells.

"We're not leaving here without you, and you're coming with us in one piece," calls Dom.

I see Skyler nodding. I turn and see that Zeke and Rake are doing the same.

"Please," Rake is now within a few feet of me. Apparently unafraid of the gun I'm pointing at his chest, he reaches out his arm. "Take my arm and come with us," he says, leaning until he almost touches me.

"We have a plan that just might work," says Zeke, walking closer as well. "Skyler's done something crazy and we'll know more soon."

Do these guys not fear death? I wave my gun at them, and they all just keep advancing like zombies. Zombies that claim to care about me and never want to let me go.

"You do?" I really hope he's not joking. "Because I really couldn't bear what's meant to happen. I would truly rather die than be sold."

"Yeah, we do. I promise," says Zeke.

"Tane will just keep coming after you, though. And me."

"Trust us," says Skyler, calmly. "Please."

"He really has a good plan. For once I'm not joking," says Rake.

As I think about what they have just shared, I take a deep breath. I don't know what to believe. I look into Zeke's eyes, and then Rake's. Glancing over to where Skyler and Dom are gazing at me, I see fear in their eyes for the first time since I've met them. But I can tell that it's fear for me, not fear *of* me.

Sighing, I reach out and connect with Rake's outstretched arms and he pulls me towards him. As soon as I'm within reach of his arm span, Zeke grabs me as well. Rake pulls me into his chest and Zeke takes the guns out of my hands.

They load me into the car, and Rake goes to get in the other vehicle. I collapse into Zeke's arms, Skyler and Dom barreling into the vehicle and reaching out to touch me and soothe me from their seats.

After a moment, Zeke starts the ignition and we make our journey back to the house, Rake following along behind.

When we get home, Zeke stops the car and comes around to the back to collect me. He picks me up and carries me inside, down the hallway, and places me on his neatly made bed.

Dom and Skyler follow, and they all climb onto the bed and hold me, clinging to me however they can, just wanting to make physical contact.

Rake joins us, the five of us in a codependent pile, panting with a combination of fear and exhaustion and relief, and trepidation about what's coming next and whether their plan will work.

I really hope it does, whatever it is. And now I know they never want to let me go.

CHAPTER FIFTY-SIX

Skyler

The next morning

The four of us wake up early, taking care not to disturb Devon, who is still sleeping peacefully, her chest softly rising and falling, accompanied by the most adorable little snores. She must be exhausted, her body wracked with stress. We'd all rather sit there and watch her sleep, but we have to get this figured out and fast.

"They said they'd do it." I rake my hands through my hair as we stand in the kitchen.

"Will it be enough?" Rake asks.

"Yeah, if we combine what they've said they'll help us with, and liquidate all of our investments, we'll just scrape through," says Zeke, who's helped with crunching the numbers.

We had some savings, and we'd been planning to buy a larger property with much better security, but that can wait. Devon is far more important than a secure building, although we'll likely need something sturdier if she decides to stay with us. No doubt Tane, or someone like him, will continue sending people after her if we don't get this taken care of.

"What were the conditions?" Dom asks. "I imagine they're brutal, and that they're going to hold this over our heads for some time. It's definitely the right thing to do, though. I'd honestly give them anything they wanted as long as we can save her."

We all nod. Devon has become the most important thing. She is our everything.

"Yeah, they're definitely doing us dirty, but if it saves Dev, who cares?"

They all nod. Deciding to prioritize Dev above all else is not in question.

"They're going to take a thirty percent cut of all of our profits until we pay off the debt, and we basically have to give them a free pass to do what they want on the isIand. They're exempt from the rules. Except the one thing they can't do is hurt her, as long as we keep paying them."

"I can't believe you reached out, bro," says Zeke. "That took some balls, reaching out to the Brixtons. I know how much you hate them, and what they did to your family. Starting a truce of sorts. Knowing they have more funds available from their mainland activities and the pieces of the business we've been unwilling to touch."

"Yeah," I sigh. "Apparently, hard drugs and murder pay a lot better than the things we try to hold ourselves to. Are we all on board that this is the right thing to do, even though it's going to change things around here?"

SEA OF SNAKES   271

I look around at each of the guys, and everybody nods em-
phatically. Nobody is unsure. We are all fixated on helping Devon.
We're collectively obsessed with her. It's happened quickly, but
sometimes intense situations bring out intense emotions, and this
feels a hell of a lot like love.

"Alright, let's head to the drop-off point."

In silence, we hop into the car and drive to the location. When
we arrive, the two guys who originally dropped Devon off at the
house are waiting as planned. The one she headbutted still has traces
of a black eye. They look confused as we approach them without
Devon.

"Where's the girl?" asks the man whose lip she split.

"Get Tane on the phone. Tell him we have a proposition for him."

"Hand over the girl." He narrows his eyes at us, trying to see into
the car over our shoulders.

"Please, call Tane. We need to speak with him."

"*Where* is the girl?" He doesn't move to get his phone.

"Her name is Devon, and we need to talk to Tane. We have a way
to pay off his debt."

"What have you got, some type of reverse Stockholm syndrome,
referring to her by her name as if she should be treated humanely?
She's a pawn, a stupid cunt that we could get a lot of money for. So
where is she?"

At the man's mentioning of Devon in a derogatory way, rage
rips through me and I can feel the same energy emanating from the
other guys.

"Don't talk about her like that."

"Or what?" He smirks. "I've been waiting for you to drop her off
so I can have a little fun with her. Get a little revenge for when she
head-butted me and kicked me in the nutsack. I bet she's got a tight

little pussy. Unless you boys have stretched it out during your time with her, that is."

He cackles, and it's enough to set the four of us off. We don't even have to glance at each other to figure out our approach. Before the man can react, Dom has his giant arm wrapped tightly around the man's neck, cutting off his air supply.

Rake approaches the man and holds a knife to his cock.

The man gasps. "Please! Don't chop my dick off! Anything but that!"

Rake cackles now as he slices through the man's trousers, and blood drips down his thighs. He collapses to the floor, screaming in agony. The yellow-toothed man runs off, deserting his partner, and we let him leave.

"Nobody talks about Devon like that," says Rake, spitting on the man as he bleeds on the floor.

Zeke grabs the man's phone, which has fallen from his jacket pocket, and dials a number. He puts it on speakerphone so that we can all hear it ring.

"Have you collected her?" A gruff, unmistakable voice answers.

"Tane," says Zeke.

"Who's this?"

"It's Zeke. I'm at the drop-off spot with my brothers."

"Where's my man?"

"I'm afraid he's had an unfortunate accident with his penis."

"What now? Where's the girl?"

"We have a proposition for you."

"I have offers on the table, and they're good ones. Where the fuck is she?"

"We can repay the debt."

"The price has gone up. The offers are more lucrative than her loser of a father owed me."

"What's the price now?"

"What it was before, plus fifty percent."

We look at each other. That's a lot of fucking money, but we all immediately nod. We're going to have to give the Brixtons a bigger cut. I knew this was a possibility, Tane changing the rules on us, so I theoretically offered them an even larger chunk of our profits, a full fifty percent.

It's going to take a long time to make it back, but Devon is absolutely worth it. I don't care if I have to work until the day I die if that means we get to protect and love on our queen for the rest of our days.

"You've got yourself a deal," Zeke replies, and I can tell he's trying not to let his voice shake. I don't trust Tane, and I'm worried he's going to continue raising the price until we aren't able to save her.

"Well, alright," he says, sounding a little surprised. "I expect payment within the hour."

"Give us two. We'll get going and wire it straight away. Text us the bank details."

"One. You have one hour. Or I'm coming for you and the girl. And this does not abdicate her father from his responsibility to pay the debt. He still owes me, but now he's become even more disposable. I may have you take care of him." Tane ends the call and within a few seconds the phone beeps. Bank account details flash onto the screen, and Zeke takes a screenshot.

It's not the time to tell Devon her father might be in the firing line, even though he should have been in the first place.

———

When we get home, Devon's still locked in the back room where we left her. We had no choice. She's pissed that we wouldn't take her with us, but we couldn't risk it. It wasn't ideal leaving her at home alone, but it was better than the alternative. We sit her down on the couch to explain what happened.

"So you guys have repaid the debt, and I'm not going to be auctioned to the highest bidder?" She looks skeptical.

"Yeah, that's right." We all nod and smile at her.

Suddenly, confusion floods her eyes. "Wait, so my father didn't pay the debt. Did... did *you* buy me? Is that what this means? Are you the highest bidders?"

"No, we paid the debt, so you would be free. We want you to stay, but you're free to go. If that's what you want." I place my hand over hers, mentally begging her not to leave.

"I—nobody has ever done anything like this for me before." Tears flood her eyes but she blinks them back. I can tell that she's processing, which is fair. This is Ia lot to take in.

"Well, that's their loss, because you deserve this and way more, and we want to give it to you. We want to spoil you for the rest of your life, and love on you," says Zeke. "But only if you want that. If you want to be free, we will hate that, but we will understand. It kills us to think about you not being around us always, but we know that you have to make the choice."

"How did you afford it?"

"We figured it out. You don't need to worry about it," I say, pulling her to me and kissing her on top of her head.

"How—how can I ever repay you?" Her voice is shallow, her eyes large as she tries to process her newfound freedom.

"I mean, you could stay with us voluntarily and let us fuck you forever," says Rake, grinning.

"I meant, that's really tempting, to be honest." She laughs. "But seriously, I want to do something to thank you. This is the nicest thing anybody has ever done for me."

"Well, you've been through enough, and we'd actually like to do something for you. One moment, please." Rake disappears down the hallway into his room and comes back with an ornately carved longboard. It's designed to look wooden, like a vintage board, and it has beautiful hibiscus flowers on it. Beautiful, just like Devon.

"This is for me?" She gasps as Rake presents her with the board, which takes up a decent chunk of the room.

"Yeah, it's a special one," he explains. "Top of the line. A really decent longboard so you can keep practicing, and spend more time out with us on the ocean."

She beams. "Wow, this is... I don't know what to say." Tears threaten to burst from her eyes as she traces a hibiscus with her finger.

"There's more," I say, getting excited. "We're taking you out to-morrow in the morning, first thing." I frown. "Even if it's for the last time." When I think of what we have planned, the frown quickly recedes. "We think it's going to be the surfing experience of a lifetime."

"Even more exciting than my first lesson?" She winks at me, and my heart melts even more as I remember that day.

"Let's just say I'm really glad we got you a longboard. It will be very important for what we have planned for the morning." Zeke winks at her and smiles.

I feel my pants grow tight, and while I try not to look at the other guys' shorts, I can see the way they're staring at her hungrily. I'm certain they're hard too, thinking about what we have planned. We're really going to spoil her tomorrow morning, and she's never going to forget it. Or us.

CHAPTER FIFTY-SEVEN

Devon

We carry our surfboards and lower them gently into the ocean. The sky has taken on a slightly lighter hue, hinting that sunrise will happen in the not-too-distant future.

The moon glows softly, so we can see each other and the hard shapes of buildings and tall palm trees off in the distance. String lights and lampposts aid our vision as we gaze toward the shore.

But we're headed in the opposite direction, out into the dark depths of the ocean. I would normally find this scary, swimming in the dark, but with these guys, I've learned to feel safe. I trust them implicitly and know they would put their lives on the line to save me.

As we get to waist height, I jump on my board and the guys do the same. We paddle slowly away from the shore until we get to the area where we know we'll be alone.

Skyler jumps off his board. I giggle as he transfers nimbly onto mine and, despite the chill of the water, I feel the warmth of his body as he presses down on me.

He lies on top of me and puts his mouth to my ear. "You're so fucking sexy, my ocean queen," he growls, his voice husky with desire.

Jesus, I swear he's the sexiest man in the ocean. Definitely in the top four.

My pussy clenches at the possibility of this morning's surf. I have a feeling it's going to be one for the books, something I'd never have thought about doing just a short while ago. I didn't know a fantasy like this existed, or that something so magical would ever be available to me.

The other men form a circle around me. "Sky, don't be greedy now. We're all here to make her feel good, not just you, bro. Just because you met her out here first doesn't mean you get her all to yourself."

"Fair enough," he replies, grinning. He's good at sharing, I've learned. Enjoys watching, too. "Let's give her something to remember us by. Lie on your back, babe."

He hops off me and returns to his own board. I do as instructed, lying on my back, my surfboard supporting me as I float calmly on the smooth ocean.

Zeke approaches me now and scoots my body down so that I'm halfway down the board. He swivels me around so that my legs are dangling off the side.

"Do you want to do the honors, man?" He gestures at Dom, who nods, hunger in his eyes as his gaze trails the length of my body, settling on my core.

Fuck, his desire is so obvious it causes my pussy to clench further. The throbbing sensation intensifies. I'm not sure quite what they have in store for me, but I have a feeling I'm going to like it.

Dom approaches me from the part of the board where my legs are dangling off the edge, and Zeke and Rake come to where my head is closest to the water.

Rake pulls the string on my bikini behind my neck and it unravels as he gently pulls the bikini top down, exposing my breasts. My nipples immediately pebble, a combination of the chilly morning air and being disrobed by this group of sexy sea gods.

Zeke leans over and cups one of my breasts in his hand. "Your tits are so fucking sexy," he growls. He lowers his face, placing his mouth over my breast and beginning to flick my nipple with his tongue. Waves of pleasure shoot straight into my pussy. I know I'm getting incredibly wet.

Rake leans in as well, taking my other breast in his mouth and beginning to tease me with his tongue. "Your nipples are like rocks," he says. I moan as the two tongues pleasure my nipples.

Dom moves closer now. While the other two continue to pay attention to my breasts, I feel him reach out and tug on my bikini bottoms. The ribbons come undone with a satisfying ping, and he pulls them completely off.

"Don't let them float away over there!" I suddenly feel anxious about losing my bikini.

He snorts, putting them to his face and inhaling deeply. "Won't let them out of my sight," he says. "Your scent is intoxicating, by the way. I'm obsessed with your cunt, and now I'm going to feast on you."

Scrunching the bottoms up and putting them carefully on his board, he moves closer to me again and forces my thighs apart. He laps at my pussy, the sounds of his tongue and my entrance mirroring the lapping of the ocean as it slaps gently against the underside of our surfboards.

I moan gently, arching my back in the moonlight as these three gorgeous men use their tongues to pleasure my tits and my snatch. Dom slides two fingers inside of me and thrusts them in and out, slowly, as he nibbles and sucks on my engorged clit. I let out a small gasp as I feel his teeth brushing against me, teasing.

"I want to taste her pussy now," says Rake, lifting his head up momentarily from my nipple. He doesn't stop paying attention to my breast though, just transfers from his tongue to his thumb and forefinger, rolling and pinching it.

"I don't blame you," Dom replies. "She's so fucking delicious."

They swap places, each continuing on with what the other had started. This time, Rake devours my pussy, while Dom starts playing with my nipple. Rake nibbles at my swollen nub, sending a pleasant shiver up my spine as he crosses the line between pleasure and pain. I cry out as Zeke and Dom both bite down on my nipples and suck them into their mouths at the same time.

I can't wait to see the marks they each leave on me, each bruise and welt a reminder of their mouths and hands and cocks, claiming me. To remind me I'm theirs, every part of me. Something to look forward to over the next few days.

Rake begins to increase the pace with which he licks and sucks on my clit, and I feel my body start to tighten in anticipation of a release.

"Hang on, bro," says Zeke. "I want a taste, too. Don't let her come yet." He knows how to read my body extremely well, knows when I'm close and how to keep me right at the edge. Right before my body gets to the point of no return, Rake pulls his face away.

"Alright, alright. You get to eat her out, too. It's only fair." He switches places with Zeke.

Now three of my four sexy guys have had the opportunity to suck on my tits at sea, and Zeke approaches my pussy with an eagerness and a desire that just adds to my arousal. He twirls his tongue around my clit, pulling it into his mouth and massaging it, and nibbling on it gently with his teeth.

I moan as he continues to flick at my clit like he can't get enough of me, and slides two fingers inside me. He spreads my legs further apart and slides his tongue inside my eager pussy.

"Mmm," he says, "Your pussy is glistening in the moonlight. You're so fucking wet, and you taste so good." He thrusts his tongue in and out of my canal, tongue fucking me while he works my clit with one of his fingers. "Should we let her come, guys? What do you think?"

Skyler sits on his board, watching with a smile on his face. I can tell he's extremely hard, but he seems perfectly content observing for now.

"Do you want us to let you come now, our little Devo?" asks Rake. "Or should we make you wait a little longer? As a punishment for not being able to decide whether to stay with us?"

"Please," I moan as Zeke flicks his tongue against my clit. "Just finish me now."

"Don't tempt us. Out at sea, in the dark. So much opportunity," says Zeke, winking at me. A short while ago, that kind of comment would have unsettled me, but now I know it's just their dark humor. A bond that I share with them.

"Not until I get my turn," says Sky. "Get her to the edge one more time, though. So she's ready for me."

"End me. Do it, please," I say, begging.

They all comply, but at this point I'm not sure whether they're going to listen to Sky or me, placing their mouths back on my breasts and my pussy, each using their tongues to twirl and lick up and down, nibbling and sucking and squeezing and rubbing.

I moan as they lick and suck, their tongues spoiling my body, the pressure continuing to build its way from my core.

Skyler suddenly says, "Fuck this. I need you right now," and dives off his board, swimming over to me and shoving Zeke to the side. He inserts three fingers inside of me, sliding them into my wetness in one go, and I moan as he begins to ram them into me, finger fucking me in rhythm with his tongue, which he flicks rapidly against my clit.

"Oh my fucking god," I yell. "You are too much. I can't—."

I cry out as an orgasm rips through my body like a freight train. Pleasure shoots throughout me as Skyler continues to lap at me with his hungry tongue, and Rake and Dom clench their teeth on my nipples.

My hips buck from the surfboard, my neck tilting back, and yet they don't stop. They keep licking my pussy and my nipples as wave after wave of pleasure crashes over me. Who thought the biggest wave today would be from my orgasm as four men pleasure me on my surfboard? I lie back, panting, as my peak subsides.

They're all looking at me now, adoration and desire in their eyes. I know we're not finished. I'm not sure of the mechanics of this over-water fucking session, but I'm here for it and eager to learn.

"Are you ready for a four cock special?" asks Rake.

"That's an offer I can't refuse."

In the past, such an offer would have intimidated me and made me laugh nervously. But not today. Today I feel sexy and confident and excited and ready to try anything with these men. My men. I am their queen and they are my gods of the sea. They can do with me what they want and I will do anything they want.

"I'm coming aboard," says Rake, and the others watch as he mounts my surfboard and climbs on top of me. With one hand propping him up, he uses the other to swipe some hair away from my face. "You're so fucking sexy," he says. "I can't believe you're ours."

I watch as he pulls down his board shorts, revealing his very hard, perfectly formed cock. "I'm going to fuck you now," he says. "What do you think about that?"

"I'm ready for you," I reply, smiling back at him. He wastes no time and glides into my pussy in one smooth movement. I cry out as he fills me up with his girth.

I'm not going to lie. This man has a fucking epic cock and he knows how to use it.

I look up at him, admiring his muscular chest and shoulders that I can barely see in the dark, although my eyes have adjusted enough so that I can glimpse his muscles ripple. He pierces me repeatedly with his hard cock, our pace dictated by the rhythm of the ocean as it gently rocks the board. He fills me up, stretching my walls as he impales me with his girth. I moan each time he enters me.

He increases his pace, thrusting harder and faster. I wrap my legs around his waist and clench his cock with my pussy as hard as I can.

I feel his body tense, and he releases, coming inside me with a groan. "Oh fuck, yeah. You are amazing, my little Devo," he says, lying down on top of me, pressing firmly along my body as I feel his dick jerk a final time inside me. "I really hope you stay. You'd be so hard to give up. I don't think I could take it."

"I'd miss you too," I say back, reflecting on how much my opinion of these guys has changed in the past while. I try to push the feelings down and worry about them later. Now's the time to be focusing on getting fucked.

"My turn, man," says Dom. Rake nods and pulls out of my soaking, freshly pounded pussy and hops off my board.

"How do you want me?" I gaze into Dom's eyes, and I'm ready to do whatever he says. I'm genuinely curious about what he picks because I don't know how many ways there are to fuck on a surfboard.

"From behind. I want to see that ass jiggle," he says, smirking. I grin and obediently flip over.

"Get on all fours," he growls. He hops onto my longboard, and it wobbles, but he quickly finds balance. Propping myself up on my knees and forearms, I look behind me as he pulls down his shorts, revealing his gorgeous, very hard cock. I back my ass up so that I'm pressing against it, looking forward to him sliding into me from behind. Which is what he does, in one move that has him inside me, right up to his hilt. I gasp as I feel his cock hit my walls.

He immediately pounds himself into me and I feel myself panting from the exertion. His thrusts are intense, like he's trying to fuck me into staying. It might work, because oh my god, his cock is amazing.

"Fuck!" I yell as he slides in, particularly forcefully. Again, riding that line between pleasure and pain.

I revel in the frissons of pain that radiate when he slams into me. My pussy clenches even more tightly around him, and that only serves to excite him further.

He slaps my ass forcefully, and I cry out as the slap reverberates across the water. He slaps me two more times. I can't wait to see the mark he leaves on me, no doubt the size of his large hand.

His pace increases and I feel his body tighten. He groans and then comes inside me. I feel his cock throbbing forcefully as he pumps his seed into me, my pussy seizing around him as the orgasm rips through his body.

He kisses me on my back as he pulls out, panting. I turn and see sweat slicked across his torso, his physical exertion outweighing the chilliness of the morning air.

"My turn," says Zeke. He climbs aboard and sits down, stroking his hard cock, his legs dangling into the water on either side. "Get on here, baby. Ride me in reverse."

I flip around so that my back is to him, and carefully lower myself down onto his girth. I moan as I impale myself on him, to his hilt. His cock is long and thick, too, and I cry out as it stretches me.

I bob up and down on Zeke, and the other guys stare at my tits as they bounce wildly in the open air. Zeke reaches around with both of his powerful arms, tweaking my nipples between his thumbs and forefingers, sending little ripples of pleasure straight to my pussy.

As a result, my pussy clenches snugly around his cock, and he groans. I feel his body tense up as he releases into me, squeezing my nipples hard.

I cry out as he shudders with pleasure behind me, my back arching. Tilting my head back, I meet his lips with mine in a passionate kiss, his tongue entwined with mine. "Fuck, you're incredible, Devon," he says. I slowly hop off his cock, taking care not to flip the board. He returns to his board with a lazy smile on his face.

"I was patient. So I get to have you now," Skyler grins, his eyes twinkling in the rising sun.

"You have been patient," I smile at him.

"Saving the best for last," he grins.

They're so good at sharing. I am enjoying being the item being shared, no complaints over here.

Skyler removes his shorts, revealing the fourth in a line of gorgeous cocks that I've had the pleasure of viewing and enjoying today. His piercing glints in the darkness, and I can't wait for it to drag against my walls again.

He hops onto my board, teasing me as if he's going to tip me into the ocean, but he grabs me just before the board capsizes and says, "Sit on my cock facing me. I want you to ride me."

I like his plan. I straddle his body, my thighs gripping against his sides, and I slowly lower myself down onto his engorged hardness. Our faces are close, and his eyes have regained their twinkle. God, he's sexy. I moan as I slide onto his cock, his piercing grazing my walls as it makes its way inside me.

I'm soaking wet and I glide onto him easily. I bob up and down on his cock, slowly at first and then picking up pace. I angle my pelvis so that my clit rubs against his pubic mound. A soft moan escapes my lips.

He holds me by the hips, encouraging me to raise myself up higher and then slam back down onto his girth. Our eye contact is intense, and I can feel six other eyes on me, admiring me as I maneuver my pussy over his cock in rhythm with the ocean.

He smiles at me, hunger in his eyes as I ride him.

"Ride me, baby," he says. "Your pussy feels amazing. Just like I knew it would when I first taught you how to surf."

"You were thinking about my pussy when you were teaching me to surf?"

"Yes, and your ass. And all the things I wanted to do to you. Some of which we've already done and I want to do again."

I grin and my pussy clenches at the thought of him balls deep in my asshole. "I found you to be quite distracting yourself. All of your muscles and tattoos and your sexy smile. I definitely jerked off at the thought of you multiple times." He winks at me and then increases the pace of his thrusts.

"We'll never get that moment back again, you know," I say as I continue to impale myself on his cock, his piercing rubbing me in all the right places.

"But now you have a neverending opportunity to keep coming back and doing it over and over again," he says, gripping my hips even harder, pinching me. I almost cry out from the delicious pain. I'm going to have bruises tomorrow, and I don't mind one bit.

"I prefer your way of thinking."

"Me too. Stop talking and ride me," he growls.

I obey his direction to zip it and continue to bounce up and down on his cock. I run my nails over his chest, leaving marks I can make out in the soft light.

"Baby, you're going to make me come," he snarls.

"That's my intention," I reply.

I ride him more quickly now, continuing to tilt my pelvis so that my clit receives some targeted attention.

Suddenly, I feel an orgasm coiling in my core and I speed up to the point of no return. I cry out as a wave of pleasure explodes from my core, and my pussy shudders wildly as I come on his cock.

"That's it, baby, come on my cock. Good girl," he says, and he groans as he reaches his own peak. He releases inside me, hard, and I feel his cock twitching as he bucks his hips and tilts his head back.

He pulls my mouth to him, our lips crashing together. His tongue swipes through my lips and intertwines with mine as he continues to twitch inside me.

After catching his breath, he gently lifts me off him. My pussy is raw, pounded by four hot men in the ocean. I've never felt better.

"Sun's coming up. I could sit here all day with you on my dick, but the lifeguards tend to frown upon it." He grins at me.

Begrudgingly, I realize this concludes our little over-water rendezvous.

"Lost your bikini bottoms. Dom must have dropped them while he tongue fucked your cunt," says Rake, a serious look on his face.

My face falls. There's no way I can get out of the ocean with no pants on. No way. I'm stranded in the sea forever. I'm going to have to hide behind my board and hope nobody notices my ass when I run by.

"You're going to have to form a circle around me!" My voice wavers. I'm not one for public nudity and the thought is mortifying.

"Just kidding, little Devo! Jeez! Calm down!" He pulls the scrunched-up pair of bikini bottoms from behind his back and hands them to me, grinning. "You'd think you'd be less uptight after being tag teamed by four guys."

They all laugh, and I snort. Here I am worrying about the potential for a nude run when I just got eaten out and fucked by three guys on a surfboard at a very public beach.

By now the sun really is rising, and other surfers making their way into the water for an early morning run, so I quickly put my bikini bottoms back on and fasten my bikini top.

We hop onto our boards and catch a couple of small waves before heading back in. The guys clap as I take a good one most of the way to shore, and they quickly catch up to me.

"Just a short one today?" says a surfer as he paddles by us. He's cute. Good god, I love the beach and the men who ride the ocean… and me. But I don't need a fifth. I'm very happy with my four sexy, protective guys. "How were the waves?" he asks, nodding toward the break further out.

"Oh, they were rocking and rolling. A nice rhythm to them today," says Rake, glancing at me and the other guys. "Built up a lot of momentum, quite exhilarating really. Orgasmic, you might say. Definitely one for the books."

The surfer gives a skeptical glance to the small waves rolling in. "If you say so, man," he says. "Anyway, have a good one." He does a shaka in our direction and then heads out towards the break.

"I can guarantee his day won't be as good as ours," says Zeke, winking at me.

"Hey now," I say, mischievously. "Maybe next time we'll ask him to join us."

All four men immediately frown at me.

"Four cocks is plenty enough for you, Ms. Good Pussy," says Dom, and the other guys laugh and nod in agreement. "And your pussy is ours. You are ours."

"Yes, you're all I want and need. I wouldn't ever ask for anything more." I smile at each of them.

I can't remember ever feeling so happy, so lucky, so satisfied. They all smile back at me, adoration in their eyes. I am home.

CHAPTER FIFTY-EIGHT

Skyler

It's taken Devon to do what nobody else could ever do before. To break down my walls.

I don't know how she did it, but she snuck through my defenses and she's helped me see what I couldn't before. I guess that's true for all of us in our own ways.

Because of her, I've been able to let somebody else into my world. For the first time in my life, I'm not ashamed of my family's legacy. Is my father's story still hugely problematic? Yes. But that doesn't mean I am too, just because I come from his sperm. He created me, and it ends there.

Because of her, I've realized I don't need to carry the weight of his misdeeds like an albatross around my neck any longer. I am not him, and I won't turn into him. I get that his behavior was his choice. It wasn't because of something that I did, or some deficiency on my part.

And I finally get to be proud of my family's historical role and status on this island, which I've inherited, for better and for worse.

She's helped me to realize that I am a good leader. And while Zeke and I co-lead effectively together, I can branch out on my own and everything doesn't suddenly fall apart. I've realized that I should consider some entrepreneurial options, and maybe make the surfing school idea happen.

There's no need for me to always feel second best, and I can be the best at more than just surfing.

And most of all, I can have a meaningful relationship with this incredible woman that I love. I don't think there's a way I could ever love someone else as deeply as I love her, and I really hope she decides to stay with us. If she doesn't, I'll be devastated, and I'm worried that I'll just go back to how things were. Maybe even worse. Because as much as she's helped me to work on myself, I've been able to do it because she's been there for me along the journey.

I am enough on my own, without the other guys. Being true to myself is the only option going forward. But I choose to continue on this path with them, and with her. I just hope she chooses the same.

CHAPTER FIFTY-NINE

Rake

I am love-struck. Plain and simple.

Devon sees right through my goofy act, to the man on the inside. The one who nobody else ever sees.

I love being her onion, and I can't wait for her to keep peeling away my layers one by one, even though it's scary.

And despite seeing me, all of me I've shared so far, more than I've ever shared with anyone else, she hasn't run away. In fact, I get the feeling she likes me. Maybe even loves me a little bit. She at least less than three's me.

My sweet little Devo, feisty and crazy and smart and funny. I just want to snuggle beside her forever.

There's a chance she won't choose us, though. I mean, this situation is complicated and unconventional. But then again, so is she, I suppose. I wouldn't have her any other way.

I'm not sure what I'd do in her shoes. If I'm biased I'd say I'd definitely stay with us, but that's because I want her to. She has freedom
now, and living with us won't be without its complications.

Hopefully she picks us, but it has to be her choice. If she doesn't, the
layers of the onion are going back on and I'll refuse to ever let anybody
take them off again.

CHAPTER SIXTY

Zeke

I can't stop smiling. It's been a really long time since I've smiled so much, and I hate to admit it, but my cheeks hurt from all the grinning.

There's something magnetic about our Dev, and I feel so different around her. It's like she's broken down my walls.

She doesn't expect me to lead her or the other guys through everything. I've felt okay about handing more responsibility over to Skyler. I mean, look at how he came up with the idea to save her, the only way it could have worked. And he pulled it off seamlessly, without needing my guidance.

Dom and Rake might both be ridiculous humans in their own ways, but they're grown men as well, and highly capable without me being their mentor.

It's like she's made me see all the pressure I was putting on myself to show everyone that I had the answers to everything. It's like she's helped to lift an enormous weight from me, sharing the load more equitably with the other guys.

And the guys, to their credit, have already been stepping up so much more. Even Rake, he's still a giant goofball, but he's letting her in to see who he really is on the inside. She knows more about his story already than I thought he'd ever tell, and I have a feeling he's going to share even more one day.

I want her to sit with me while I work, to ask me questions, and to be my thought partner. I value her perspective. She brings something special to each of us, individually and collectively.

I'm not sure how she's done it, but now I know we can't live without her. She needs us, just as much as we need her.

I just hope she realizes that.

CHAPTER SIXTY-ONE

Dom

"You make me feel safe. In a way that I didn't think would ever be in the cards for me." I smile at Devon and trace her palm with my thumb.

She smiles at me and interlocks her hand with mine. "You're this big, burly guy who can fight off just about anybody, and *I* make *you* feel safe?"

I can't help but chuckle. Yes, it sounds strange, but it's important for her to know how I feel.

"Yeah, after I lost my family, I guess I haven't ever been able to relax. I get shit from people for being so serious and cold, but that's why. I'm terrified that if I ever am not 'on', something bad might happen."

Jesus, I don't know how she does it. So many years of bottling up my emotions, shoving them so far down and taking out my rage on everything and everyone. That had become comfortably uncomfortable for me. I had sunken deep into my darkness and had no desire to pull myself out. And now, here I am, talking about the terrible memories. And I'm okay with it. This woman is magical.

"That makes sense. And you are safe with me. You always will be." She smiles, looking up at me through her gorgeous, long eyelashes.

I pull her in close and kiss her on the top of her head, inhaling her intoxicating scent that I associate with positive memories. Who knew this small, feisty woman could provide such comfort, such warmth?

I just hope she doesn't choose to leave.

Like a moth to a flame, I just can't get enough.

CHAPTER SIXTY-TWO

Devon

A while later

After the most amazing day, one that I will certainly never forget, I have a lot to think about. I never expected to find anybody who loved me unconditionally, who didn't abandon or reject me. But now I see that the people who did that to me did it for selfish reasons.

It was never because I was bad, or less than, or not good enough. It was because of their own demons that they were fighting, that they were too weak to overcome.

And now, I have a found family. I have chosen four men and they have also chosen me. It may have been an unconventional way of meeting, and it has all happened very quickly. But sometimes you just know.

They know my demons, my pain, and my flaws. And they still want me, and nobody else. Are they perfect? No. But they are perfect for me.

They're all so special in their own way.

My brilliant Rake, so bright, but so scared of showing it to the world, so he hides it behind his comedy, and doubts his own judgement. The one I know least about because he keeps it hidden. My big tall onion.

My caring Dom, kind and gentle underneath his brutish exterior. He would kill for me without blinking an eye. His story is so dark, and I hope that one day he can forgive himself. He's thinking about looking into volunteer firefighting. He knows he can't go back and save his family, but it might rebalance things in some way.

My smart, analytical Zeke, who always seems to know what to do or say, yet somehow isn't complete without his brothers. Finally, giving himself a break, no longer trying to be everything to everyone. But still, a phenomenal leader when he steps up.

And my Skyler, the one who started it all. Just intensely sexy and wise and ageless and strong. Occasionally mean, but he seems to keep that more to the bedroom now, which is just fine by me. He really seems to have come into his own. He can talk about his family without snapping. His soul seems lighter, somehow, if that makes sense. He's even talking about starting his own surf school business, and I am so excited for him, but I will keep a close eye on the clients he takes out. I hope he does itI, because he's going to be amazing. He already is amazing.

I'm so incredibly obsessed with him. With all of them.

All of them are my loyal protectors who adore me unconditionally, despite and maybe *because* of the darkness that everybody else always seemed to run away from, to reject me and abandon me for.

And all of them are hot and kinky as fuck.

I don't know how I got here, but I am one very lucky girl. How could I give this up?

But this was quick. And I have fears that, as quickly as it has all happened, that our love has built, something could quickly rip it away.

Do I really know these men? Can I honestly trust them? Do we have what it takes to make it in this unconventional relationship? I'd like to think so, but I'm just not sure.

I haven't met one person who hasn't let me down in some way, some of them brutally, and I'm relying on four entire humans here. Four humans who say they love me, but who also held me captive and could one day destroy me. They've built me up and strengthened me. I don't know myself anymore without them and can't picture each of them being in my life.

How do I know they'll never change their minds and sell me to the highest bidder themselves? What if they regret their decision to prioritize my life and my safety? What if I'm just another woman in their lives and they'll be onto the next one in a few weeks or months? There are so many questions that I don't have answers to.

The island might be beautiful, but living here with them wouldn't be without its challenges. I'd be signing myself up for a life where I'd be protecting the island, too.

And, instead, it might be easier to just go back home to the life I was so desperately trying to get through. Although it always felt a bit crazy, I now think of it as a simpler time.

CHAPTER SIXTY-THREE

Devon

"I feel like I've finally found a place where I truly belong. I never thought I'd find that, ever. I don't know how I'll ever beat that."

My eyes threaten to flood as a wave of emotion sweeps over me.

"You're my found family. That fills the emptiness, the void, but also digs deep into it, excising and vanquishing it. That lights up my darkness but also celebrates it."

I want them to understand this is a decision I'm not taking lightly. They need to know how much they mean to me, but why I can't just agree to stay because it feels good right now.

"I guess you've got a decision to make," says Zeke, a sad smile on his face tinged with hope.

Skyler nods. His eyes are kind. "You've got to do what's right for you, but if there's anything we can do to help you decide, please let us know."

Rake doubles down on Skyler's comment by winking lasciviously, and staring in the direction of his cock. Typical, and slightly compelling.

Dom just pulls me to him, wraps me in his big, burly arms and kisses me on the top of my head. "We'll never find anybody like you, you know," he says, softly.

"Likewise," I reply.

———

I spend the night tossing and turning, unable to sleep with such a massive decision weighing on my mind.

The past few days have been a whirlwind, and the intensity of the situations I've been in with the guys has sped up and sharpened some emotions. Maybe they'll fade just as quickly when I go back home, but I doubt it. I don't think I could ever replicate our time together. Nobody else could make me feel the way they collectively do. This is so hard. I am so torn.

My logical brain, used to abandonment, points out all the reasons this won't work. These guys held me captive, against my will. I'm still processing being kidnapped and almost sold to goodness knows who. Clearly, there's some trauma I'm going to have to work through, inI addition to all the unresolved bullshit I've left untreated for so long.

I have a life back home on the mainland. Maybe not the best life ever, but still a life. Donkey would miss me if I stayed here.

If I stay, I'll always be at risk of Tane deciding to sell me again. It sounds like he changes the rules on a whim, and he knows he could get a good price.

I'd need to accept my role in helping to protect the island, and I'll always have a target on my back being associated with these guys. It won't be a simple life, and I'll have to be okay with that.

As I contemplate whether to follow my heart or my head, it feels like my heart is trying to claw its way out of my body and attempting to run back to the four of them, and my mind is booking a ticket back home so that when this all falls apart it doesn't have to pick up the pieces.

I really don't know which part of myself will prevail.

Earlier, I packed a bag with my things, just to see what it felt like. It's not heavy, because all I have are the clothes Rake picked out for me, but it may as well be on fire and weigh twenty tons.

I carry it into the living room, dragging my feet, and feel eight eyes on me. The tension is palpable.

Noticing the bag, they all look at me and then at the floor.

"I see that you've decided to go," says Zeke, the first to speak after a prolonged silence. "It's a real shame you're leaving us, but I understand why it might be too hard for you to stay."

He looks destroyed. Dom looks like he's about to cry. Skyler twitches his foot and cracks his neck. Rake stares at the ceiling and blinks repeatedly.

Suddenly I know. The decision is obvious. There is only one choice.

I drop the bag and their eyes widen. They look at me expectantly as I gaze at each of them. I can't hold it in any longer. "You know what? I've been thinking, and... I've decided to prioritize myself and my own needs. What makes me happy. Not living life based on what might go wrong or expecting things to fall apart."

"Are you saying you want to embrace your darkness? Finally admit that you're one of us and that you belong here?" Skyler looks at me, his eyes full of hope.

"Oh baby, I embraced my darkness long ago. I just never dreamed that anybody else would, too. Let alone four men like you."

"You want to be with us?" Rake asks.

"Yeah, that's what I'm saying," a smile slowly spreading across my face. "I've found my family, and it wasn't where I expected it to be, but I couldn't imagine doing anything differently."

"So you're here to stay?" Zeke raises an eyebrow.

"If you'll have me." I smile at each of them, my doubts melting away as I see their love. At this moment I'm the most vulnerable and the most confident that I've ever felt in my life. I know I am loved. I know I am home.

"Oh, believe me. We will have you. All at the same time. Over and over again." Rake grins, and I see his pants are growing tight.

I feel a pleasant twinge between my legs. "That's what I was hoping you'd say. I'm glad this isn't the end."

Ready for more? Check out a spicy bonus scene here

Heidi Stark is an indie author who is increasingly falling in Iove with the craft of writing, almost as much as she loves the characters in this book.

She is inspired by the locations she visits on her travels, and the people she meets along the way.

When she's not writing, you can usually find her reading, listening to podcasts, or dreaming about her next book.

Learn more about Heidi Stark at her website. Sign up for exclusive content and my newsletter here.

You can also find out more about Heidi and her upcoming books on social media:

Facebook Page

Facebook Group

Instagram

Twitter

BILLIONAIRE'S TAKEOVER SERIES

- Irreversible Decision

- Compelling Proposal

- Love Merger

NOVELLAS

- Love in a Seedy Motel Room